THE MEMORY FOUNDATION

Also available by Amanda West

Writing as Amanda Reynolds

Her Husband's Lie
The Wife's Secret
The Assistant
The Hidden Wife
Lying to You
Close to Me

THE MEMORY FOUNDATION

A NOVEL

AMANDA WEST

NEW YORK

Books should be disposed of and recycled according to local requirements. All paper materials used are FSC compliant.

This is a work of fiction. All of the names, characters, organizations, places and events portrayed in this novel are either products of the author's imagination or are used fictitiously. Any resemblance to real or actual events, locales, or persons, living or dead, is entirely coincidental.

Published in the United States by Crooked Lane Books, an imprint of The Quick Brown Fox & Company LLC.

Crooked Lane Books and its logo are trademarks of The Quick Brown Fox & Company LLC.

Library of Congress Catalog-in-Publication data available upon request.

ISBN (hardcover): 979-8-89242-570-4
ISBN (paperback): 979-8-89242-572-8
ISBN (ebook): 979-8-89242-571-1

Cover design by Danielle Mazzella di Bosco

Printed in the United States.

www.crookedlanebooks.com

Crooked Lane Books
34 West 27th St., 10th Floor
New York, NY 10001

First Edition: May 2026

The authorized representative in the EU for product safety and compliance is eucomply OÜPärnu mnt 139b-14, 11317 Tallinn, Estonia, hello@eucompliancepartner.com, +33757690241

10 9 8 7 6 5 4 3 2 1

For Mum. Miss you. x

He holds out his hand, but she's not ready to leave. Not yet. This is all she knows . . .

CHAPTER

1

Tash

A FLICKER ON SCREEN and a musical chord, dramatic, heralds the eerie blue glow of my laptop as it boots up. The unnatural light floods the loneliness of my tiny tenth floor city apartment, casting shadows into the corners of the boxy bedroom. It's the deepest pit of night and the sleep I so desperately need eludes me in this witching hour. I can't get comfortable, my stretched stomach competing for space with the balanced laptop, my back aching as I prop myself up on plumped pillows and type "The Memory Foundation" into the Google search box. The results are too many, too scattergun. I add a name—Dr. Wade Hunter—and filter the results by date, newest first, looking for a diversion from the future and all that now holds for me. I am back to being "Natasha Walker, Investigative Journalist," researching a source of information for an exposé. A possible line of inquiry pursued as my fingers fly across the keys. It could be nothing, but the thrill of the chase wicks deep in my belly, competing for space beside my unborn child. I miss everything of my old life. I cannot believe it is over, at least for now, so I cling to the one part of me that I did not leave behind at the office today—along with my security pass and the last fifteen years of a career-led life—my ability to write a damn good story.

The Memory Foundation's website is little more than a landing page. It has a corporate rather than medical feel, which pleases me as I have no expertise in Big Pharma, but give me a corrupt CEO or a dodgy company ethos, particularly with a feminist angle, which usually go hand in hand, and I'm in my element. I have no idea if that's what I'll find at the Memory Foundation, if anything. All I have is an email from a potential whistleblower who claims to have been a volunteer there. I don't even know what the Memory Foundation does, let alone why "Patient A" saw fit to reach out to me. I'm an odd choice given my lack of expertise in tech-based medical research, which appears to be what the Memory Foundation is into, but I've learned to proceed with hope if not expectation. My mother taught me that, among many other things. Like independence and resilience. My heart squeezes at the thought of how depleted Mum is now. I need her former strength, her resourcefulness, her experience. I fight for breath, adjusting myself against the pillows, but the Memory Foundation's website has finally booted up and a video is now playing. Dr. Hunter's somewhat hesitant voice filling the silence. He's in his late thirties to early forties at a guess, square-jawed and clean-shaven. Good looking, although not my usual type. I prefer a more open expression. His is intense. I pause the frame and study the setting. There's no foreground but behind him is stacked what looks like gaming equipment—virtual reality headsets with visors, discarded on an old-fashioned looking wooden desk, as well as multiple pairs of clunky headphones—and there's a large window framing a snowy backdrop of mountain peaks and above them bright blue sky. The camera tracks his hand movements. The wobbly image inducing the nausea that has returned in my third trimester. I swallow hard and it thankfully passes. The remote mountaintop location intrigues me as much as he does. It feels like a secretive facility, which suggests they have something to hide, or protect. I pause the video and get up to go to the bathroom. When I return it's exactly six AM. Too early to start the day, too late to sleep. Dr. Hunter's frozen face watches me, his mouth open mid-word as I take a sip of flat ginger ale and tap the video back to life.

"My father, Dr. Hunter Senior," the blond-haired, blue-eyed Dr. Hunter Junior tells me, subtitles accompanying his speech, "began this journey many years ago, when I was still a child. A dream formed in his once brilliant mind that I have vowed to carry through to its thrilling conclusion. A legacy I am destined to fulfill, which is why I established the Memory Foundation here, high in the mountains. A place to live, work, and dream."

He glances over his shoulder at the mountain vista, then looks back at me. "A beautiful and inspiring setting to make my father's dream a reality. A dream to return dignity and quality of life to millions, even billions of people suffering with profound memory loss: something that, sadly, my father succumbed to himself."

Wade Hunter rubs at his eyes, then looks down the lens. "By fusing the technology available in the world of virtual reality with developments in AI and our understanding of memory storage and retrieval, I have been able to trigger and return recall to those who have lost that function through dementia, trauma, or brain injury. My groundbreaking techniques will ensure that our full span of years is not only endured but enjoyed, whatever disease or accident may befall us. The dream is now close to a certainty: a way to imprint memories that will stave off cognitive decline and provide hope that we can not only live longer but live well."

I glance at the photo beside my bed. My mother, a decade ago, smiling and happy. Eyes bright. She is wearing a pale blue blouse, one of her favorites. Her dark brown hair is showing the first signs of gray; her glasses, a new addition at the time, lend her a distinguished air. She has applied the same makeup she always wore, never leaving the house without the apples of her cheeks rouged, long lashes coated with mascara, lips stained red, and teeth checked for smudges. Her blouse is ironed and stain-free, not even a hair out of place. I pick up my phone to message her, knowing there is no point. Hasn't been in a long while. Instead, I email the matron at the care home to let her know I'll visit Mum later today.

"Each of our loved ones deserves to be a fully functioning member of our society for their entire life-span," Wade advises. "One that can bring a wealth of experience to us all. Age should be a number, not a protracted decline. Trauma a moment in life to move on from, not forever defining our futures. Our brains do not have to crumble to dust. Not if my work, begun by my late father, is supported to its conclusion. But I need your help."

He looks straight at me.

"If you are interested in changing the world for the better, either as a volunteer or as an early investor, a pioneer in either case, please click the contact button below. Together, we will make a difference. Together, we can change the course of history. Together, we can change the world."

My forefinger slides over the trackpad, moving the cursor until it hovers at the link. I have no money to invest, just a small pot of savings to eke out until my return to work for the magazine. And I can hardly sign up as a volunteer at the foundation, not in my present condition. But maybe I should make contact anyway?

The small red light of the webcam at the top of my laptop's open lid winks at me. I blink, clear the sleep from tired eyes, and the red light is gone. I snap the cover closed, the room plunged into near-darkness as my heart bounces around my constricted rib cage. Only a few hours into my maternity leave and already I've got sloppy. I should have checked the webcam was disabled.

Odd though, as I was certain I had.

CHAPTER

2

Lydia

THE WHIR OF the motorized blinds opening wakes Lydia Hunter from a deep and protective sleep. An eiderdown of pure glittering white that covers every speck of the Alpine panorama revealed. The floor-to-ceiling windows of their third floor suite slowly unveiled, along with the view.

She shakes her sleeping husband, then walks to the window and presses a palm to the toughened glass. The mountain road snaking up to the Memory Foundation will soon be indistinguishable from the rest. The journey to and from the airport even more dangerous for the bad weather. Lives have been lost on that road. Many more of them in the valley below. The inhabitants of the nearest village, a tricky ten-mile drive down from here, renamed it Ghost Valley after three seasons of avalanches decimated the entire area thirty years ago. But it's not only the unexpected early snowfall that unsettles Lydia. It's her husband's fallibility. In the five years she has known Dr. Wade Hunter she could count on the fingers of one hand the times he's been proven wrong, and he was adamant last night that it was far soon for their first snow of the season. Promised her, in fact. She should have trusted her gut. She'd felt it in her bones as they'd walked out under the stars. Shivered at the thought of what those heavy clouds might bring come morning. And now it's here. And still falling.

"It'll be fine," Wade reassures her, a hand to her bare back as she stands naked at the window. There's no fear of being observed up here, so far from humanity. "The Tank can deal with a few inches of powder, and I can drive that road with my eyes closed. You know I can."

The Tank is their affectionate term for the ancient four-by-four that Wade drives up and down the mountain to get supplies from the nearest store, way down in the valley, and to the closest airport, two hours away, to collect and return the steady stream of volunteers who come to the foundation each summer. The volunteers are confined to the satellite building across the ravine—in Wade's laboratory—but the four guests flying in today are to be welcomed into the Memory Foundation's main building for an exclusive and luxurious week of "the ultimate in destination travel." An immersive program showcasing Wade's patented Memory Flights, which will offer each guest an exclusive preview of the wonders possible here at the foundation. *If* Wade can get the Tank to the airport and back in this weather. The challenge to car and driver is not to be underestimated. The roads are dangerous at the best of times, the steepest section only passable until the snow comes, and rock falls are a year-round hazard. The terrain is not for the fainthearted, even in good weather.

Maybe the arrival of snow is a sign to abandon the whole scheme, which has always felt to Lydia like a prostitution of Wade's brilliance and in contravention of the foundation's true aims, but if there had been any alternative they'd have taken it. Their previous investors have grown tired of the wait for official approval. The funding needed for the foundation's research and development, which is massive, now withdrawn. "The suits," as Wade calls the bureaucrats he is forced to appease, have also abandoned them until "proof of concept," which will be impossible without a robust volunteer program.

Many sleepless nights have been spent trying to come up with a way to carry on the foundation's vital work. A week-long vacation-friendly experience was eventually devised by a reluctant Wade, who presented it to Lydia as "a bitter pill, but one I fear we must swallow." The guests will receive first-hand access to the foundation and their home. The week offering each of them a chance to imprint a treasured memory in vivid detail and take it home with them, returning to it in full technicolor whenever they choose. The years will not dim their happiest recollection or their ability to relive it. It will live in them, untainted and as permanent as a tattoo.

It's just a week. A week to paint on a smile for their wealthy guests and earn themselves enough money to make their dream for the foundation a reality. A dream she and Wade share. To return memories to those who have lost them through dementia, trauma, illness, old age. And in turn gift meaning and dignity to those patients: a quality of life no one should be denied. But that's not what their guests are here for this week. They want to be made to feel special when all they are is wealthy and likely entitled too. It is a frivolous waste of Wade's precious time and the foundation's already limited resources, but hopefully a means to an end.

Wade starts pulling on the warm clothes he'd hastily discarded after their walk the night before, and the loneliness of their imminent parting creeps up on her. This place is huge, but Wade fills it up, and without him, even for a few hours, there are too many thoughts, too many empty spaces. She longs to hunker down in their cozy third-floor suite as they always do when the weather turns. Just the two of them for months on end. She is prepared to risk everything to keep this place going, but is this a step too far?

"Last-minute doubts?" Wade asks, reading her thoughts as he often seems to.

Their closeness is her most precious possession. Built gently and with care after she arrived here in traumatic circumstances five years ago. They don't need anyone but each other. Except sadly, it seems now they do.

He's sitting on the end of the bed, already dressed in jeans and checked shirt and holding out his hands to her as he asks, "We have no other option, do we, my love?"

He knows the answer as well as she does. They have been through every potential investor, scheme, alternate idea, and this was the only one either of them could see working. "No," she replies, looking back at the snow before she adds, "We don't."

Her genius if slightly eccentric husband pulls on thick socks, frowning as if it were a puzzle to him how they fit, then he stands beside her at the window, their faces reflected in the glass.

"I assume you will spend your day hunting for any last-minute specks of dust you may have missed on your hundreds of inspections of the guest suites?" Wade asks.

He's teasing, of course, but she has been fastidious in the renovations, which have not been easily accomplished in such a remote location. She's also had to acquaint herself with modern etiquette and sensibilities, which have moved on in the five years she's been isolated from the rest of the world. Although not all the planet-friendly trends she's discovered have been echoed in their privileged guests' requests. Lab-grown meat and plant-based foods do not feature heavily in their dietary requirements, and they are all flying here by private jet. Well, all except one.

"I'll do a final walk-through," she replies, smiling at him. "Once you let me know you're on your way back."

Four guests, plus the two of them. Six people to mix and match and keep happy. Each visitor to the foundation, as with the volunteers, carefully vetted. Plenty of applicants were rejected along the way. Potential rivals, Wade told her, who saw this week as an opportunity to send in spies. It pays to still have friends in high places who can run extensive searches, a reassurance to them both. Then the work began to adapt the tech to provide something more recreational than therapeutic. A chance for their paying guests to relive a chosen moment, simply for the pleasure of experiencing it over and over. A magic carpet ride during which their rich clientele will never leave Wade's lab, while the memory will feel as real as the first time it happened. Maybe even better. Each memory flight providing a more in-depth experience that imprints the psyche until the memory is stored permanently and in vibrant detail. It's turning their serious work into a theme-park ride, but it's just a week. A week to get enough money to save this place and hopefully some high-profile advocates for the foundation as well.

The short video Wade posted on the Memory Foundation's website cleverly managed to sell the concept without giving too much away. The mystery only serving to heighten curiosity so they could name their price. An eye-watering sum neither of them thought they'd achieve and then wondered if they should have asked for more.

Wade stands up, and she smooths the rumpled bedsheet, then shakes out the thick feather duvet, piling on cushions and throws. There was only a bare mattress and a scratchy blanket to lie on when she arrived here, in terrible pain and yet soothed by Wade's concerned expression and gentle care. Dark days followed, many of them. But she has made this place—this man—her home.

"The guests' e-tablets are charged and in their rooms?" she asks as Wade hunts in the bottom of their shared closet for his snow boots.

"Yup, all done," he says, finding the padded boots he hasn't needed since March. "They can message me directly with all their questions about the memory flights, so no need to bother you."

"Great. I'll have my hands full with the catering."

The app Wade devised for their guests can adjust everything from the mood lighting in their suites to the temperature of the rain showers—which he installed with the help of YouTube videos while she passed tools and encouraged. And there's a private messaging interface for the guests to contact Wade wherever he is but most likely in his lab. Wade is both practical and clever. His medical training, followed by years as a scientist and an engineer, means he can turn his hand to most things. Although he does have a tendency to overengineer a nonexistent problem, like devising the complicated app which then required expensive iPads, one per suite, any connectivity beyond the foundation disabled. Surely, she'd suggested, their guests could switch on their lights and run their showers in the old-fashioned way, and basic cell phones could be provided for their stay? Apparently not. Their wealthy and tech-savvy millionaires will be used to the best of everything, including the latest tech with everything at their fingertips, and direct access to her husband at all times. And any cell phones, even ones they provide, are far too risky, security-wise. Wade will ask their guests to surrender all their electronic devices at the airport, confiscated for the duration of their stay. All it takes is one careless post on social media and the world will find them. And neither of them is ready for that.

The preparations have taken up far too much of their time and emptied the limited pot of remaining funds that should have over-wintered them. It will be a relief to look ahead to more financially secure times after the guests have gone and wonder what this large injection of cash might mean for the final push. The culmination of Wade's life's work is so close, they can both taste it. A game-changing development in memory retrieval that could well take the field of dementia and trauma care to new and unprecedented places. The results have been incredible, each cohort of volunteers more successful than the last. She cannot understand why their investors pulled out so close to the finish line, but as Wade says, it will be their loss.

She returns to the view, looking up at the highest peak rising up behind the foundation, Mount Dunkler, "Darker Mountain." That is where the avalanche began. The one she almost lost her life to the day she arrived. No warning other than a terrifying sound that rumbled loud and deep as her car approached the last bend at the top of the mountain road.

"Hey," Wade says, circling her waist from behind, the warm layers of clothing he's bulked up with for the journey soft against her bare skin.

The view she has seen literally thousands of times is pure unadulterated white. She's witnessed every kind of weather up here. Observed the snow melt and return, watched blue skies and wild blizzards, and yet it still fascinates her: the sweep of the epic mountain range that surrounds the foundation and the drama of the highest peak that buzzards and eagles circle. The foxes and rabbits that burrow in soft earth and then deep snow. And the sparsely populated and inaccessible village nestling way below them in the valley. Her favorite walk is through the patch of forest just beyond the high gates, the evergreen fronds drooping now with their cargo of snow. It is staggeringly beautiful, through every weather and season. A balm to her soul despite its claws, but she has never ventured farther than she can run back. And hopes more than anything she will never have to leave this magical place.

"Come with me," Wade says, as he tries to fasten his incompliant jacket. "To the airport, I mean. What is wrong with this zipper?"

She shakes her head and then brings the two ends of the zipper together and closes it to the top, just beneath his chin. "How would you manage without me?"

"Very badly," he says, kissing her, then his expression darkens. "Having strangers here, Lidds . . . I know how scary that is for you. Are you sure you can cope?"

She nods, unable to verbally give the reassurances she knows he needs.

He looks at her and then grabs his phone from beside their bed. "I'll message them now, say we're not quite ready, the tech is glitching, last-minute issue that means they won't get the full experience we promised."

She almost gives in to her fears and allows him to do just that, but they'd have to refund the guests' money, half of which they've already spent and the rest desperately needed. That would leave them with no choice but to abandon the Memory Foundation, and that's unthinkable.

"No, if someone was . . ." she says, clearing her throat. "I mean, if they were here for me . . . It'll be fine, I'm sure."

Wade nods and pockets his phone. "Yes, such low odds of any of these four being in any way connected to—"

"Exactly," she replies. "You've had them all vetted so thoroughly."

Wade had told her, several times in fact, that despite the investors withdrawing funds without warning, he still has friends in high places who remain interested in their work. Contacts he can call up who will feed a name into a computer that mere mortals have no access to. Secret dossiers containing confidential intel of a nature that eliminates all doubt about a person, or confirms it. Friends who will support them financially again, when the time is right, and in the meantime still keep a careful eye on what will hopefully soon be an enormously profitable asset.

"Wade?" she asks as he turns away, avoiding her gaze. "Please tell me you had the guests thoroughly vetted by your contacts?"

"Oh yes, great idea," he says. "'Can you just check out these VIPs I'm asking here so I can continue the project you've told me to shut down as you've got cold feet?'"

"Cold feet about what?"

Wade shakes his head. "No idea."

"But I thought the investors' withdrawal was a financial decision, budget cuts? That's what you said."

"All I know is they had a change of heart, but we have to keep going, Lidds, we're so close. This is too important to give up because a few venture capitalists and bumbling bureaucrats don't have the stomach for it. We're pioneers, you and I."

"The stomach for what?"

"To share what we have achieved with the world. To win this race and save millions from further suffering. It's time to go public, at last, but they always want more checks, more data. It's never-ending and someone will get there before us if we don't show our hand soon, I know it."

The goal has always been, since day one, or at least for as long as she has known Wade and the foundation, to relieve the burden on the public health service by providing a proven treatment for dementia. It could save millions of people from a truly dreadful disease, and probably billions a year in social care, not to mention the rehabilitation of all kinds of memory trauma victims. And of course the foundation's contract, should they get official ratification to provide memory flights to patients, would be worth a fortune. But that's not the point. It's the difference it could make to so many lives that drives them both.

"No proof is ever enough for those number-crunching suits, Lidds. More forms, videos, logs of cases—it's endless."

"So what checks *did* you make on our guests?" she asks, processing the fact that the rigorous vetting she believed would protect them both, and the foundation's secretive work, has apparently *not* happened and they are on their own.

"They all seemed genuine from what I saw online."

"You're saying you googled the guests? Is that the extent of it? I could have done that."

"I'm sorry, Lidds, I didn't want to worry you, stress always brings on your anxiety and then the panic attacks."

"For God's sake, Wade, you should have said something. You can't protect me from everything."

"I can try."

"Okay, so what do we do now?" she asks, acutely aware that it's already far too late to be unpicking this. Their guests are all in the air by now.

"It's fine, I'm sure it is. You could still come to the airport, though, good distraction?"

She shakes her head, but just for a moment she imagines traveling down the mountain road in the Tank, safe at Wade's side. He's an excellent driver, he'd get her back in one piece. She doesn't doubt that, and she wouldn't need to see anyone other than the guests. It's only a few hours, and she'd be with Wade the whole time. It might be good to push herself a little and make her way into the outside world, at least as far as the airport. It would also be a distraction, as Wade says. Much better than being in this vast building alone, only her anxiety for company. She has been tempted to leave before, even climbed in beside Wade a couple of times, ready to be driven down to the village store to collect supplies. Much as she loves this place, it can close in on her. The winters are harsh and dark, her nightmares bleak and overwhelming. She looks out at the snow, heavier now if anything.

"Might do you some good?" Wades adds, encouraging again.

"No." She gently pushes Wade away, blood thumping through her ears. "I can't. Not in the snow, you know that. In fact, not at all."

She turns from Wade and closes her eyes, forcing away the memory. Then she hears it. The whumping sound of snow on the move. She squeezes her eyes tight, knowing it's not real, but the avalanche that roared toward her the day she arrived at the foundation is coming for her again, as it does every day. She crouches down, hands over her head, waiting for it to engulf her. She will not escape it this time. She deserves to die in the river of snow that pulls everything with it down the mountain. It's her destiny. And a fitting punishment for the decision she made that allowed her to survive. A selfish hateful one that she regrets every day and with every fiber of her being.

"It's okay, it's okay," Wade says, crouching beside her. "Lidds, listen to me. You don't ever have to leave. I promise. I will never let that happen. Just the two of us against the world. You and me. Look at me, Lidds. I'm sorry I asked. I shouldn't have pushed you."

"But it won't be just the two of us, will it?" she pleads, looking up at him. "Not with strangers coming here. What were we thinking, Wade? What if they know who I am? Or recognize me once they're here? What if they spot the grave, or they've come here to find it, or find me? What then?"

CHAPTER

3

Tash

I WATCH THE DOOR of the North London coffee shop with hawklike vigilance as I stir my decidedly average and massively overpriced cappuccino. My domed stomach touches the edge of the table and the froth wobbles, the dusting of chocolate sloshing into the saucer. I am a ridiculous waddling creature who cannot sit in a café without making a mess, or go more than half an hour without needing the bathroom. What was I thinking arranging an interview with my source for the Memory Foundation story while I'm in this state? Except I know what I was thinking. I was thinking of Mum. A notion in my head of some divine plan for this strange hiatus in my professional life. As if there were a way to find order in the chaos and a purpose beyond birthing this enormous baby that kicks and rolls and presses into every molecule of soupy space between my squashed ribs and widening hips.

I take another sip of the lukewarm brew, allowing the buzz of caffeine to do its work as I push away thoughts of my latest visit to the care home. The smell of the place always stays with me. The cloying scent of decay. And Mum: her blank face, tissue paper hands, fine yet wild hair, all of it so compromised until there is now almost nothing left of the woman I adored. She was once full of life, full of me. I want to share this pregnancy with her, the pain and the pleasure. I want her in the delivery room, her hand squeezed by mine. I want her to say it will all be okay, that we can do this parenting "malarky" together. I want her to promise I will be as good a mother as she was and that I won't be alone. That I'll have my mum with me.

I drink every last bit of the milky coffee and spoon in the remaining froth. The one cup a day I allow myself is precious. Aside from the coffee, this meeting allows me to push aside the never-ending parade of emails and texts about birth plans and positive parenting, and for the next hour or so, subdue the worries about how on earth I will manage a career that involves last-minute and often dangerous travel. A career I must resume to pay for the bigger apartment I will soon need. Although the reminders of those responsibilities follow me here too, a text pinging onto my phone that invites me to join an prenatal group that will no doubt contain loved-up couples who make every decision jointly.

I delete the text and look around for anyone who might be Patient A. She claimed in her email to have been a volunteer for the Memory Foundation, but other than that I have no idea of her reason for contacting the hard-hitting magazine I write for, let alone why she asked for me by name. I don't even know what she looks like, but hopefully I will spot her when she arrives. She's certainly piqued my interest in an area of medical research that hadn't blipped on my radar before now.

Which is odd given Mum's condition, but the prognosis had been so absolute from the start. And denial had been our friend before that. Keys mislaid, names forgotten, but that happens to everyone as they get older, right? Then meals left in a lit oven, front and back doors wide open, calls in the night from concerned neighbors, police at the door. Mum hated the idea of a nursing home. Told me I was wicked for making her move there and she would be fine on her own. She wasn't like those other residents who had no idea what day of the week it was. I was desperate for her to accept the situation, and now I wish she had an ounce of that fight left in her.

Is it foolish to hope Wade Hunter's claims may be true and a preventive technique, or even a cure, is as close as he suggests? It must be worth this meeting with a potential source to at least ask that question, even if she turns out to be a time waster. Although, why would she ask to speak with me of all people? This is definitely not my wheelhouse, despite my vested interest because of Mum. I write about child labor and women's rights in the workplace, and most recently, the trafficking of underage girls. But of course, I am interested. Alzheimer's is the most common form of dementia and the one that has attacked my mother's brain, leaving holes so wide there is barely anything left. I wish I hadn't googled the odds of developing it myself, but in fairness, who wouldn't look that up? I am determined to do all I can to stave off this cruel disease, but I have a feeling daily Wordle and regular walks will not be enough. I need this meeting to be the start of something more concrete. But first I need Patient A to show up. My usual tolerance for lateness is fifteen minutes, but I'll allow her another ten.

I'm on my phone, in the Notes app reviewing my interview questions, when the café door swings open. A mousy woman wearing dark glasses and a raincoat edges in. I told her I'd be wearing a red jacket, but it's so hot in here I've taken it off. She stares through her oversized shades, scanning the tables. If she's trying to attract attention, then she's doing a terrific job of it. Everyone in the steamy café is watching the redhead in a bad wig with bright red cheeks and a nervous disposition.

"Are you Ms. Walker?" she asks, marching over.

"Yes, hi, but call me Tash," I reply, getting up with some difficulty.

"Oh, you're pregnant." She points at my ridiculous stomach. "I didn't know that."

"Why would you?" I reply, perplexed by her reaction, which appears to be annoyance, and to add to her consternation I then have to tell her, "I'm sorry, but I need to . . ." I glance at the sign for the bathroom.

"Now?"

"Yes, sorry." The urge is sudden and imperative. "Can I just . . . ?"

She nods curtly and lets me pass. I look back, and although she's taken a seat I have no idea if she will still be there when I return. I'll have to be quick, which is not easy when you're the size of a small car and the bathroom is tiny.

* * *

Patient A is sipping a tea and checking over her shoulder when I get back. I assume looking for me, although the sunglasses make it hard to tell and her general surveillance of the café continues after I sit. I offer to swap seats so she has a clear sight line of the door, and weirdly, she accepts. She then apologizes for her paranoia but says she thinks she's being followed.

I crack that stupid joke about it only being paranoia if it isn't true. "Sorry, followed by who?" I ask as she frowns and hands me my jacket from the back of the chair, the swap completed with some difficulty.

"Do you have any idea how much dementia care costs our government, let alone in the U.S.?" she asks, the non sequitur coming, as they do, out of nowhere the second we are settled.

"I do, as a matter of fact. Been doing my research, and although I'm on maternity leave, I can assure you I'm still a working journalist."

She nods, adding a tight smile. "Right, good. Then you will understand the potential contracts for a viable treatment are worth a fortune."

"Yes, sorry, can we just backtrack a bit? Your full name, please?" I ask, taking out my phone. The email was a series of numbers and letters that gave nothing away.

She shakes her head. "You don't need to know all that. Not yet. Like I say, have to be careful. There are competitors who send spies. You could be one of them for all we know."

"You represent the Memory Foundation?"

"Dr. Hunter's been looking for the right journalist to speak with for a while," she replies, avoiding my direct question. "He feels it's time that he took control of the narrative. Planted his flag, as it were, before the chance is stolen away by a competitor. But he needs to be sure he can trust you."

"Trust me?" I think of that flashing red camera light on my laptop. "How does he even know who I am?"

"By reputation," she replies enigmatically, although the red wig then slips forward, which detracts from her serious tone, and her hands shake as she adjusts it, her raincoat still buttoned up to the collar. She's clearly nervous and someone *has* hushed-up pretty much every shred of information about the Memory Foundation's volunteer program, evidenced by my failure to find out any more than the website gave away. That kind of blanket news suppression takes a lot of money, or friends in high places, but maybe this is all bullshit and she has no more connection to Dr. Hunter than I do. Although I've seen enough frightened whistleblowers to recognize this woman is living in fear of something. What's curious is that her tone when speaking about Dr. Hunter and the Memory Foundation is sympathetic. Not a whistleblower then, but maybe a bona fide messenger from the main man. There's a flutter of excitement in my tummy, or it could be the baby kicking my bladder again.

"Can I get you something to eat, or another tea?" I ask. "Settle your nerves with a slice of cake before we get started with a few basic questions?"

She shakes her head. "I can't stay long, but just to say that Dr. Hunter's pre-interview checks will be extensive, although that puts a bit of a crimp in the plan." She gestures to my stomach again.

I look down, although I'm used to the bump now, kind of. "Why is my being pregnant an issue? I've told you I'm still working, and I will right up to—"

"Logistically."

"Logistically?" I ask, feeling an eyeroll coming on to rival one of Rowena's. Ro is not only my editor but also my oldest friend, and yet she'd seemed reluctant to share the email from this woman, her doubts about this supposed source for the Memory Foundation now amplifying my own.

The email from Patient A had come through to the general contact address at the magazine's website but marked for my attention. Ro screens everything first, and when she finally mentioned it, on the day I was leaving to begin my maternity leave—desperate for something to take with me other than a potted peace lily and a good luck card with a voucher for recyclable nappies—she'd asked the same question I had. Why would Patient A have asked for me by name? I'm not exactly high profile or known for this kind of story. My best guess is they must have seen my recent award nomination—my first and for a little-known *Women in Journalism* prize—and the goofy photo that accompanied the press release.

"Duh." Patient A says, eye-rolling me herself. "You ain't going nowhere on a plane anytime soon, are you? Third trimester, right? You can't fly."

"I can fly short haul up to thirty-six weeks," I reply, trying to keep up now that a meeting with Dr Hunter himself seems to be a possibility.

"And you're . . ."

"We can conduct the interview with Dr. Hunter by email and video call," I reply, fudging the issue as I'm about to hit thirty-five weeks.

"He can't trust someone he's never met, can he? Even the most extensive screening can't always . . ." Patient A glances around and drops her voice to a whisper. "He has been let down in the past. Lies spread. It's a face-to-face interview, or deal's off."

"What deal?" I ask, suppressing a smile at her dramatics. "And what kind of lies?"

"The kind that cause unnecessary damage." She scrapes her chair back and stands up. "Seems we've both had a wasted journey."

I place a hand on the table and get up too, but more slowly. "I know it's not great timing, but give me a few weeks and I will be able to fly again, or maybe we could meet next time he's in London?"

"There's no way he'd leave the foundation, and you gonna leave the baby behind straight after you drop?" she asks, folding her arms. "Make a journey to a remote Alpine location with one flight in and out a week and a two-hour drive up a mountain? It's a dangerous place, believe me, I've been there enough times to have a few scares on that road."

"You've been there, as a volunteer?"

"Yeah, course I have. Plenty of times. Don't you believe me?"

"Of course. So where is it, exactly, and are the claims on the website true?"

"It's in a former cable car building, right at the top of—" She pauses and mimes zipping her mouth, looking around the café again before she adds, "And yes, course they're true."

"What's it like, then, the memory retrieval technique, I mean?"

"Amazing. As is Dr. Hunter, but that's all I'm saying for now." She turns and heads to the door.

I grab my jacket and follow or try to, negotiating the narrow space between the tables with difficulty. "Please, don't go yet." My pleading tone draws stares as I apologize for spilt coffees.

"What's the point?" she asks as I catch up with her outside, her hand to the wig that's lifting in the strong breeze. "You're clearly about to birth that bump, and we know you don't have anyone in your life to look after it, so—"

"What did you say?" I ask, trotting to keep up with her along the busy shopping street, buggies and screaming toddlers hampering my progress. "How do you know that?"

"That you're on your own, Tash?" she asks, turning to me.

"Yes! How could you know that and who exactly is this *we*?"

She looks sheepish but soon recovers, her tone imperious. "Obviously, you have been looked into you before this meeting. Although this baby stuff . . . You have kept it pretty quiet. Unplanned, was it?"

I take a deep breath to quell the rage as I pull on my jacket. We are by a convenience store, the unmistakable scent of weed wafting past and inducing a wave of nausea, or maybe that's the pregnancy hormones? But most likely it's the possibility that my privacy has been violated by this odd woman. I sink down on the low brick wall next to the shop. It's damp, and there's a dodgy looking alley behind me, a hooded man exchanging some kind of goods in its shady depths, but right now I couldn't care less about that. I need to know what she knows about me. If anything. She could well be bluffing, although she's right. I am on my own, and I have kept this pregnancy as quiet as I could. No social media posts. Although in my line of work I'm not much of a sharer anyway. It's usually best.

"You okay?" she asks, sitting beside me.

"Yes, just tired."

She looks around, then back to me and nods her head, her red wig flopping forward again so she has to push it back. "Must be exhausting, all that." She points at my stomach. "Such a shame."

"I do want this baby."

"I didn't say you didn't."

"No, I'm sorry," I reply, smiling at her. She looks so defeated. "Are you being coerced in any way? Feel threatened by Dr. Hunter?"

She laughs. "No, of course not. I'd do anything for him. What Dr. Hunter has achieved is—"

"Right, sorry . . . Hang on a sec."

Patient A follows my eyeline to a guy on the opposite side of the busy road. He's on his phone, but he looks familiar. I think he was in the café, on a bench by the window, his back to us and dressed in business attire, a pinstripe suit. I can't be certain it's the same guy, but if it is, he is likely watching us again now.

"Look, I will protect you as my source," I tell her, whispering now. "Whatever has happened, I promise you can trust me and if you are being pressured, I can help you."

She looks at me. "You have no idea what you're dealing with, do you, Tash? The level of interest, the rivals who would do anything to have what the Memory Foundation has to offer, the money at stake, you simply wouldn't believe it. Dr. Hunter is an honorable man looking to share an incredible advancement with the world, and maybe you were a good choice, maybe not, but either way I'm sure we can find someone else, and just like that." She snaps her fingers, and the man in the pinstripe suit looks up from his phone.

"Can you at least give me your name before you go?"

She shakes her head. "I'll be in touch after I've had another think. You know that phrase? You've got another *think* coming? Lots of people say it wrong. But it's *think*, not *thing*. Mum taught me that."

I smile. "Mums teach us a lot, don't they?"

She scowls, then walks away, and thirty seconds later the tall man in the pinstripe suit follows.

CHAPTER

4

Lydia

Lydia sits at her desk in her cozy office at the very top of the Memory Foundation's three-story building. The tiny room was originally a lookout station for avalanches, hence its name, the Crow's Nest. And she loves it up here. Her safe place.

"They would listen for avalanches as much as watch for them, often snow-blind," Wade explained on her first visit to the room in the eaves. "A flask of brandy-laced coffee keeping them warm on long lonely shifts."

The half-moon window is too high for her to see out, which usually suits her well. She has no desire to be watched over by the mountains, or watch them, but she can't help but listen, as those workers did all those years ago. It's been five hours since Wade left for the airport and according to his last message, sent two hours ago, he is on his way back with four passengers and a "mountain of luggage." Soon they will be here, and she longs for his return as much as she dreads the arrival of their guests.

She drags her chair to the window and with a hand to the corner of her desk, then the back of the swivel chair, climbs up. There's something vertiginous about the familiar view from up here, and her vision swims as her gaze swoops down to the snowy forecourt between the slab of curved concrete that's the main building, and the tall steel gates. She grips the dusty sill and peers out of the eye-shaped dirty glass window, looking for the pinpricks of the Tank's headlights coming up the mountain road. The shadows are deepening and the snow still falls, but the only light comes from across the abyss of the ravine, the domed glass roof of Wade's laboratory lit up in the darkening sky. The swaying covered walkway that spans thc gap between the main building and the lab induces another wave of dizziness so she has to hold on even tighter to the crumbling sill. Memories return. Of the first time she crossed the ravine, clutching Wade's hand so tight she drew blood with her nails. Hard to conceive of a time before she arrived here and found her purpose, leaving behind a life she has no recollection of or desire to return to. Five short years, and yet a lifetime too.

The hardware Wade was using back then for his now patented memory flights was far from the refined experience they will offer to their guests this week. The lab is also transformed from the dilapidated state she found it in five years ago. Although the redecoration has not been as extensive as she would have liked. Wade covets his privacy over there. She concentrated her efforts on getting the guest suites on the second floor of the main building up to scratch, while the satellite building has remained virtually untouched. Wade has been locked in his lab across the ravine most days and some nights, working on the guests' chosen memories. She did manage to persuade him to upgrade the old dentist chair he was using for the volunteers, but it's still pretty basic over there, although she loves the glass-domed laboratory. Not least because it was where she and Wade first declared their feelings for one another, lying together on the cluttered floor surrounded by VR headsets and looking up at the canopy of stars. That is one of her most precious memories, and she has very few of those. Everything before her arrival at the foundation is gone. Not even a flicker of the past remains.

She'd hoped that her total amnesia would make her an ideal candidate for Wade's volunteer program. A great way for her to repay his many kindnesses over the weeks and months of her convalescence. The physical injuries she sustained when she jumped from her car seconds before it was hit by an avalanche were expertly tended by the talented Dr. Hunter, but her memories were gone; she can't even remember why she came here in the first place. He had saved her life, so it was the least she could do to offer herself as a volunteer on his testing program, and she'd hoped it would also reawaken something of her past. The process would, as far as she understood it when Wade tried to explain the memory flights, "trigger" lost recall by use of stimuli fed through one of the sets of headphones and visors strewn around the lab, thus re-imprinting the data. The testing program was proceeding with mixed results back then—but for her it proved especially tricky. There was no history for Wade to feed back to her. No online history to mine for stories and photos and her favorite songs and paintings. All the things Wade had found worked with his past volunteers, she was lacking. She was a blank canvas. A lone woman who turned up in the snow, half dead and traumatized after surviving an avalanche, with no idea who she was or why she had come to this remote place. She didn't even know her own name.

"I don't understand. Are you saying I'm of no use whatsoever?" she'd asked him, frustrated and feeling like a burden. One she knew she would soon have to remove. A thought that filled her with panic for so many reasons.

"I deploy visual cues, often from phone records, photos, and social media comments too," he'd explained, absorbed by something on his laptop as she paced the lab, trying not to get caught in the cables that zigzagged the floor back then, a health and safety hazard. "But in your case we don't have any access points," he said, reaching out a hand to still her as she passed his desk. "Sorry, you're an enigma, my darling Lydia."

"Lydia?"

"It was my mother's name and I thought . . . But you choose of course."

"No, I like it," she'd said, touched by his tenderness as he'd looked deep into her eyes and pulled her to him.

The euphoria of their first moments of passion together had soon burst like a bubble, however, when Wade reiterated that he was sorry, but there was definitely no way she could take part in his volunteer program.

"No, *I'm* sorry," she'd told him, morose as she found her discarded clothes on the lab floor and dressed. "I should probably think about leaving soon, in that case."

"Leaving?" he'd said, pulling her to him again. "Not yet, surely? Not after what we just shared. And where would you go?"

"No idea, but there's no reason for me to stay here."

"Actually, maybe we can work something out," Wade said, eyes lighting up. "If you feel up to it?"

Physically she was on the mend by then, maybe eight weeks or so after her arrival, although the pain in her back and neck from the impact of flinging herself from a moving car was and still is debilitating. Mentally, however, she was a wreck, anxiety-inducing flashes of the moments before the avalanche and the choices she'd made, dogging her to this day.

"Yes, anything," she'd told him, feeling more hopeful as she joined him at his desk where he was scrolling through pages of indecipherable coding on his monitor. He was such a gentle lover and with such a brilliant mind. "What did you have in mind?"

She climbs down now from the window and drags the heavy chair back to the desk, sitting down and then pulling herself closer to her screen so she can flick through the spreadsheets she compiled for each of their picky guests: dietary requests, pillow orders, drinks preferences. She knows these four strangers as well as anyone might without having met them. Next she opens up the welcome speech she prepared on her phone to read it through one last time, but the words jumble before her. It happens like this sometimes, her brain simply switches off, or at least is running on less than full capacity, especially when she panics, but it is no less disconcerting for its regularity. Wade assures her that severe trauma will do that to a person, and the absolute best thing to do is to take a few deep breaths and wait until the fog clears.

"Many of the volunteers have experienced brain freezes as a result of previous trauma, just like you," he'd explained, adjusting this and that on his laptop as she lay back in the old dentist chair for Wade to "try a few things" that first time. She'd stared up at the glass roof to a night sky, and then blue skies or scudding clouds, then finally snow. So much snow. These flights soon became a regular thing. Their trips to the lab providing a way for him to keep the testing program alive when the volunteers couldn't get up the mountain because of the bad weather. Wade had managed to devise something special for her. A bespoke experience that invented a backstory which they built together, piece by careful piece, the flights providing valuable data for Wade despite her lack of a known history to mine, or at least one she could recall. So instead they created a new one for her, together.

"I have a duty of care to every one of my volunteers," he'd told her as he made notes and tweaked the invented narrative, adding more detail each time. Specifics that added tiny but significant layers. Her new biography soon felt so real that she started to believe in the "facts" they'd come up with together, despite knowing they were a work of fantasy. She was a scientist, they decided, who'd come here to help with Wade's important work. It made sense, at least on paper, and it reinforced her desire to stay. Wade was her soulmate by the end of that first winter together. And if at times the story didn't feel right, it was because they were both scratching around in the dark for something that simply wasn't there. Literally making stuff up. Which was bound to confuse and at times upset her, but they both remained excited by the idea of living and working together. A brilliant opportunity to test his AI generated reels, which were increasingly sophisticated. The augmented VR grew even better too, with each flight more realistic than the last, the hardware updated too. The trouble was she always came back to reality with a bump. No longer "Lydia Hunter" as he'd named her—a little weird as it was his late mother's name, but still an honor—the PhD student arriving at the mountain top in brilliant sunlight ready and able to assist in the vitally important test flights. Instead, she was back to being the woman with no name who'd made a terrible decision in order to survive an avalanche. A decision that saved her life, but left her wishing she were dead. Thank goodness Wade was always there to comfort her. Always making it better. Always patient. Always promising he would protect her and she would never have to leave this place, or him. Never have to face the world, or the true consequence of actions taken in the split seconds she had, but which would haunt her forever.

The trajectory of their love affair is a lavender haze of falling in love with Wade and the Memory Foundation's work and this place, all at once, one inextricably connected to the other. She wanted to be his everything right from the start and became insanely jealous of the volunteers who arrived at the lab after the first thaw. She never meets them, never wanted to, for obvious reasons—if someone recognized her, reported her to the authorities, it would be catastrophic—but she's thought about the visitors to Wade's lab a lot, quizzed Wade too, which he finds amusing. He's assured her there are no trysts with eager students as bedazzled by him as she is. His work is his only passion, besides her. A dream he inherited from his late father and honors to this day.

It inspired her love and admiration even more that Wade took on this challenge in his father's name. Dr. Jeremy Hunter was, in a dreadful irony, searching for a cure for dementia when the disease took hold of him too. But Wade's dedication to that legacy has come at a price. He'd neglected his needs as well as the comfort of his volunteers before her arrival—they were slumming it in back of the lab in very basic accommodation for weeks at a time, all in the name of research. Turning the lab into a welcoming space for the volunteers was her first task the next winter, despite Wade's claims it really wasn't necessary. Students lived in halls and went traveling to grubby hostels, they didn't mind. But she did, and besides, some of the volunteers were older, and trauma victims, they deserved a comfortable bed, even if it was a bunk. The following summer she sorted out a suite for them on the third floor. Then more recently she oversaw the renovation of the guest suites on the second floor, and a lounge on the floor below that, turning the foundation into a luxurious venue befitting the five-star price tag, or as close as possible to that aim given their limited means and remote location. She's found having a project has helped her to cope, or at least survive.

A flash of light at the high window snaps her back to the guests' imminent arrival. She drags the chair back in time to catch a glimpse of the Tank winding its way up the last visible section of the twisting mountain road, then it's gone again, round the dark side of the mountain. The snow is settling on the window ledge thickly now, fat flakes falling as the half-moon eye blinks into the darkening sky. Invisible black wings beat hard against the frosted glass as the Tank's tires track ever closer, bringing four strangers into her secret world. All she can hope is that they truly are strangers. The alternative, that one of them is coming to find her, is unbearable, so she pushes it away along with the rising panic. There's no time for that now. They are almost here.

CHAPTER

5

Tash

I'D HOPED TO hear from Patient A soon after our initial meeting in that café, but it's been weeks now. Long enough to safely assume the trail has gone cold. Likely I was too pregnant for her taste, which is a new one on me. I've been threatened, warned off, stonewalled, and doubted as a woman, but never rejected as a pregnant one. I should have moved on to something else by now, but for some reason I cannot give up on the Memory Foundation.

I am therefore delighted to see Patient A's contact details appear on my phone. Although the timing of her call is spectacularly bad. Not only because it's almost midnight—although night and day are a continuum right now, and if I've had two hours sleep in the last twenty-four I'd be amazed—but because my newborn is screaming the place down. And yet I take the call with no hesitation but a complete lack of dexterity as I juggle my daughter, almost dropping her as I switch to speaker and place the handset on the kitchen table by the window.

"It's been a while," I observe as I gently lower myself into the chair and try to settle Nova to the breast. Feeds are not something either of us are adept at, but it's the only hope of having a decent conversation. "Thought you'd decided I'm not the woman for you."

There's a deathly silence, other than Nova's snuffling. I hold my breath, waiting for Patient A to speak and Nova to latch on. This story represents so much more to me than a way to usefully pass the time before I can return to full-time work. Assuming I can find a nursery place and therefore resume my demanding travel-filled seat-of-the-pants role at the magazine this side of my daughter's graduation.

"You've had him then?" Patient A asks as Nova produces an anguished cry, frustrated by my ineptitude as I jab a sore nipple her way.

"Yes, last week. A girl, in fact." London is lit up far below as I expose my other breast and brace for the pain of my daughter latching on, or trying to. None of this is easy. Every task hard won, and often incomplete. My phone screen stares up at me. Silence again. I should hang up. This is ridiculous. I have no idea who Patient A is, or why she has called again after so long and at a such an unearthly hour. She could be high, drunk, delusional, any or all of these. And I have no time for this. And yet, all the time in the world.

"Last week?" she asks, her tone sober and abrupt. "I thought you were further on than that."

"Well, no, I wasn't. . . . But I used the time before she arrived to research the Memory Foundation."

"Yeah?" she asks, sounding doubtful. "You still interested then?"

"Of course," I reply, bravado carrying me through as it always has. "But I'd given up on hearing from you again. Assumed you'd found someone else."

"Yeah, I was hoping to, but you are exac—"

Nova falls from the breast and wails. "Sorry, I missed the end of that."

"This is clearly a bad time, so—"

"Please don't go. You must have had a reason to call back?"

The deep pull as the milk flows brings with it a warmth that tugs me away from the call, beats of silence passing.

"You *have* spoken with Dr. Hunter about my keenness to still meet with him?" I ask, afraid she's no longer there.

"He's been very busy. Volunteers there all summer."

"Is that where *you've* been?"

"Not this time, but I will be back at the foundation again soon."

"Maybe the two of us could go together? Just give me a few more weeks and—"

"How many weeks exactly?" she asks, sounding off. "Time is kind of the essence. Once the weather closes in the journey will be impossible."

"Maybe three, four?" I suggest, no idea how I will feel by then, physically and mentally. And there's Mum to think of too. No one has put a time frame on it, but I get the impression we are talking months, maybe even weeks. And this is all assuming I get the go-ahead from Ro. I'll need her to cover my travel expenses and provide me with a platform for the story. I've been keeping quiet for now, until I have something concrete to show my boss, knowing she will require more than a hunch. I need proper evidence to convince Ro to back this trip. Facts that so far have been very thin on the ground to nonexistent. And I'm exaggerating my research to Patient A. All I've managed to do is skim-read a couple of articles about the "positive side of AI" and how that might, one day, provide the breakthrough needed to stimulate lost memories. Mainly, I've been busy failing at preparing for and then being a new mum: morning, noon, and night. The fatigue is unbelievable and with my limited brain capacity pre and post birth—thirty-two hours of labor and a ten-stitch episiotomy would take it out of anyone—I feel woefully underprepared for an interview with Dr. Hunter that may well never happen. I glance at the card that Kitty, Ro's wife, wrote and sent. It's the only one I received. Patient A was right, I am on my own, and I feel that this is the story I am destined to write. Sometimes it feels as if it's the *only* story I might ever write, and if I don't I will succumb to an abyss of cluster feeds and exploding nappies. Even worse than that, I will let Mum down in some abstract way I cannot explain but which feels tangible and guilt-laden and as full of regret as my own selfishness and fear of the disease that's already taken her from me in almost every sense. A ghost all that's left.

"So what do you think?" I ask Patient A. "If I can organize myself by say a month's time, are we still on? Will that work for Dr. Hunter?"

After a long pause, which I deliberately resist filling despite a rising panic at my audacious plan, she says, "You said in one of your *many* voice notes that you love-bombed me with that we mustn't ever let fear get in the way of what's right. That we should be brave. Protect ourselves and others. Whatever the personal cost. Do you still stand by that?"

I'm amazed at my sanctimony. I don't even recall thinking all that, let alone saying it. It must have been in one of my more lucid moments, or maybe a desperate attempt to rattle her into returning my messages.

"Yes, I do, and I can protect you as my source if that's what you're worried about," I add, as if that were in any way true. The only person I should be promising protection to is Nova.

"You're the one who needs to be brave here, not me," Patient A responds, her voice loud in the small apartment. "I'm fine."

"This is my job. I've traveled to some pretty—"

"Even now you have a child to think of?"

I take a beat, surprised by her perceptiveness. She's been, in my limited experience, emotionally cut off and direct to the point of rudeness. I glance down at Nova, who is rooting for more milk.

"Finding the truth and reporting it has been my life's work," I reply, finding the words from somewhere in my past self. "I want my daughter to be proud of me."

"I wouldn't know about that."

"You don't want kids?"

"Would have loved them, but life had other plans for me. Well, Mum did."

"I'm sorry to hear that," I reply as Nova's strong suckle proves painful and I stifle a wince. "Being a carer to a parent is a tough gig, isn't it?" I ask, taking a punt on her situation.

"Yes," she replies absentmindedly. "Thought for a while things might change, but . . . Anyway, let's get off this call now just in case."

"Just in case of what?"

"I'm away for a few days," she replies, ignoring the question. "I'll be in touch when I get back, see what we can do."

"Are you going to the Memory Foundation?" I ask, desperate to keep the conversation going, but she's ended the call.

* * *

As soon as Nova is sleeping, I start my research proper, bookmarking everything I can about Dr. Wade Hunter and the Memory Foundation. It's two AM when I look up from my screen. Common sense would dictate I should get some sleep while I can, especially as concentration remains a challenge with a cotton-wool postpartum sleep-deprived brain, but I knuckle down again and start to finally make some progress.

As far as I can make out from the limited press coverage of the foundation, the tech Dr. Hunter claims to have developed can harvest and then collate, possibly even reproduce, lost memories. Again, not sure, but I think by utilizing data from documented histories compiled using personal testimony, if available, as well as secondhand accounts and any photos or video history on social media, he claims he can implant lost memories using what is referred to more than once as a "digital harvest." There's very little about how the foundation then uses this data, or detail of him or his company's success stories, or reports from volunteers, but I do stumble on his father: Dr. Jeremy Hunter, who began the foundation's research into a cure for memory loss decades before. He looks like something out of a World War II biopic in his three-piece suit with his dark hair parted at the side, cold eyes boring into me from a Cambridge University alumni magazine. He was a pioneer in the use of MRI brain scans to detect early signs of dementia but also a somewhat controversial figure who died of the very disease he had hoped to cure. His techniques and ethical practice are also questioned in the few documented reports of his research. Participants and their next of kin were apparently not aware their data was being used for study, but he wrote a paper that paved the way for future advancements and has obviously inspired his son to carry the flag in his name.

Nova is fractious and needs my attention, forcing me to leave my laptop and pace the small apartment while bouncing her up and down on my shoulder. I lay her in her crib and watch the short welcome video of Dr. Hunter Junior on the Memory Foundation's website again, sound turned down so as not to disturb Nova, the captions appearing as I slide the cover over my webcam this time, just in case.

"If you are interested in changing the world for the better, either as a volunteer or as an early investor, a pioneer in either case, please click the contact button and apply. Together, we will make a difference. Together we can change the course of history. Together, we can change the world."

I lay my head on the kitchen table and close my eyes, but instead of sleep I think of the night I spent with a stranger in a hotel room in LA. The one that led me to this circumstance. The one that changed everything. It was a foolish and rare lapse in my usual scrupulousness regarding birth control, but—and I have gone back and forth on this—maybe on some level I wanted to fall pregnant. I am thirty-eight years old. Classified, delightfully, as a "geriatric mother." I wasn't aware of my biological clock ticking away, but I never for a second considered not having her. I only wish that decision hadn't cost me so much. Is that the usual price of motherhood and what Mum sacrificed too in order to keep me? Her chance at professional fulfillment forfeited in favor of being a good mother, as she undoubtedly was. Maybe I am simply following her path to its logical conclusion.

I lift my head from the smeared kitchen table, saliva on my chin. My reflection in the steamed-up window is alien. A version of me that spirals into the one I fear most. I look old and alone, lost and confused. I look like my mother.

Nova sleeps cherub-like in her crib as I run a crooked finger across her cheek and know in my heart I cannot run off to a remote mountaintop location to interview a scientist in pursuit of an exclusive story, however important that feels. Even if I had anyone I could trust to look after my daughter, it's just not practical right now. Mum needs me. Although she has no idea who I am when I visit. Nova cries and I hold her to me. My precious girl. I won't let her down, but maybe being a good mother is about more than sacrifice. Maybe it's about being brave. Leading by example. Whenever you get the chance. Each generation doing better than the last, seizing those opportunities rather than living a life laced with regret and resentment.

I console myself with the thought it's academic for now. I have no way of finding the Memory Foundation's secretive headquarters without Patient A, and who knows if I'll ever hear from her again, or if she's a reliable source. But the gut instinct I've always relied on is telling me she is credible, and I just need to hold my nerve a little longer.

CHAPTER

6

Lydia

PANICKED BY THE Tank's imminent arrival, Lydia runs down from the Crow's Nest to change into the smarter outfit she laid out ready on their bed—a shift dress and blouse underneath—then down another floor to make her final checks on the guests' suites. The rooms were already perfect, at least to her eye, but seeing them through the lens of her discerning guests she now doubts every choice. Are the cushions and throws luxurious enough? The towels in the en suite bathrooms too fluffy or not fluffy enough? It had been difficult to source everything in time. Too many trips down to the village for Wade to collect deliveries, so she'd felt guilty every time she ordered another lamp or ornament. The guest suites take up the entire second floor, one room on each side of the building, then a larger one at the end of the carpeted corridor. She goes into each in turn, using the guest iPads to adjust the lights and close the motorized blinds. They can also personalize the locks on their doors to a code of their choosing on arrival, as long as they are tech savvy and, unlike her, can remember the code. She's not great with tech generally, learning pretty much everything from scratch, although she was blessed with a few muscle memory cues to ease the way back to computer literacy. She instinctively knew her way around a keyboard, while other basic skills still elude her, like retaining the four-digit codes required to unlock the internal and external doors. Wade alternates the codes between his mother's and father's birthdays, day and month, but there's no significance to those dates for her, or any dates for that matter. It's impossible to know for sure if her memory loss is attributable to her injures or PTSD, maybe both. It's frustrating, but she is lucky to function as well as she does and that is mostly down to Wade's patience and care. She's grateful to him, of course, and tries to take his advice not to "spiral about the past" although some curiosity remains about who she was before the foundation.

She used to search online for herself almost daily, but how do you find someone when you don't know who they were? With only the jeans and shirt Wade cut off her to treat her injuries—mainly cuts and bruises other than the whiplash that has permanently affected her back and neck—and no sign of a coat or bag that would likely have contained her phone, wallet, driver's license, there was no place to start the search, let alone resolve it. The only possible lead was the rental car company, but the risk of opening up the trail was too great and the car she'd driven up the mountain, when Wade eventually located it, was damaged to such a degree it would be hard to trace to the point of collection. Although the rental company would likely be at the nearest airport and have records of the one that never came back. But what would that have achieved other than highlighting she was accountable for someone other than herself who had not survived the journey. Much safer to bury the evidence as Wade reassured her he had. She shivers at the thought of the makeshift grave he described. He did his best to be respectful, but it feels wrong, in so many ways. The guests will be driven past it, twice, but Wade assures her it is discreet. No one would ever know it was there unless they were looking for the small pile of rocks deep in the valley.

For a long while she imagined a search party traveling through the snow to find her. A heavy knock at the door waking them, angry recriminations followed by the inevitable demands she face the consequences of what she did to survive that avalanche, but no one has ever come looking for her. No thuds on the doors, no rattle of the locked gates. No flashlights shone in their faces as they lay entwined. She has got away with it. In that sense, at least.

She is in the largest suite now, the one at the end of the second floor corridor, when headlights sweep across the closed blinds, quickening her last minute checks and her heart rate. She has assigned this room to the Bentleys who have flown in from New York. Nick, seventy-three, is a native New Yorker, and Rachel, his wife of almost ten years, thirty-six, originates from the UK. The other suites are smaller but have better views. The one at the front she's allocated to Jack, forty-two, a California entrepreneur. And the smallest room opposite that is earmarked for their scholarship place, Zoe. Another Brit.

Wade suggested they offer a free place to assuage any negative press should the crazy price tag of this week's stay somehow get out. All visitors to the foundation must sign stringent nondisclosure agreements, but nothing is ever watertight. They have ended up paying Zoe's travel expenses too, but she does sound like a deserving case. Wade has hinted at a lost loved one who died in a tragic accident, so regardless of the possibility for damage-limitation, if needed, it's good to know someone will benefit in a more meaningful way. A nod to the foundation's true aims.

Room checks done, Lydia runs down another flight of concrete stairs to grab the canapés she'd left in the kitchen. The tiny galley fridge is stuffed to bursting. She then hurtles across the hallway toward the guest lounge with the slates of food in hand. It's a large sitting room with a fully stocked bar to the left, where she places the food, and comfy modular sofas under the curved windows. The Tank should have made its way round the mountain by now, but there's still no sign of those twin beams in the panoramic view over the valley. They must be on the final section where the road twists most perilously into dark shadow. That was where Wade found her, less than a mile from the gates, describing how she'd buried her head in the crimson snow, pain creasing her forehead when he'd tried to lift her. She was close to death, hypothermia setting in, but she'd begged him to leave her there to perish. She'd wanted to die. She recalls that much.

There's a distant and sparse sprinkling of lights from the tiny village in the valley far below. Night descends fast at this time of year, but the view will be an impressive greeting for the guests come morning. She shivers, hugging herself, then holding her hands out to inspect them. They are chapped despite the gloves she wore to scrub this place top to bottom, her nails rough and broken. They'd had no concept of the enormous amount of money, energy, and emotional turmoil required to get the foundation ready for this enterprise, but as with all things, this too will pass. It's only a week, after all. A week to turn their fortunes round and prove the foundation's worth, securing their future here.

The headlights come round the mountain first, then the Tank itself comes into view pulling up on the other side of the tall metal gates, where it stops. The snow has drifted and is blocking the gates, piles of it caught in the glare of the headlights. Why hadn't she thought to go down and clear it? It's such a bad start for their VIP guests, trapped in a steamed-up old car in danger of rolling back down the steep track, and after such a long and arduous journey.

Wade gets out and looks up at her. She steps back from the window, curious for that first glimpse of the four strangers about to enter her home, but she is also afraid to be seen. She can't hide for much longer, but the habit is ingrained. Like when the volunteers come and she barely leaves their suite.

Wade rattles the gates now, coaxing them to move. Then he glances up again, his face illuminated by his lit phone, his grin reassuring. He waves, then turns and walks back to the car as the gates finally move, a scraping sound as they carve arcs into the mounds of snow before they clang shut again behind the Tank.

This will be the first chance for their guests to get a proper view of the Memory Foundation, and she hopes their impressions are good. It may not appeal to everyone, but the brutalist three-story concrete construction is undoubtedly imposing, and she has softened the path up from the forecourt with fairy lights wound around potted baby fir trees that Wade plucked from the forest. She should go down to greet them, but then the Tank keeps going, cutting deep tracks into the snow as Wade drives it straight down into the basement carport. This was not the plan, although maybe it is sensible given the amount of snow outside. She should have cleared the path for the guests too. She's strong enough now, muscular from the hard labor of the lifestyle here, although her neck and lower back pain means she has to be careful when using the snow shovel. It's a shame, though—the basement is a tangle of cables and noisy with the whine of the generator. Not the most auspicious of welcomes.

She waits, listening for the cut of the Tank's engine and then the first signs of them coming up the metal staircase from the basement. Strange voices soon travel to her, quickening her breaths. Sounds that produce no clear words through the locked metal door but move in unfamiliar patterns, and are too loud, or soft, to be Wade's. Then the sound of the door from the basement being unlatched, and then footfall across the parquet flooring in the hallway. These last few seconds of anonymity stretch out. She takes a deep breath and reminds herself of all the benefits these guests bring with them: money, mainly and hopefully positive word of mouth. They are now the only hope of the foundation's survival and her only chance of remaining here with Wade. And she is, she prays, as much a stranger to them as they are to her. All she has to do is stick to the agreed story and all will be well. She is Mrs. Lydia Hunter, scientist, wife, hostess. Nothing else. Four guests in a world of nine billion. She repeats the odds that Wade told her and takes another deep breath, trusting, or trying to, in the math. It's been five years. No one is coming to find her.

She paints on a smile as the unfamiliar voices get louder: female, high-pitched, then a man, older. This is a good thing. All will be well. Better than that. It's going to be an amazing week. It has to be.

CHAPTER

7

Tash

IT'S BEEN THREE long weeks since that midnight call from Patient A. I assume she's at the foundation, or maybe she's investigating better prospects for her story? Or maybe she's a deluded nut-job who's catfishing me. I message her most days, listen to her voicemail, send an email or two. You'd think I'd have better things to do with my time, but the days are long and the nights even more so. I seem to have birthed a nocturnal baby, so while I should be catching up on sleep when I can, or taking the chance to brush my teeth or hair, or tidy my impractical tenth-floor apartment, I instead choose to spend the precious few bursts of quiet time getting a better feel for Dr. Wade Hunter and what his foundation does. It's likely a pointless exercise, but it's the only connection to previous me that I have. And I miss her. Natasha Walker: Investigative Journalist.

I've always thought of myself as alone, but not lonely. There's a very distinct difference, and one I am now acutely aware of, as well as how my life choices have limited my options. Choosing work over friends. Travel over company. Sex over relationships. Choices I no longer have. I should have made more effort with the other new mums. They could have sympathized or offered practical tips. And while I know I'm fortunate to have Nova and I love her more than life itself, my daughter reflects and amplifies my ineptitude and resultant sadness. We are drowning slowly but surely in one another's dull and yet demanding company. All that keeps me afloat after another soul-destroying visit to see Mum is a fine thread of hope that one day I may get the opportunity to write this story.

I read over my notes, opening the foundation's website as a gray drizzle descends the plate glass window that runs down to my bare feet beneath the kitchen table. The drop to street level is scary, but the rain softens it to a painterly haze, and being in Dr. Hunter's world is my comfort blanket. Like chatting with an old friend, or Mum. Although it's always a one-way conversation.

My aim is to nail down what his tech not only claims to achieve, but how it works in practice. His explanation of "fusing the technology available in the world of virtual reality with developments in AI" is frustratingly vague but to my layman's brain, sounds credible. I can imagine, given the right stimuli and environment, you could reactivate lost memories held in dusty synapses. Like the moments of lucidity Mum occasionally exhibits, recounting with clarity things that happened years ago, decades even. Proving that everything is within us, somewhere. Just this morning she looked at me when I took her hand and rested it on Nova's downy hair, then she asked me if a slice of my favorite homemade treacle tart would stop me crying.

Dr. Wade Hunter is the only person mentioned on the foundation's single-page site, aside from his late father, but there must be a larger team handling the flow of volunteers and the logistics of running such a remote facility. I'm guessing they all sign an NDA, but it would be good to meet with other personnel too, when I go there. *If* I go there.

Wade Hunter's handsome if disheveled appearance in the welcome video puts me in mind of an eccentric but brilliant English professor I had a yearlong crush on. I guess I've always had a thing for an older man, although Nova's father was . . . Well, I don't know for sure, but definitely quite a bit younger than me. Dr. Hunter's voice has a deep resonance to it that suggests maturity, but his physique, as far as I can tell from his seated position in the video, is muscular. I've searched everywhere for more photos, but the only one I have unearthed is of Wade as a diffident teenager outside Edinburgh University, his father's scowl beside him as they stand stiff and at least a foot apart.

I leave the sound on low and lean in to listen to Wade's welcome message again although I could recite it word for word. There's no date stamp on the video, adding another cloak of mystery that also piques my curiosity. I slide the webcam cover back to see if the red light comes on. Something I've taken to doing of late. As if I were flirting with a potential date. I feel closer to Wade Hunter in these moments, my desire to know more about him floating me out the tenth floor window and into his snowy mountainscape. Sometimes the webcam light flashes, or I think it does, but not now.

Maybe I'm losing my mind. It's a distinct possibility. I'm certainly losing my heart to that vista of white peaks that he lovingly contemplates before he looks down the lens at me again with those intense blue eyes.

The webcam light illuminates, startling me. I sit up straighter. A dot of red reflected on my forehead like a sniper's target. My breath holds for the second or two the light is on, then it's gone, and I let the air flow from my lungs. I could have imagined it. Probably did. But it felt thrilling while it lasted.

My phone rings, and Nova shrieks and writhes so I pick her up first before answering.

"Hi, is this a good time?" Patient A asks.

"Yes, of course. How are you? I'd given up on hearing from you again."

Never one for small talk she says, "Dr. Hunter wants to meet you, soon as. So shall we talk in person, say tomorrow?"

"Yes, yes, of course. Wow. Really?"

"Few hoops to jump through first, but basically yes. May as well get on with it before the weather turns, as I said it gets dangerous up there."

I feel nauseous but excited as the call ends. This is crazy. And yet it's also the news I've been waiting for and the only thing that's energized me in days, other than imagining Dr. Hunter is watching me as I watch him, which is ridiculous. That's not even possible, is it? I push away the intrusive thoughts, the guilt, and the overwhelming practicalities, pretend I am old-me. The one who would be telling Ro my plans. Which of course is exactly what I now must do.

She's my safety net, always has been since the day she took a chance on an overly confident graduate with a useless master's in creative writing who smoked and drank as much as she did. Ro will have my back on this, and if not I will walk away, even at this late stage. Her instincts are always spot on. If she says it's a no-go, then that's it. There won't be any discussion or debate. I will simply give up on this story.

CHAPTER

8

Lydia

"Lydia!" Wade says, finding her hiding at the back of the guest lounge. "Didn't you hear us come up from the basement? I thought you'd come out and meet the guests, as agreed."

"Sorry, yes, I should have."

Beyond the door she can hear the chatter of unfamiliar voices growing more distant as they go up the concrete steps, cases bumped with them.

"I've told them to head straight up to their rooms," Wade says, grabbing her by the hand. "I wanted to check on you first, see how you are doing. Have you been all right on your own? No panic attacks?"

"I'm fine." She pushes past him. "I'll show them which room is which."

"No need, I've told them. Come here, I want a hug."

Her husband is still in his coat, his boots covered in melting snow and wet prints running from the door on the polished wooden floor. He has the tightness of cold about him but a flush of color from coming inside. His face is warm as he presses his cheek to hers and pulls her close. She hugs him back, wanting more than anything for the guests to never come down.

"What are they like?" she asks, pulling back. "Any red flags?"

"Not really, much as expected, although . . ."

He heads toward the bar, shedding his coat on one of the high barstools. She picks it up and drapes it over her arm, feeling the icy cold damp of it through the sleeve of her blouse.

"Although what?"

"Nothing, all okay, I think," he says, forcing a smile. "You look lovely, by the way," he remarks, taking a beer from the fridge behind the bar and popping the cap. "I like that outfit on you."

"Really?" she asks, looking down at her smart attire. She lives in sweats, Wade in his favorite checked shirt. "I wasn't sure."

"Yeah, you look good, although it's . . . you know, a bit strange. All of this."

She'd settled on a black fitted shift dress and a caramel silk blouse layered underneath. She'd wanted to feel put-together and stylish, imagining herself as a capable host in the guests' company. Various secondhand purchases from online auction sites now fill her wardrobe, the latest box arriving just in time at the village store. And he's right, it does feel strange.

"What are your first impressions of them, then?" she asks, handing him his wet coat to stow behind the bar. She takes the nearest of the four stools the other side and watches him swig the beer as if he drinks one every day, which he absolutely does not. "I need details, Wade. Quickly before they come down."

"Nick likes the sound of his own voice," Wade observes, wiping his mouth with his hand. "He sat up front with me. Bit of a distraction, to be honest. Roads were dicey."

"Really?" Lydia hooks her sneakers on the barstool. She'd ordered some heels but guessed the size wrong and prefers her comfy sneakers anyway. "The road is bad already?"

"Yeah, pretty much covered in thick snow from the valley up."

Wade looks at the door and drops his voice as he describes the state of the steepest section of the road. The part she remembers from her arrival here. She shivers, and he reaches his hand across the bar to hers. He's looking gorgeous in his smart shirt and jeans. He even let her cut his blond curls. He also shaved off what was a very bushy beard. Her wild man of the forest is gone. He squeezes her hand, then releases it to steal a canapé from one of the slates she'd set on the bar, everything a last-minute rush despite the weeks of preparation.

"Oh my God, this is amazing, Lidds," he says, crunching down on a duck parfait quenelle wrapped in a leaf of crisp iceberg lettuce. He reaches for another, roast beef in something called a Yorkshire pudding, a puff of batter that looks delicious.

"Leave those for the guests," she says, gently tapping his hand then rejigging the configuration on the slate to look neat again. "We don't have that many." They'd come frozen from an online delivery service that charged a fortune plus extortionate shipping, but the selection does look pretty if disappointingly small.

"I'm starving, Lidds. It's been a long day. First Zoe kept us waiting at the airport, then that drive . . ."

"Zoe's flight was delayed?" she asks, stealing a canapé too and licking her fingers. The paté is velvety smooth with a depth of flavor she's not used to, which it should be for that price.

He shakes his head, still chewing. "Nope, the weekly scheduled flight landed bang on time, but she didn't come through with the other arrivals."

Wade had asked the Bentleys and Jack Myrtle to synchronize their flights—on separate private planes—with Zoe's, which was due within minutes of theirs. "So where was she? The airport is tiny, isn't it?"

"Not so tiny that she was AWOL for almost an hour," Wade explains, reaching for another canapé and thinking better of it as she swats his hand away. "Which did not go down well with the other guests, particularly Rachel bloody Bentley who is quite frankly—" Wade stops talking and looks at the open door. There's no one out there in the hallway, but they would have heard him if there was. They need to be more careful. "Her case was searched."

"Oh no, poor Zoe," Lydia says, passing Wade a napkin and using one herself.

"Yeah, it's usually just the same guy waving everyone through, but of course, not today."

"But they're all here now?" she asks, checking behind her again.

"Yeah, all present and correct."

"What's Jack like?"

"Quieter than the others, but he seems okay, I guess."

"What does that mean?"

Wade places a finger to his lips, his focus moving past her again and toward the door. "Sorry, thought I heard someone coming down. Must have imagined it, but we do need to remember it's not just us here now."

She nods, wishing that weren't true. "Are you worried about Jack?"

"Well, you know what they say about the quiet ones," Wade replies, smiling.

"No, what?"

Wade's smile fades. "Sorry, something Dad used to level at me a lot, but I'm sure Jack is—" Wade sprints from behind the bar to the door, right hand outstretched. "Nick, Rachel, come and meet Mrs. Wade Hunter."

Lydia slips from the barstool and crosses the room too, her ability to walk toward the Bentleys, let alone with confidence, hampered by the tight feeling in her chest. This is the first time she has seen anyone but Wade in five years. And before that she has no recollection of meeting anyone. It's surreal, her movements forced and unnatural, and yet she knows these faces well, has studied them at length, but never in the flesh. She opens her mouth to speak, say anything, but all she can think is how odd a choice of introduction it was: *Mrs. Wade Hunter.*

Rachel Bentley's frosty expression doesn't help. The taller woman's eyebrows, perfectly arched, have ridden halfway up her wrinkle-free forehead as she notices Lydia's sneakers. Her jet black hair is pulled into a ponytail so taut the skin at her temples is puckering. She is wearing a tailored charcoal waistcoat as tight as a corset, forcing her small breasts up, and her heels are even higher than the ones Lydia rejected. The red soles just visible beneath the long hems of Rachel's immaculately cut trousers that swish as she closes the gap between them with purposeful strides. There's a waft of something heady and expensive as Rachel leans down for a double air kiss, no physical contact made in the quick exchange. The second Mrs Bentley married her billionaire at the tender age of twenty-six. Nick Bentley is almost four decades his present wife's senior. It doesn't take a genius to work out the dynamic, but maybe that's unfair. And the gossip online is that Rachel stands to inherit not a penny unless they are married for another five years, the prenup she signed legendary. Perhaps she loves him with all her heart and the money is just a bonus. Who knows.

"Do you have a name of your own, Mrs. Wade Hunter?" Rachel asks, throwing a smile to Wade over her shoulder while Nick grins in a frankly annoying manner at his wife's snarky opener.

"Yes, of course, sorry, I'm Lydia," she replies.

Nick Bentley then moves in and kisses Lydia sloppily on one cheek. He has bad breath and his palms are rough as he pumps her hand, face like leather with pure white veneers that clack as he says in a thick New York accent, "Hey, Olivia. I'm Nick, pleased to meet you."

"*Lydia*," Rachel corrects him, frowning. "Your hearing is getting worse."

"It's the flight," he tells them, taking the comment with good humor and then jabbing a stubby finger into his right ear and waggling it. "Stiff drink usually sorts me out." He eyes the bar greedily and Wade takes the hint.

"What can I offer you folks, beer, champagne, cocktails?"

Folks? The role of host is an unnatural one to Wade, but he's taking on the part well.

A woman with fluffy blond hair is hovering at the threshold of the guest lounge now, eyes stretched in nervous alarm above the neck of the equally fluffy pink sweater that she shrinks her chin into. "Hello? Dr. Hunter?"

"You must be Zoe?" Lydia says as she approaches their third and most nervous guest. The scholarship place. "I'm Wade's wife, Lydia."

Zoe looks at Lydia's outstretched hand. "Yes, you are."

"Right," she replies, somewhat bemused by Zoe's response as she withdraws the proffered palm.

"You're not what I imagined," Zoe says, looking her up and down. "Shorter."

"Why would you—?"

"Zoe!" Wade says, joining them. "Everything okay with your room?"

"Yeah, very swanky," Zoe replies, looking directly at Wade and beaming, her expression entirely changed from the frown Lydia received. "Thought you might, you know, change your mind about me joining in."

"You are most welcome, Zoe," he says, glancing at Lydia. "Isn't she?"

"Yes, of course, we look forward to making you comfortable during your stay with us," she adds, echoing Wade's welcome.

"Exciting!" Zoe says, again to Wade.

"How was the journey from the UK, London, isn't it?" Lydia asks, hoping to establish some kind of a rapport. Wade has hinted at a great tragedy in her past, so allowances must be made for the damage trauma can inflict.

"Yeah, Stratford Way," Zoe says. "You know it?"

Lydia shakes her head. "Sorry, no, I . . . Is it nice there?"

"Not particularly. And sorry again that I held everyone up at the airport cos of my bloody case being searched, I'm such an idiot bringing all those meds." Zoe looks at Wade. "They thought I was a drugs' mule."

"I'm sure it wasn't your fault," Lydia assures Zoe who looks crestfallen as Wade heads back to the bar without further comment. Not even a smile.

"So, what can I get everyone to drink?" Wade asks, directing his question to the Bentleys who are waiting by the bar.

"Champagne for me," Rachel replies.

Wade nods and extracts an expensive bottle of vintage Veuve from the fridge behind the bar. The one that Rachel requested in her rider, claiming she's allergic to cheaper brands. He peels the foil and then twists the cork, which releases with a dull pop before he takes a stemmed glass from the shelf behind him and fills it to overflowing. He wipes the base with a napkin then hands it to Rachel with a flourish.

"You'll have some champagne too, Zoe?" Lydia suggests.

"God, no," Zoe replies loudly. "I daren't drink, not on top of my meds. That would *not* be a good idea. Just a diet Coke, please, Dr. Hunter, if you have one?"

"Wade, honey?" Lydia prompts as her husband scowls across the bar at Zoe. "Diet Cokes are in the fridge."

Wade nods and crouches down to look. The repeated comments about her medication are inappropriate of Zoe, but the meds themselves are not a surprise. Zoe declared a cocktail of antidepressants and mood levelers for her "nerves" to Wade, which he'd assured Lydia present no contraindications to the memory flights. Zoe will be also be under Wade's trained medical care and monitored constantly, as are all their guests, both before and after this week. You can't take any chances with people's mental health.

Wade grabs a can of diet Coke and hands it to Zoe, thumping his forehead as if he's an idiot for not asking her himself what she'd like to drink, and making Zoe laugh. Rachel touches the fluffy pink shoulder of Zoe's sweater, telling her she loves it, which feels disingenuous given the contrast to Rachel's designer look, but their chatter relieves Lydia of any further hosting obligations for now, especially as Nick is bonding with Wade over shared beers.

Then their final guest arrives.

The tall and handsome California entrepreneur, Jack Myrtle, cuts a striking figure at the door, although Lydia seems to be the only one who has noticed him. At well over six foot with black closely shorn hair, dark brown eyes, and an easy smile, he holds her gaze before she drops hers to the floor and taps her finger to thumb to calm her nerves. The room feels crowded already, although there are only six of them in the generous space: Zoe and Rachel on the sofa now, while Wade is chatting to Nick at the bar. She should say something to welcome Jack, but she's too hot in her stupid shift dress and fussy blouse, pulling at the bow to try and loosen it. She slides her hand round to where her hair feels damp with sweat, rubbing the painful spot at the back of her neck that throbs.

"Jack!" Wade calls over, saving her yet again. "Come join us guys for a beer."

"Yeah, great," says Jack, walking toward the bar. "A beer would be good."

CHAPTER

9

Tash

THE SIGHT OF the familiar office building, thirty stories high, induces a wave of nostalgia as I approach. It's only been a matter of weeks since I was last here, but this building was home to Tash the globe-trotting investigative journalist who wrote long-form exposés on corruption for a tiny but mighty publication that I was proud to represent for fifteen fulfilling years. I felt purposeful inside this glass box reaching to the sky. I yearn for that again, even more so now I'm here.

The dozen shallow marble steps up to the entrance are the first obstacle. It's early, no one around to help with the pram, but hopefully Ro will already be at her desk. She cycles in each morning with her dog up front in a wicker basket. It's a thirty-minute pedal from the Chiswick semi she owns with her wife, Kitty. They bought it back when prices were, if not affordable, then more in reach. I cannot wait to see my boss, if not her feisty and stinky canine companion, Agatha, who always snarls at me despite the fact I am also Ro's oldest friend.

I bump the pram up behind me and then park it behind one of the low-slung leather sofas in reception and carry Nova toward the security officer. He looks as tired as I feel and frowns at Nova, now squirming in my arms, then he recognizes me and waves me through despite the lack of a security pass.

Nova settles again as we ride up in the elevator. I kiss her forehead, inhaling the sweet smell of her hair as her head lolls into my chest. Ro is not a baby person. In fact, she's not that keen on being interrupted at the best of times, let alone this early. At least there's no one else around as the doors open. I can't be bothered with colleagues' questions about the birth, and Nova is not looking her best, her sweet face plastered with baby eczema. Luckily everyone else rolls in midmorning, much as I used to.

I head past the banks of empty desks to tap on Ro's closed office door. She's never been a fan of hybrid working. The office is where work happens, not at home. She looks up through the glass door and mouths, "What the fuck, Tash?"

"Hello to you too," I say, stepping in. Ro's glass walled office smells of dog farts and cigarette smoke.

"What are you doing here?" Ro says getting up, cigarette in hand and ignoring Nova to settle the snarling pug back in her basket.

"Thought I'd catch up, remind you who I am."

"Yeah, right . . ." she says, blowing out smoke. "Sorry I haven't visited. You got the . . . ?" She waves her cigarette around. "I want to say flowers and a card?"

"Close enough," I reply, laughing at Ro's honesty. "Please thank your lovely wife for the care package and beautiful card."

Ro exhales and smiles, reminding me of a fire-breathing dragon. It's a nonsmoking building, but she's always been a maverick, and anyone who challenges her gets short shrift, including security. She's smashed multiple smoke detectors, either with a spiky heeled boot or an empty vodka bottle, depending on who you ask. I worry about Nova in the smoky atmosphere, but I came to talk to Ro and this is her turf, so I take the seat opposite her, the desk a mess of papers and old copies of the magazine, my name inside them all.

"Yeah, sorry I haven't been around to visit as yet," Ro replies. "But you know how it is here, always manic, and I'm not that into . . ." She looks at Nova for the first time.

"Yes, and obviously I'm keen to get back to work soon-as, in fact on that note . . ."

Something slips in Ro's smile, a worrying expression crossing her lined features. Agatha picks up on it too and growls louder in her basket, teeth bared. Ro shushes the dog. "It's Tash, Agatha, you remember her."

She offers me a cigarette and I shake my head. "I don't anymore, remember?"

Ro nods, and I bounce Nova on my lap, hoping she will be a good girl. Ro isn't tolerant of babies, but she was surprisingly supportive of my decision to go ahead and have this one. A deep well of shame rises up at how poorly I'm doing, tears threatening. I don't want to cry in front of Ro. I never have, except for that one time when she'd found me weeping in the office bathroom and marched me round the corner to our regular drinking spot. I'd thought she was going to fire me. I hadn't been on my best form for weeks, and the tears would be, I assumed, the last straw, but Ro had instead offered a bony shoulder to cry on. Perceptive as ever, she'd guessed what was going on even though I'd tried so very hard not to let the fact I was pregnant affect my performance.

"Course I bloody knew," Ro had told me, grabbing my untouched glass of Pinot that she'd ordered, as confirmation, and downing it. "You've been a zombie for weeks. And that story about stomach flu . . . Hardly the most convincing excuse for throwing up every morning. And no one is on antibiotics and off the booze for that many weeks."

"Oh God, does everyone know?"

"I'd imagine so," she'd told me, picking up her vodka-lime-soda. "So what happened? And please tell me it at least involved a handsome stranger and a night of wild sex, not a bloody turkey baster and a sperm donor?"

"What?" I'd asked, confused by her sly smile. "No, of course not, this was not planned."

"Good. So I'm assuming from the permanent smile on your face after your last assignment it happened then?"

I'd wiped my nose and nodded.

"Makes sense, you know that powerful orgasms pull in sperm?" she'd explained, undeterred by the barman's interest in our conversation, or his warning that dogs were not allowed in the bar, let alone on it. It was an ongoing argument he would never win.

"And how exactly would you know about sperm?" I'd asked, laughing through my sodden tissue.

"Not exactly my area of expertise, I'll admit, but I never thought you'd let one slip through, not in a million years."

I had no answer for that, other than a shrug and more tears. But she was right, the orgasms had been multiple. But why the carelessness about using a condom? That was harder to explain. Sheer drunken stupidity didn't really cover it. He'd offered, but I'd lied, told him I wasn't able to have kids, so as long as he was happy, so was I. What was I thinking, beyond the immediate sensation of him inside me, skin to skin? Was that all it was? A moment of recklessness in the name of risky pleasure. Or did I, even then . . . want this to happen?

"So," Ro asks me now. "Let me see it properly."

"Nova," I prompt, turning my daughter round so Ro can see her gorgeous if blotchy face. Agatha looks over too. Neither of them appear impressed. I've sent Ro multiple photos and even asked her to be godmother, to which she'd replied one word, *Srsly?!*

"But you know who the father is?" Ro asks now. "I mean, no doubts?"

"Yes, of course I do. I'm not . . ." I shake my head, undecided how to finish that sentence. "I hadn't slept with anyone in a while, and no one since."

"You've told him?" Ro asks, taking off her leather jacket and chucking it on the floor as she comes round, leaning over Nova and holding her cigarette away.

"Yes, I have, but we've agreed he's not going to be involved."

"Bullshit," Ro says, eyes wide through her thick glasses as she straightens up. "Don't lie to me, Tash. I know you far too well."

"He basically *was* a sperm donor," I say, hoisting Nova onto my shoulder which unfortunately means the audible sound of her then filling her nappy is amplified in the small office.

"Married?" Ro asks, lighting another cigarette from the first one, disgust written all over her face as she covers her nose and sits back down. In fairness the smell emanating from Nova's sleepsuit is revolting. Even Agatha can't best that.

"No, nothing like that. But he lives on the other side of the world and he's a confirmed bachelor, as far as I know, and you know, she's here now and he has no idea, so . . ."

"He still has a right to know."

"I can manage perfectly well on my own."

"I'm not big on the rights of men, but in this case . . ." Ro replies, exhaling. "He is the father. And I also think it might be good to get some support. Frankly, Tash, you look like shit."

"Thanks," I tell her, raking my fingers through matted hair I'd neglected to brush in my haste to get us out the apartment. "You wanna try it?"

I hold Nova up and Ro shakes her head, then she looks at Nova properly, regarding her as if she is an alien being. Nova stares back, eyes unfocused. I get up and open the door wider to let in some fresh air, collecting leakage in my cupped hand under Nova's bottom. I am on borrowed time before the nappy situation is untenable.

"How's your mum?" Ro asks.

"The same, or worse, and talking of which, I need to run something by you, if that's okay?"

"Anything except for child care." Ro's eyes narrow as I attempt a grin. She's the only person, sadly, I could contemplate leaving Nova with. Well, Kitty too, but they come as a pair and it would be Ro's call. "Sorry, Tash, but we both know I'd drop her on her head within minutes."

I laugh. "Yeah, you would."

"I could sub you for a child minder, if you need a break."

"No, I can afford one, it's just . . . I'm sorry, I shouldn't have asked you for that. You're my boss, it's just the thought of leaving her is so . . ." The tears I've held on to begin to flow, hot and shameful. I can't cope on my own, Ro is right, but neither can I imagine leaving Nova with a paid sitter, not with all the stories about neglect and infant deaths in the news that I torture myself with. It seems to be happening everywhere, although likely I'm hyperaware of it, now I'm the one making those kind of impossible choices, and on my own.

"What can I do to help?" Ro asks. "Other than that." She gestures at Nova with her lit cigarette.

"I need your advice, actually. It's about the story you gave me."

"What story?" she replies, distracted then by the ping of an email. A reminder of those days when all I had to think about was my next coffee and email. What bliss.

"The Memory Foundation. Patient A."

Ro's head snaps up from her keyboard. "That nut job?"

"Not necessarily."

"Come on, Tash, that was clearly the work of an attention seeker. Plus there's nothing on the website that substantiates—"

"So why pass on the lead?" I ask, my jaw clenching. "I've been obsessed with it."

She raises her hands in surrender, cigarette in one, pen in the other. "You looked a bit . . . lost, I suppose. And that was weeks ago, Tash. You haven't mentioned it since."

"Right, well, no, we haven't exactly been that in touch, have we?"

Ro squashes the cigarette butt into the overflowing ashtray. "Sorry, there's been a lot going on here."

"Such as?"

"Nothing," she replies, worrying me.

"Okay, so let me pick up some slack for you," I suggest. "I can do a few hours from home at first and still work on this story." Ro has taken a deep breath, brow creased. "What is it? What's wrong?"

Ro places her palms down on the desk and clouds of ash and dust rise up in the early sunlight as she stands up. "Tash, sweetheart, I'm so sorry, but you can't come back right now, and I definitely cannot pay hours on that story, let alone expenses."

"What are you saying, that I'm out of a job?"

She sits back down, Agatha leaping with impressive athleticism onto her angular knees. Ro's always been thin, but she's lost even more weight. "Maybe you could try for some freelance work, or copyediting?"

"Ro, what's going on? Are you sick again?" Ro had a scare, few years back, but she'd seen that off and come back even stronger.

"God no, strong as an ox," she says, waving away my concern. "It's just you know, this place . . . Having to make a few cutbacks, but I can put out the word. Something that will suit your circumstances better. Regular stuff, women's magazines are still a reliable—don't look at me like that. It's good honest work. Well, good pay. Maybe."

I look at Nova, squirming in her stinky nappy, poor lamb. She'll get sore if I don't change her soon. "I have a contract, Ro. Maternity pay, period of notice."

"Which of course I'll honor."

"I can't believe you're doing this," I say, not sure if I mean her giving up on the story or giving up on me, maybe both. This isn't the Ro who told me I have the best instincts of any of her staffers. I came here to bolster my crumbling ego and get her support as I edge nearer to the prospect of a meeting with Dr. Hunter, but instead she's firing me by stealth, because I have a baby. I walk out, Nova's shit-filled nappy leaking all over my jacket now as I cradle her to me.

"Tash, wait, let me explain." Ro catches up with me by the elevators. "I am being a friend, or trying to. No one else knows but you."

"Knows what?"

"That the magazine is in trouble."

"It's always in trouble. Am I'm the only one getting fired?"

"I don't know . . ." she replies, reaching out.

"You don't believe in me now I'm a mother, do you? You think I've lost it. Chasing a crazy dream because I'm a crazy new mother."

"Don't put words in my mouth, Natasha Walker."

"But you don't believe in me, do you, or trust my judgment on this?"

"Why does this particular story matter so much?" Ro asks evenly, despite my rising hysteria.

"You really have to ask me that when you know how Mum is?"

Ro looks down, inhaling deeply. She was there when Mum started to forget things. Names at first, eventually mine. She saw the pain and worry I went through trying to get Mum into a decent nursing home. How the money ran out and I had to fight to get funding sorted. How it's stretched me to breaking point to see my mother, a woman who cared for others her whole life, reduced to a shell. How dare Ro question why this story is everything to me.

"I'm sorry, Tash, truly I am," Ro says, touching my arm. "Of course I understand why this matters to you so much, but it's not about you, there's other stuff—"

"I get it," I tell her, jabbing the button again. My tears have been replaced by anger, Agatha's yelps echoing my distress. "I thought we were friends, but clearly not."

"Tash, wait, you don't understand."

"What don't I understand?" I ask, rounding on her as I support Nova by her heavy nappy, which is leaking onto my dress now, a mustard stain across the printed cotton. The only semi-smart thing I could find to wear that accommodated my rock-hard boobs and was vaguely clean. "Tell me, what's really going on here?"

"Just that I have no idea what the next few months hold."

"How convenient that you would hide behind vague statements of doom when what's really happening is it's problematic to have me here now. You truly are a coldhearted bitch."

Ro looks shocked but takes a deep breath, then replies, "I know you don't mean that."

"Don't I?" The empty elevator arrives, doors opening and I go in.

Ro steps forward and sticks a high-heeled boot in the way of the closing doors. "You're super-talented, Tash, the best of all my reporters," she says, finding the words I came here for, finally. "But I've learnt the hard way that this kind of journalism is a lost art. No one has the time, money, or patience for the long game. Trust me on this. It'll work out for the best for you. You're a bloody good writer. Something will come up, but not this story. The old Tash would have known that."

"Fuck you!" I shout back as I kick her boot out the way and the doors close.

CHAPTER

10

Lydia

"YOU FEELING BETTER NOW?" Wade asks Jack from the other side of the bar, opening him a beer.

"Better?" Jack asks, taking the squat bottle.

"You were quiet in the car, mate. Travel sickness, or something else on your mind?"

"Oh yeah, much better now that white-knuckle drive is over, thanks," Jack says, turning to smile at Lydia standing behind him. "That is quite the journey to get up here."

She takes the barstool next but one to Jack. Nick, seated at the other end of the bar, looks down the counter at them both, his deep-set eyes meeting hers before he gets up and joins his wife and Zoe on the sofa.

"That was nothing," Wade tells Jack, laughing. "You should see it in the depths of winter."

"I'll pass on that," Jack replies, taking a mouthful of beer. "How do you find that drive?" he asks, turning to Lydia.

"Me?" she asks, shaking her head.

"My wife is a better passenger than driver," Wade replies on her behalf. "Isn't that right, sweetheart?"

She smiles, grateful for Wade's timely intervention. "Can I have a drink too, Wade?"

"Of course, darling," he replies, squeezing her hand across the bar. "A glass of bubbly?"

"Yes, just a small one," she tells him, mindful of the many courses she has to reheat and serve. It's simple enough, but there are wine pairings too. Although drinks are Wade's responsibility.

"You're not much of a drinker?" Jack asks as she takes the half glass of champagne from Wade. "Me either. This is about my limit," Jack explains, raising his beer.

"Not really a good idea for me," she explains. "I suffer with migraines, since the accident." As soon as the words are out, she regrets them. Her headaches are connected to the brain injury that also wiped her memory. Not a subject she wishes to discuss so soon or at all. "I mean, only occasionally, but—"

"Indeed they are," Wade adds. "Only occasional but enough to be careful. Doctor's orders, right, Lidds? My wife's well-being is, of course, very precious to me."

Jack frowns. "Yes, of course."

Wade takes the bottle of champagne to the guests on the sofa where he refills Rachel's glass, then he offers round the slates of canapés. Lydia should have done that herself, but she's pinned to the barstool, still flustered. Rachel refuses the food, while Nick and Zoe help themselves to a napkin and pile them with one of each type of canapé.

"Save room for dinner," Rachel tells her husband.

Nick nods, stuffing in two. "A juicy steak I hope," he replies, mouth full. "I'm joking, Rach." Then he informs the room, "I have high cholesterol, need to look after my heart." He taps his chest. "Which my wife is always happy to remind me of." Nick laughs, while Rachel does not. "I think we can all tell I got the better end of the deal," he says, reaching for Rachel's free hand, which she pulls back. "She keeps me young."

"Well, I can assure you the catering is going to be magnificent," Wade says, looking directly at Lydia, then to Nick as he adds, "But the food isn't why you're here, is it?"

Nick laughs loudly and taps the side of his large nose. "No, it sure ain't."

Rachel looks at her husband. "What exactly *are* we here for?"

Nick laughs again, but Rachel's comment is a worry. Surely, she knows exactly why she's here. Lydia tries to catch Wade's eye, but he's busy serving more drinks. He picks up Nick's empty beer bottle and lobs it into the bin behind the bar. The glass bottle clatters noisily to the bottom—a slam dunk—making Lydia jump. She swallows the bad taste left in her mouth and puts her glass down. A full program of memory flights, one per guest per day, takes a lot of prep. The guests have all had to provide Wade with as much information as possible of their chosen memory. Rachel's question must therefore be about the specifics of the flights, how they work, which Wade has kept very much under wraps, rather than the purpose of her stay.

"Another beer for you, Jack?" Wade offers, but Jack says he's good, thanks. "Anyone else need another drink?" Wade looks over to Zoe, nursing the can of diet Coke that she apologized asking for and has barely touched. Poor Zoe, must be tough being the only freebie.

Lydia looks beyond the guests to the vast empty sky, now a deep navy. The stars will soon appear, a dusting of diamonds so startlingly beautiful they would be an impressive diversion for the guests, and something positive she could add to the conversation, except the snow will likely obliterate that light show for tonight. Hopefully tomorrow night will be clearer, although the thought of yet another evening spent together, then more after that, is overwhelming.

"If there's anything's left in that bottle I'll take a top-up," Rachel says, holding her glass up again. Wade does the honors, emptying the bottle of expensive champagne into her glass, but he looks fed up as Lydia catches his eye. They need to ration the booze, the supply is limited, plus at altitude alcohol passes into the bloodstream faster. If it were just the two of them she'd ask Wade to explain the science of that again. He never minds. However many times she forgets something. That's part of being in love, he always says. In sickness and in health. For richer or poorer. 'Til death us do part.

She pretends to sip the flattening bubbles in her glass, allowing them to touch her lips without taking too much onto her tongue as she chances a look at Jack's left hand, resting on the bar. There's no wedding band, but not everyone wears one. Nick Bentley does, and Rachel does too, a diamond-encrusted monstrosity beside an enormous canary yellow solitaire. She and Wade have no such tokens. They said their vows under a canopy of snow-covered pines in the small patch of forest just beyond the gates. It was an icy day four years ago and no one was there to see it, no rings, no flowers, no champagne, no anniversary they observe, but it meant everything; still does. Just the two of them. Married in all but the legal sense, and every sense that matters.

"I'll take another diet Coke now," Zoe says, holding up the empty can and stifling a burp.

Wade bows. "Of course. I am here to serve your every desire." Zoe blushes, then laughs. "Nick, you ready for something stronger?" Wade asks.

Nick cups his ear, and Rachel frowns deeply, although her forehead remains smooth as she looks up from her seat on the sofa between Zoe and Nick.

"Maybe something stronger would be good?" Nick replies, looking hopefully at the decanters of spirits on the bar. "You got a decent bourbon in one of those?"

"Have to say, I'm lost without my phone," Rachel tells Zoe, her back now turned to Nick. "I'd usually be posting every five minutes for my followers."

"I'm not one for Insta, but I like Facebook," Zoe replies. "You got many followers?"

Rachel shrugs. "Almost a million. When do we get our devices back, Wade?"

"As I explained at the airport," Wade says, pouring Nick a large slug of whiskey. "We need to ensure no trade secrets escape with a careless photo or thoughtless text. You'll get everything when you leave, okay?"

"Can I have my phone if I promise not to post anything?" Rachel asks.

"Absolutely not," Wade says, handing Nick his drink as he joins them at the bar. "Another beer, Jack?"

Jack looks up. He'd been tearing the label from the empty bottle, a pile of paper curls in front of him. "Um, no, thanks, but maybe some water, please?"

Lydia leaves her stool and grabs the jug from the other end of bar, then pours Jack a long glass.

"It comes straight off the mountain," Wade explains. "My wife's first job of the day. She goes to a mountain stream close by, don't you, Lidds?"

"You carry the drinking water supply up here on your own?" Jack's expression is filled with concern as he takes the filled glass. "Thanks."

"There's running water, of course," Wade replies. "But we love the fresh mountain water and we thought our guests would too."

Lydia nods, pouring a glass for herself and gulping it down.

"But that must weigh a ton?" Jack asks.

"Lidds is a warrior woman," Wade says, laughing. "She's out there at the crack of dawn, in all weathers and usually half naked."

"*Wade!*" She shoots her husband a warning look as she notes Nick's sudden interest. He heard that, all right. She wipes her mouth. "I am not half naked."

"Snow boots and a coat but not much underneath," Wade adds, still laughing. "Sorry, I am of course exaggerating," he says, relenting finally. "Although when it's just the two of us we don't worry too much about clothes, do we? No one around for miles to spy on us."

"Exactly how many miles to civilization?" Rachel asks.

"About ten miles to the nearest village," Zoe pipes up. "You saw it on the drive here."

"Those wooden huts we passed?" Rachel asks, and Zoe nods. "That wasn't a village! We didn't see another living soul. There must be somewhere closer, the other side of the mountain?"

"Shame about the coat," Nick says, laughing in the throaty way he has as he swallows another mouthful of whisky. "I'd have enjoyed seeing that naked water run every morning."

Rachel ignores her husband and looks instead at Wade. "Ten miles to even basic humanity, is that right?"

"The Memory Foundation is indeed remote," Wade explains. "But it is also a truly magical place, and we want you to feel it's your home away from home for the week."

"We are not staying the week," Rachel replies, addressing her husband then. "You said two nights tops, Nick."

"The thing I'd love you to do, Rachel, is really embrace its uniqueness," Wade says, intervening in the Bentleys' brewing argument. "Relish the quiet and majesty. No distractions from phones or laptops, so you can be in the present when you are not in the past." He laughs at his own joke and pours himself a slug of whiskey, then clinks glasses with Nick, who leans heavily against the bar. Wade never touches spirits, says they lower his inhibitions, but he knocks the whole measure back.

"No problem for me, but my wife?" Nick quips. "She is *very* attached to her phone."

Rachel scowls. "I'm not, and you're a dinosaur." She smiles as if it were meant as a joke, but the delivery was deadpan and the smile is fleeting.

"I *am* a dinosaur," Nick concedes. "Which is why I need my youthful wife to remind me of that." He looks at Rachel. "We all need little reminders of what we mean to one another, don't we, babe?" His comment sounds heartfelt, but Rachel's expression is frosty. "Let's see how it goes,

Rach, you never know, you might actually enjoy yourself here."

Distracted by Rachel's murderous expression, Lydia only catches the end of Wade's exchanged look with Nick, something unspoken but conspiratorial traveling between the two men across the bar that speaks of a prior understanding. Or is she imagining Wade's subtle nod that she only caught in profile?

"So why set up the foundation here of all places?" Nick asks his drinking buddy as Wade pours them both another generous measure of whiskey from the emptying decanter. "In the middle of nowhere."

"I wanted to be well away from prying eyes."

"You're certainly that," Rachel responds, setting down her emptied glass on the side table by the sofa.

"I searched for a long while," Wade explains. "The building was a wreck when I stumbled on this place, but very solidly constructed." Wade is directing his comments more generally now as he paces the room. "It's withstood everything thrown at it over the last fifty-plus years and since Lidds' arrival has been transformed into a home filled with creature comforts and, most importantly, love."

"When was that?" Jack asks Lydia. "I mean, when did you arrive at the foundation?"

"Why so curious?" Wade asks.

"No reason," Jack says, looking genuinely perplexed by Wade's defensive response. "I'm just a naturally inquisitive person, sorry if that's been misinterpreted, but I love to hear people's stories."

"Ooh, me too," Zoe pipes up. "How *did* you two meet?"

"Lidds came here to help with my research," Wade replies, scowling at poor Zoe. "My wife is a talented scientist in her own right."

Lydia smiles, nodding along to the invented backstory, which he's embellishing. She's an assistant at best, the passer of tools and bringer of moral support.

"I'd been languishing on my own for far too long," Wade explains, still talking. "I was a skinny beardy mess, wasn't I, Lidds?"

The version of Wade she'd opened her eyes to after the avalanche was much as he's described, or at least, she thinks so. Mainly she recalls blood and snow and pain.

"I was a sad fuck until this one came into my life," he adds, joining her by her bar and kissing her cheek almost as clumsily as Nick did, his breath pure alcohol. "But now I am the luckiest guy alive and definitely not worthy of her frankly crazy choice to stay here."

"Must have been a tough decision to leave your whole life behind," Jack says, looking at her.

"I was drawn to the work the Memory Foundation was doing," Lydia says. "Then of course I couldn't leave." Wade leans toward her and they both smile, but she takes the chance to ease the glass from his hand and place it beside them on the bar.

"Ah," Zoe says, also smiling but looking less than convinced. "How lovely."

"Yes," Jack says. "That is a nice story."

"I reckon you got this place pretty darn cheap?" Nick asks, voice booming as he stands up straight, whiskey glass in hand, pontificating with it. "Considering it's up the top of a fucking mountain and miles from anywhere."

"For the square footage it was very reasonable," Wade replies as he grabs the decanter and tops up Nick's glass. "No one had lived here in decades and no one else wanted to buy it."

"On account of all those deaths," Zoe pipes up, silencing the room.

"What did you just say?" Rachel asks her companion on the sofa.

"I assumed you all knew?" Zoe responds, eyes wide as she looks up at Wade. "That's why they call this area Ghost Valley. Isn't it, Dr. Hunter?"

CHAPTER

11

Tash

THE LOCATION PATIENT A suggested for our meeting is way across town. I set out early, determined to shrug off a lingering malaise since my visit to my ex-boss this morning. Ro's messaged me a few times since, asking for a chance to explain, but what's the point? She's revealed her true colors, and now my only friend in the world is gone and also my job. At least the motion of the London bus and a second outing in one day sends Nova to sleep. My eyelids droop, but I'm too wired to sleep, and I can't risk missing my stop.

Patient A is waiting for me when I arrive at the small café in the Strand I suggested, but she's in an odd mood. Manic and talking nonsense as we sit at a cramped corner table, our knees touching despite my efforts to angle mine away. I'm so tired I tune out Patient A's rants about her mother, who sounds a complete harridan, the warmth of the café soporific. I nod my agreement with her observations, that I assume come through the filter of an acerbic elderly woman's unilaterally negative opinion of life, until Patient A notices my attention is wavering and asks, "Am I keeping you up, Tash? You don't seem quite yourself today."

"No, I'm okay, but we didn't come here to discuss the cost of living crisis, did we?"

"Nah, guess not." She looks at Nova. "How's it going, then, motherhood?"

"It's magical," I reply, immediately regretting the sarcastic overshare, but I don't have the headspace for circumspection or small talk. She's the only person I've spoken to in days other than the argument with Ro, and I don't have the energy for game playing. I came here to arrange an interview with Dr. Hunter, but if that's not on the sticky table, then I will give up on this nonstarter of a story and look for paid rather than speculative work. Although it will pain me to do so. I'd love to prove Ro wrong and break the story of the century. That would show her.

Patient A scratches her head through the bad red wig, which wobbles side to side. "So Dr. Hunter *is* amenable to a meeting, but you cannot take anyone with you."

"Oh, you mean Nova?" I say. She nods, and my heart flips over, as does my stomach. "That's great news, though, about the interview, I mean."

"Yeah, but I cannot emphasize enough that you are not to bring her." She points at Nova as if she were an unpinned hand grenade.

"No, I mean, I wouldn't, obviously," I reply, ignoring the fact that if I can't take Nova, I likely can't go at all. And there's Mum to think of too. But it would only be a short trip. A few days tops. That could work. "I passed all the foundation's checks then?"

"Yeah, must have." She looks behind her, then takes her phone out from her bag. "The suits will have organized that," she says, glancing up at me as if I should know. "They can do anything."

"And who are these suits, exactly?"

She shrugs. "Let's not question the process. You're in and that's all that matters."

"Do they work for Dr. Hunter?"

"Well, that's what he claims. Nasty, though, some of them. Threatening. Mum never liked them when they came to the house—"

"Hang on a sec, you're saying these suits threatened you and your mother in your home?"

She shrugs. "No, not threatened. But like I said before, there's a lot of money at stake. Government contracts up for grabs that could be worth billions to the first company to prove their technique works. Dr. Hunter thinks the bureaucrats are in his pocket as they were *sooo* keen at first, but I reckon it's the other way around now. You need to be careful. If they think you're endangering the program, or their precious reputations, who knows what they're capable of."

"Don't worry about me, I'm used to this kind of stuff, but you and your mother, that's out of order. Did you report this harassment to the police?"

"Why would I do that? They were offering me a place as a volunteer. I wanted to go."

"But your elderly mother, she would need protecting?"

"Yeah, like I'd want to protect her after what she did."

"Sorry, what?"

"God, Tash, you call yourself a reporter? The tragic circumstances of the fire that killed my fiancé."

"Oh gosh, I'm so sorry, that sounds awful. What happened?" I ask, scrabbling to keep up with the scattered conversation. "And how does that involve your mother?"

"Look, it's fine, I mean it's not, but you can't wallow in the past, can you? I mean, I did. For a while. Which has actually been massively helpful to Dr. Hunter in compiling my digital history. And that's how the suits found me, you know the algorithms, so in a way without them—"

"Which algorithms?" I ask as if I'd know one bit of code from another, and I'm still trying to fathom what she's talking about. Government officials recruiting volunteers for the foundation on the back of social media searches for trauma victims, is that what she's saying? And what about my interview with Dr. Hunter, when will we get to that.

"Mum called them ambulance chasers," Patient A explains.

I nod in a rare moment of solidarity with Patient A's mother. Targeting a grieving woman and her elderly mother definitely smacks of ambulance chasing. And I've being doing much the same as Patient A lately, hankering after a past that's gone.

"It's hard not to dwell on what might have been, though, isn't it?" Patient A says, as if she's read my mind, but she's talking to her empty teacup. Her eyes flick up. "We were going to get married, have babies, me and Steve." She looks at Nova. "It's been hard, processing the fact that's never going to happen. Then I was accepted into the testing program, and now I get to be with Steve every time I go to see Dr. Hunter." She sighs. "Only wish it could be all the time. But I try to remain positive and look to the future."

"I don't want to live in the past either," I tell her. "And I *really* want to write this story. These testing programs sound incredible."

"Right, so let's get things going," she says, grinning.

I hug Nova to me, my arm protectively around her as Patient A scans the small café. She's right, I do need to be careful, but of her more than anything. It's a short road to Crazy Town, with few road blocks to slow down a sleep-deprived new mum who should know better than to trust this woman in a bad wig with all my hopes and dreams. I spot a man in a suit a couple of tables over. He is just a businessman, having an espresso. Probably a father himself. He smiles at Nova and I smile back.

"Earth to Tash?" Patient A asks, waving a hand in front of me. "You still with me?"

It's a good question. "So what happens next?"

"I'll be in touch soon with the specifics. Let's stick to messages from now on, unless we absolutely *have* to meet up. But when Dr. Hunter says go, that's it. Believe me."

"Can you at least tell me the name of the closest airports so I can book the flights?"

"It's tiny. Can't remember the name, mainly consonants. I'll message you."

"Right, I see."

She rubs the back of her neck, the wig shifting around. "Look, I know I must sound flaky on the details, but I promise when you get there it will all make sense. The memory flights are the best drug in the entire world ever, you'll see."

"I don't want to volunteer, just want to see what's on offer."

"Sure," she says, turning on her heel, the wig flapping around as she leaves.

* * *

I push Nova home through the incoming rain, riding up to my apartment in the empty elevator. The people who live here relish peace and solitude. They come and go in their dry-cleaned clothes with carry-on cases and takeout for one, ready to catch up on lost sleep and banish jet lag. There is a strict no children or pets policy. I would have been the first to complain about a screaming baby.

When Nova finally sleeps, I open up my laptop and stab in the same old Google searches, wishing I had a direct line to Dr. Hunter, cutting out Patient A. The Memory Foundation website appears with another click and there he is, Wade Hunter, waiting for me in his snowy lair. I just need a bit more information how to find him. That and a minor miracle in terms of childcare.

CHAPTER

12

Lydia

"PEOPLE DIED HERE?" Rachel grabs Zoe's hand and pulls her closer to her on the sofa. "How many? When? What happened?"

"Um, lots of them, I think. Hence the name: Ghost Valley."

"Did you know about this, Nick?" Rachel asks, snapping her gaze up to her husband, who is handing his empty whiskey glass to Wade over the bar.

"No, of course not," Nick slurs. "Is this true, Wade?"

"Sorry, I thought you'd all know," Zoe says, voice soft, childlike.

"No, we did not," Rachel replies. "At least, I didn't."

Wade pours Nick's drink, then puts the half-empty decanter down, slowly. "Shall we all calm down so I can explain," he says, shooting Zoe a warning look.

Lydia shares her husband's annoyance at Zoe's comments, entirely misinformed, but Wade's obvious irritation, brows knotting, is not helping. Not that Zoe is picking up the signals.

"I was chatting to someone on the plane who spoke a little English," Zoe tells Rachel. "And they asked me why I was coming here, to what the locals call Ghost Valley, as they rarely see any tourists since the avalanches wiped out the entire—"

"*Avalanches*?" Rachel repeats, getting up to join her husband at the bar. "Call our pilot, Nick, ask him to turn back."

Nick shakes his head. "Not without my phone, I can't." He sticks his chin out at Wade. "You gonna explain what this is all about, or do I need to make arrangements to leave now with a full refund?" Nick's tone, although equally stern, lacks commitment and he's definitely slurring his words.

"Maybe I shouldn't have said anything," Zoe says, catching Wade's eye. "But I can't get that name out my head, *Ghost Valley*."

"Did you hear this? We're staying in a place named Ghost Valley?" Rachel asks Nick, shaking him by the arm as he slumps over his drink. "Are you serious? We need to leave."

"Sorry if I'm speaking out of turn, Dr. Hunter." Zoe grimaces. "It's just, I thought the other guests should know."

"And thank goodness you told us," Rachel says. "Because we *are* leaving!"

"You are not in any danger," Wade interjects, his response faltering at first until he clears his throat and adds, "The Memory Foundation is a fortress. This is the safest place to be."

"So we *are* in danger?" Rachel demands, raising a hand to the falling snow beyond the darkened windows. "You admit that much? Look at it out there."

"That's nothing," Wade tells her.

"Doesn't look like nothing to me," Rachel replies, walking over to the window. "What do you think, Jack?"

"It is pretty heavy," Jack says, standing up from the stool and joining her. "The forecast was for more snow too. I checked before we left."

"And yet you brought me here," Rachel replies turning round to look at Nick. "To a place called Ghost Valley that's prone to avalanches!"

"Okay, let's all calm down," Wade says, walking round the bar to stand in the center of the room. "What Zoe has failed to tell you is that these avalanches happened over thirty years ago, and we haven't seen another one in the whole time we've been here, have we, Lidds?"

"Um, no," Lydia replies, startled into a quick and not entirely truthful answer. "There are small avalanches regularly," she adds, standing at her husband's side, their guests' attention now on them both. "But nothing on the scale of the ones that decimated the valley all those years ago, and nothing that will trouble us here."

Nothing like the one that almost killed her the day she arrived.

"The valley *was* like a ghost town as we drove through," Rachel observes, pointing down to the black void where the pinpricks of light from the few inhabited dwellings have now been obliterated by the whirling snow. "Even the store was shuttered."

"The store was closed as it was late, that's all," Wade tells her. "It opens for a few hours each day."

"Hundreds died," Zoe explains, plowing on as she joins Rachel and Jack at the window. "That's what this woman on the plane said, or at least I think she did, it was you know, lots of miming . . ." Zoe waves her arms around. "On account of the language barrier."

"Dear God," Rachel says, hand flying to her throat.

"Okay, that's enough," Wade says, tapping his phone so the motorized blinds slowly close and Rachel, then Zoe and Jack, are forced to turn round again and look at him. "There is honestly no need to panic. Even if . . . *Even if* . . ." he repeats as Rachel looks like she's about to walk out, which would be pointless without her phone to summon their private plane. "In the *extremely* unlikely event of another avalanche, which as I have said will not happen, there is zero risk to us within these walls. This building has been around longer than any of us." He glares at Zoe. "It is much safer than a return journey down the mountain in the dark, which I for one am not prepared to risk. Safety is always our primary concern at the foundation, so I would appreciate it if you'd stop spreading half-baked rumors, Zoe. I don't really understand what you hope to achieve?"

Zoe looks suitably chastised. "Sorry, must be the excitement getting to me."

"That's true about the dark," Nick says, piping up from beside the bar. "Be safer to leave in the morning, babe." He walks unsteadily toward his wife and clumsily places a square palm on her angular shoulder. "Nothing to be lost by staying the night, yeah? You might feel differently tomorrow."

"I very much doubt it," Rachel says, shrugging him off as she joins Zoe back on the sofa. Then under her breath. "Can't believe this was my husband's idea of a fun break. I am out of here first thing."

"Great." Wade smiles, as if it were all resolved. "And to be clear the road is *always* passable in the Tank, but only in daylight."

Lydia looks at Wade and smiles, nodding her agreement, although that's not strictly true either. There are weeks at a time when they are stranded here, but not because of avalanches. The main issue is heavy drifts on the steep road caused by prolonged snowfalls. But that's not the case now, or at least not yet. Although if the bad weather doesn't let up, they could be in trouble. And Jack's right, the forecast is for more snow. They've weathered much worse than this, of course, weeks living off tinned soup and jars of preserved fruit, but the catered food in their freezers is only enough for the week, no more, and with six of them eating their way through supplies they'd soon run out of store cupboard staples. She takes a deep calming breath, forcing aside the panic. It's a bit of snow, not the onset of winter.

"So you *could* still get us back down?" Rachel asks. "In the morning? You just said that, right? And you will?"

"Yes, of course," Wade responds. "But why make the long trip here and then leave before you've seen what's on offer? Especially as the snow will likely have cleared by morning or soon after. You have an incredible week ahead of you. If you still want to leave, then fine, but in daylight."

"Seems I have no choice in the matter," Rachel replies, folding her arms and shrugging off Nick's clumsy embrace.

"I tell you what," Wade says, smiling at Rachel, then Nick. "How about I take you two over to the lab now? I'm sure if you see for yourself what's in store, you'll feel much more excited."

"Great idea," Zoe says, getting up.

"Sorry, just the Bentleys for now," Wade replies, patting the air to get her to sit down again. "Lidds, okay to leave you for a few minutes while I show the Bentleys round the lab?"

It's not what they'd agreed, but Wade's tactic to show off the lab is a good one, although Rachel's claim she has little to no idea why she's here is still a worry. How on earth is Wade going to satisfy Rachel enough to convince her to stay if she's not been collaborative so far?

"Lidds? Okay to hold the fort?"

"Yes, of course, sorry," she replies. "But could I have a word first?"

"We won't be long," Wade tells her, headed to the door. "Just a quick guided tour of the lab, okay?"

Lydia nods, placing her trust in Wade as she always has. They need the Bentleys to stay, and knowing her husband he already has something in mind that will dazzle Mrs. Bentley as much as he dazzled her all those years ago when she took her first flight with no idea what to expect. He better had, or this week could be over before it's begun, and much as she would love to have the foundation and Wade to herself again, that would be a disaster.

CHAPTER

13

Tash

WE'VE ENTERED WHAT the matron at the care home has advised me are "the final stages of Mum's illness." The wait is agonizing, but I have no choice. And in among that confusion of guilt and impatience, I wait for further instructions from Patient A for a trip I cannot now take, and carry on my research for an interview I will surely have to forfeit. As if everything will be fine if I can get to Dr. Hunter and break the story of a cure. It's too late for Mum, but for others like her who might be affected in the future, I have to try. Me, for instance, and one day, God forbid, even Nova. Mum is often sedated when I visit and unresponsive but at least not in distress, which is something. I drag out my laptop and make notes as I sit a silent vigil beside her. Sometimes—well, a lot of the time—I feel quite mad, my obsession so deep I fall into it, and days pass and Mum is still here. Well, sort of. And so am I.

Predictably, Patient A hasn't been in touch as promised, but she was spot-on about one thing. Untold riches are at stake in the race for a reliable and proven memory retrieval technique. The applications would be countless and extremely profitable, from recreational "time travel" to a longed-for cure for dementia. And there have been glimmers of hope, if you look hard enough, which I have time for in between feeding Nova and gasps of fresh air in the pleasant garden of the care home.

Like the man in Texas who was part of a large pharma company's trials—a combination of drugs and immersive VR, as far as the limited "facts" of the article go—which sound similar to Dr. Hunter's program and ties in with the few details Patient A shared. Initial results were good, but the volunteers then experienced "false memories," which relatives claimed were deliberately planted. Bizarrely, these "ghost memories"—a sudden recollection that comes out of nowhere—occasionally belonged to a different gender, which must have been, as the reporter said and somewhat understating the case, "discombobulating." Especially as they were so convincing the patients believed in their authenticity.

In Canada, a new wonder technique—where volunteers were helped via therapy, hypnosis and augmented reality to "re-experience their trauma"—initially looked promising too. Flashbacks were reduced "significantly," and participants reported feeling "much more themselves," but further investigation showed worrying patterns of increased forgetfulness and the program was quietly disbanded. Rumors emerged post-trial of side effects, including PTSD, characterized by horrendous nightmares as well as depression with severe anxiety and even physical pain reported.

But it's not all been doom and gloom. In Australia, trials took place just last month where a patient suffering from dementia was fed "enhanced" memories through a program of VR-based "movies" created using artificial intelligence, mining the subject's archive of photos and online content. The procedure sounds remarkably similar to my rudimentary understanding of Dr. Hunter's data harvesting. The elderly woman involved was able to recall names and recognize faces of family members after years of blankness, but the results faded within hours, which must have been a cruel blow not only for the developer but also for the loved ones involved. A flicker of hope ignited and then immediately snuffed out.

I leave Mum and come home to sit at my kitchen table as the light fades and day slips into night, wondering if a proven process were available would I put Mum forward? She's far too frail now, but maybe a year or two ago? The lead scientist on the Australian project described brief moments of "bittersweet lucidness," but then the disappointment of a return to a catatonic state within hours. It must have been unbearable for loved ones to have that glimpse of the person, only to lose them again. I'd do anything to have another meaningful conversation with Mum, but what would be the point if it was only transitory? Would it still be worth it to share some of what life has thrown at me. "I got pregnant, Mum. I'm a single parent, like you were with me, and it's hard, but I love Nova, and so would you."

It's tough to know what I'd do, given the choice, but if the Memory Foundation is offering something more permanent then I'm determined to see it firsthand and report it widely. Dr. Hunter is right to want to get the word out, and right to choose me. I *am* the woman for the job, but aside from the practicalities of my situation, Patient A is ghosting me again. It's like being in a toxic relationship. I'm constantly checking my phone and refreshing emails.

I grab my laptop and sit on the uncomfortable sofa I inherited with the rental and search for something that if I'd been less sleep-deprived and worried sick about Mum, I'd have done straightaway. I type in everything I can think of to narrow the search, but nothing fits neatly enough to match Patient A's story of her fiancé, Steve, who she claimed died tragically in a fire. And even if I find that it is true, what does that prove? I scroll through the names and faces of the seventy-two tragic victims of the Grenfell Tower fire in London, but it's a sad and pointless task. I have no idea what happened to Steve or even if he existed other than in Patient A's imagination.

I change tack and return to a map I've saved on my phone. The pins I've dropped in the vast expanse of the Alps look like the random guesses they are, although I've spent hours scrolling thousands of acres of snow and ice to drop these markers in the icing sugar wilderness. All I know from Wade's welcome video on the website is the Memory Foundation is located somewhere high up in the mountains, and that Patient A said it's roughly two hours from the nearest airport, which is tiny, and up a steep twisting road that leads to a former cable car station. It's amazing how many abandoned cable car stations there are. But then I find it. Or something that could possibly be it. The Memory Foundation's headquarters.

The satellite image is grainy and old, but the building fits all the criteria. Abandoned, impressive, high up, and far from humanity. I bookmark the map ref and the nearest airport, the name perfectly easy to spell, pleased to find there are regular flights. Then I lie down on the too-short sofa with an agitated Nova on top of me. I'm living on borrowed time. One more noise complaint and I'll be asked to leave the building, which I plan to do anyway. I need somewhere my daughter and I can breathe. A place to call home beyond this polluted city. There's nothing left for me here now. No job, no friends, no reason to pay the crazy rent. Nothing but this story.

* * *

I wake at five for the next feed and as Nova suckles I make a decision. My sudden purposefulness propelling me and my startled daughter out into the pouring rain of a gray London morning an hour later. I'm not usually prone to making threats, but in this case, needs must.

CHAPTER

14

Lydia

WADE LEADS THE Bentleys out of the lounge and across the hallway, toward the heavy steel door on the other side. Lydia follows, Jack and Zoe close behind. Wade taps his phone and the door unseals with a soft sucking sound as the vacuum is broken and cold air whooshes in.

"You are joking?" Rachel asks, looking out and then back at Wade. "There's no way I'm going over on that, it looks like a death trap!"

Like a speeding bullet train through the snowstorm, the suspended walkway is an impressive piece of engineering magic. Held taut by steel wires far above the glistening valley it's a manmade suspension bridge that spans the gap between the main building and the lab. A distance of roughly two hundred feet. But it's also a wind tunnel with leaking windows and a cracked roof, and the only way to get to the glass-domed lab glowing dimly on the other side of the fathoms-deep ravine. Having said all that, and much as Wade described the rest of the building to the group, the walkway was built to last, despite appearances.

Wade holds out his hand to Rachel and offers a winning smile, guiding her toward the open door. "You'll be perfectly fine with me."

Rachel stops at the precipice, an icy draft blowing in as she grips Wade's outstretched hand. Nick nudges her from behind and Rachel screams. She is literally digging her heels into the parquet, leaving nasty little scuffs behind.

"Come on, babe," Nick says, pushing his wife this time, or trying to. "Let's get going."

But Rachel is not about to budge, her tall thin frame completely stiff from her high ponytail and tense neck right down to her flexed heels, clamped hands holding on to either side of the door frame as Wade goes out onto the swaying bridge and tries to persuade her to join him. The walkway is surrounded by a swirling maelstrom of snow, visible through the windows that punctuate either side, strong gusts buffeting the bridge and forcing Wade to plant his feet firmly and bend at the knees.

"I promise, this bridge will outlive us all," he calls back. "It's been here longer than any of us."

"I don't care, I'm not going," she says, palms raised as she sidesteps Nick's clumsy efforts to push her forcibly from behind.

Manhandling her is never going to work. The woman is terrified, and Lydia understands that feeling. She was, and to some extent still is, just as intimidated by the crossing as Rachel. It's exactly a hundred of her paces, she counts them every time, and the only way to experience the memory flights, but no one is going anywhere like this. Least of all Rachel.

"I know it is a bit daunting," Lydia says, easing herself into position beside Nick and behind Rachel. "I found it scary at first, but I promise it's more than worth it to see what's over there, and when you've done it once, it will be much easier next time."

"Why is it moving around so much?" Rachel asks, looking past Wade down the length of the covered metal bridge. It's listing to one side, then the other, as if a giant's hand were twisting the metal ropes tethering each end. "Is that usual? Or safe?"

"Yes, it is," Lydia replies as Rachel shrieks at yet another blast of cold air laced with flakes of ice that have detached from the frozen windows. "It's designed to move with the weather. In harmony. I know it looks rickety, but the structure is more than sound."

"No way, sorry," Rachel steps back, a spiked heel digging into Nick's loafer so he curses loudly.

"Okay, how about if you and I do it together?" Lydia says, catching Rachel's hand. "Prove these guys wrong about us girls."

Rachel's resolve weakens, her expression betraying her. It looks like she is about to step out, right foot raised, then she backs up, pulling away from Lydia's grasp. "Sorry, there's no way."

"We can take it a step at a time," Lydia explains, beckoning to her to follow as she steps on the moving bridge. "Totally at your pace. You'll regret not trying, I can tell that about you."

Rachel looks at her and nods. "That is true. I've tried most things, at least once."

"Okay," Lydia says. "So let's try this. You can hold my hand, okay? And if you want to turn back, so be it. But at least try, yes?"

Rachel takes a first tentative step onto the walkway after Lydia, grabbing for her outstretched hand, then she screams as the bridge lurches, but they keep going. Wade steps aside, allowing them through, and then Nick follows and encourages his wife from the back. Lydia glances over her shoulder as Wade slips behind Nick to bring up the rear, or so she thinks. Instead he doubles back and pushing Zoe away, he then slams the door on her and Jack. It's not ideal, abandoning two of their guests like this, but for now the mission is to get Rachel over to the lab and convince her to stay. The Bentleys represent two-thirds of the week's income. Without them they won't even cover their costs. Wade was right to suggest this. She can see that now. Lydia rubs at the back of her neck, hot despite the chill wind in the walkway and continues on, dragging Rachel with her.

"That's perfect, keep your knees soft, Rachel," Lydia tells her, trying to ignore the pain in her squeezed hand as Rachel's long nails dig in. "Another step? Great. Keep going. It will move around, but it's meant to, engineered to tolerate the extremes of weather up here. I'll get behind you now, more room, but I won't let go, I promise."

On cue, scoops of snow from the mountain are picked up by the wind and thrown against the oblong windows that line either side of the covered passage. Rachel ducks and screams, turning to go back, but Lydia manages to keep her going, albeit slowly, her hands on Rachel's narrow waist now, guiding her from behind, which feels intimate but is definitely working.

"It's okay, babe, I'm here, right behind you," Nick calls out. "Same way we build skyscrapers," he observes to Wade. "To withstand movement in earthquakes," Nick adds, ignoring his wife's shrieks as the walkway swings sharply toward the valley, tugged by another strong gust. "I used to walk the girders fifty floors up back in the day, before health and safety went mad," he says as the wind drops and there's a lull. "Those were the days."

Rachel leads the way, albeit reluctantly staring ahead, Lydia's hands still resting on the waistband of her tailored trousers but more lightly now. Progress is painfully slow and Lydia shares Rachel's concerns about the bridge, despite her show of bravado. It's been a long while since she crossed in such bad conditions, and the bridge feels different, although she can't put her finger on why.

"Keep going, you're doing great," she reassures Rachel, as Nick goes into unhelpful detail about motion dampeners and mesh construction and the compromise between the recommended seismic tolerances and the creative visions of his architects until Lydia almost wishes the wind would pick up again and drown him out.

The calmer conditions settle Rachel a bit, the stiffness in her raised shoulders slackening off until Lydia senses she can drop both her hands and Rachel will keep walking unaided and at a semi-decent pace. They are almost at the halfway point now, the longest drop into the ravine beneath them and snow still falling. It's then that Lydia notices what it is about the crossing that feels unfamiliar. They are walking downhill, just a little, the bridge hanging lower at the center, the four of them now headed toward a worrying dip. It's never done that before, not to her recollection. And she has no idea why.

"It's creaking really loudly," Rachel observes, eyes ahead as the bridge groans. "You sure that's normal?"

"It is honestly fine." Lydia chances a quick look back and catches Wade's eye as he brings up the rear. He nods encouragingly, but that noise is also unfamiliar. Nick is looking invigorated by the crossing, cheeks ruddy as he follows the women's lead to the bottom of the slight slope, then Rachel's foot slips and she slides the next few feet, screaming.

"You okay, babe?" Nick calls ahead, jostling Lydia to push past. He reaches Rachel and helps her up.

"No, Nick, I am not, and none of this is fun."

Nick presses flattened palms into his wife's back. "Keep going, babe, almost there, then the fun begins. Best pick up the pace, though. Bloody freezing."

"I'll do this at my own speed or not at all," Rachel replies, shaking him off, but she does start walking again.

They have now traversed the deepest part of the ravine, the dip behind them, the end drawing closer, although still a way to go. They are on the incline now, the locked door at the other end in sight, although eddies of snow continue to plaster themselves over the regularly spaced windows on either side, making Rachel gasp every time a thud of snow lands. It must be compacted on the roof, which maybe explains the way the heavy bridge is dipping, although that's never been the case in the past, even in the depths of winter. It is always taut and level. At least, as far as Lydia remembers, which is always the caveat as she can never fully trust her recall.

"You're doing great, babe," Nick says, but then Rachel stops and he barrels into her.

Lydia is forced to stop too, Wade right behind her. This is not a good idea. You have to keep your focus on the door at the end, the pace even but relentless. If you stop, look around, you can be drawn to look down.

Rachel and Nick are walking again, but Lydia has made that mistake and glanced out the nearest window. Just a peek, down into the vastness below, which now bounces up to meet her, then swoops to where the snowy base of the valley calls to her hundreds of feet below, weakening her grip on reality. She should have kept her eyes on the door to the lab, as she always does, but those tiny twinkling lights from the few inhabited houses in the valley, pinpricks in the dark ravine as the snow swirls, had tempted her. Then it was too late. She was out there, on that road. The avalanche coming for her. No time to escape, at least, not with her passenger.

"Lidds, listen to me," Wade says, arms tight around her now. "You're safe, honey. You just need to look at me."

"What's wrong with her?" Rachel asks, her voice distant as she calls back.

"Is she sick?" Nick shouts over the gathering wind.

"She's having a panic attack," Rachel explains, turning round and pushing past Nick. "Anyone can see that."

Lydia closes her eyes as her knees give way. "I'm sorry, I can't . . . I just need to . . ."

"Lydia?" Rachel is crouching beside her now, so close she can smell the expensive perfume on her. "Can you get up? I can help you. We are almost there. Just a few steps. What happened?"

She opens her eyes. "I'm sorry, I looked down, just for a second and . . . Stupid of me."

"Take my hand," Rachel says, their roles reversed. "Come on, I'm fine now."

The floor bucks beneath them as snow and wind batter the nearest window, but somehow Lydia manages, with Wade's help too, to stand up.

"What the heck was that?" Nick asks, staring at the three of them from a few paces along the bridge. "I thought you were a safe pair of hands for Rach, not the other way around."

"Sorry, I—"

"Apologies," Wade says, interrupting. "Touch of vertigo, that's all. Let's get to the end now, shall we? Keep those eyes ahead!"

Rachel looks at Lydia with obvious concern, then follows Nick, who strides ahead.

"What happened, Lidds?" Wade asks, rubbing her cold hands in his as she shivers. None of them are wearing coats, and it is freezing out here. They need to keep moving, but she is still weak with fear.

"I saw it, Wade." She looks at Mount Dunkler, behind them now, the peak rising up behind the main building.

"Saw what?" he asks, looking past her to the Bentleys, who are thankfully forging ahead. "The avalanche again? You know it's a flashback. You're safe now."

She drops her voice to a whisper. "The grave, down in the valley, I know you said it's unobtrusive, just a pile of stones, but could someone have noticed them, or the wreck of the car?"

"No, of course not. I told you, they are well hidden. Can you keep going?" Wade asks, looking past her again to the other end of the bridge.

"Yes, I think so. Sorry."

"You don't have to apologize," he says, smiling at her. "Look! You got her over, Lidds."

The Bentleys are almost at the door to his lab. It's locked, so they'll have to wait, but Wade is right, she did that.

Lydia grins and starts to walk again, slowly at first, concentrating on the remaining steps to get to the door. The trouble is however hard she pushes away the intrusive thoughts that floored her, they won't completely budge. Visions of the avalanche the day she arrived, the makeshift grave somewhere in the valley below her, hidden from prying eyes, she hopes. The body, now just bones. The car, a mangled wreck. She gasps, and stumbles. Wade grabs her, holding her up by one arm until they join the Bentleys by the heavy locked door, both looking at her for an explanation she is unable to provide. At least, not truthfully.

"I'm fine," she says as Wade lets her go and she almost collapses again, leaning against him for support.

"You don't look it," Nick says.

"Honestly, just low blood sugar, that's all. Forgot to eat today and like Wade said, a touch of vertigo. Been a while since I was over here, I stupidly looked down when we stopped, should know better."

"Can we please get inside?" Nick asks, wrapping an arm around Rachel, who looks frozen in her inappropriate outfit, arms bare and a low-cut top all the protection she has from the subzero temperatures, which are dropping by the minute.

"Yes, of course," Wade replies. "Let's get inside and I can show you where the magic happens. This is the start of the real adventure."

CHAPTER

15

Tash

"I TOLD YOU I was dealing with it," Patient A says, throwing me a withering look from her end of the chilly park bench. "No need to threaten me with writing the story without an interview. That is not on. And I said no more face-to-face meetings, they are far too risky." She scans the park, as she has many times already.

"If your definition of 'dealing with it' means being ghosted, then frankly—"

"Frankly what?" Patient A asks.

"Look, I'm sorry, but you've given me very little evidence of your credibility and then you vanish for weeks despite saying the weather could turn at the foundation and then it will be next spring before I can go there. What am I supposed to think? I have enough shit going on in my life right now and frankly . . . Well, frankly I'm fed up of waiting for you to come through. It's been long enough now."

"The forecast is fine for weeks, no snow expected, and *frankly* . . ." She labors her point with a long pause. "I thought you'd be glad of the delay?" She looks at Nova, sleeping peacefully under her waffle blanket. "Gives you more time to you know . . . sort things out."

"I said I can leave her for a few days," I reply, although it's still bluster.

"There's one flight in and out a week."

"No, I looked up flights. They're every other day."

"Then you have the wrong airport," she tells me, folding her arms. "Because there aren't regular flights, they are weekly."

We regard one another. A standoff.

"Look, I'm sorry I forced you to come here," I say. "And of course I don't want to write this story without an interview with Dr. Hunter, but we don't seem to be making much progress with that, and that's frustrating in the extreme. I do have other things to do, other stories to write."

It's a lie, but it seems to have given her pause.

Patient A looks at Nova, then at me. "You do still want this, don't you?"

"Of course."

And I mean it. Nova isn't that reliable on the bottle and the prospect of employing a total stranger to mind her for several days, maybe even a week, is daunting, to say the least. But equally I cannot bear the idea of one day spotting this story with someone else's byline. It will juice the last drops of hope from me. I wish I could talk to Ro about it, she'd have an opinion and one I'd value, but I'm still too mad at her to pick up the phone or read her messages that are now becoming less frequent. I was hopeful when Patient A agreed to meet again, albeit grudgingly and only after my threats to go it alone, but I'm still not sure it's going to accomplish much.

She gives me one of her best if disconcerting grins. "Look, if the weather holds, which it looks like it should—and only if you can move fast—I'll see what I can do to pin down a firm date of travel."

"Really? That would be great."

She shrugs. "It depends on whether I can get hold of Dr. Hunter. He does disappear into his work for days at a—"

"But you'll try?"

"Course." She takes the lid off her coffee cup and downs the remaining froth. "I have to earn my keep like everyone at the foundation. No such thing as a free lunch, as Mum would say."

"Are you saying you were tasked with recruiting me in exchange for future visits there?"

She scratches the skin above her top lip that is just starting to line and feather. In a few short years the wrinkles will be much more pronounced, but for now they are only visible because she is so close to me. "Yeah, I guess that's roughly it. Not that I mind. I'd do anything for Dr. Hunter."

I check on the straps fastened beneath the waffle blanket. The buggy is a new thing, and much easier than the cumbersome pram, although Nova's less impressed and rarely sleeps for long before she wants to be held. She grizzles and grinds a fist into her open mouth. I take the opportunity to process what Patient A has said, that I have been targeted by her, not Wade Hunter. The doctor hadn't heard of me by reputation as I'd imagined, or taken to observing me through my laptop, both ridiculous assumptions on my part. The woman in the red wig is recruiting me, much as she was recruited herself. Another ambulance chaser.

"So, how did you come across me?" I ask, attempting an air of disinterest. "I'm not exactly high profile."

"Oh, that was my Steve," she says, beaming. "He worked at the care home where your mum is a resident."

"Wait, *what*? Your fiancé knew my mum?"

"Yeah, Steve used to talk about her a lot. Said she'd given him all your articles to read when she first moved there. She was so proud of you."

"She said that?" I ask, emotion welling. "My mother, you're sure?"

"Yeah, certain. That's how I thought of you when Dr. Hunter asked me if I knew of any journalists who might be—" She catches herself and looks up at me. "Available. He's pleased, though, thinks I've done well. You know, because of the dementia connection."

"So let me get this straight, you chose me because my mum has dementia?"

She considers this. "Yeah, in a roundabout way, I suppose I did."

"What was my mother's name?"

She shrugs. "Mrs. Walker?"

That's wrong. My mother was never married. When I don't respond, she tosses her empty coffee cup toward the bin across the path. She misses and gets up to retrieve it, slam-dunking it from a pace or two away before she comes back to stand in front of me. She could well be making this up for all I know, although Mum did talk about the night staff and how she'd chatted to one of them, a young man, about me. I just wish I'd paid more attention now, asked for his name.

"So the volunteer turns recruiter," I tell her, shielding my eyes from the bright sun as the clouds part. "Is that how it works?"

She shakes her head, looking confused.

"The ambulance chasers?"

"Oh yes, that's what Mum called the suits. Ambulance chasers."

"Exactly. And what does she have to say about all this?"

"Who?"

"Your mother. She seems to have an opinion on most things."

"Mum is dead," Patient A tells me before she strides off.

* * *

I catch up with her by a lake populated with scrapping seagulls and a pair of swans with three brown-feathered babies as large as their parents. Patient A is standing by the water, staring into space. She doesn't acknowledge me as I speak.

"I had no idea your mother was dead. You talk about her all the time, what she says and thinks. I just assumed . . ." She looks at me, just briefly, then walks to the nearest bench.

"Was your mother in the same care home as mine?" I ask, parking the buggy and careful to kick on the brake before I sit down. "Is that how you met your fiancé? Steve, wasn't it?"

She doesn't respond.

"You've always talked about your mother as if she were a presence in your life."

"She is," she says, still staring at the water. "Refused to go into a home, said it was my job to look after her. *Bitch*!"

A young mother is by the lake with a child and dog. She looks over, then pulls them both away, walking off fast despite their protests.

"Don't looked so shocked, Tash," Patient A says, calmer now. "She was a complete bitch, and yes, I hear her all the time. Her nasty little comments. The way she belittled me and Steve. She was the one who set the fire. The one Steve died in trying to save her."

"Oh my God, that's—"

"She warned me she would," she says, taking out a sodden tissue from her coat pocket. "Not so out of it she couldn't strike a match and turn on the gas, was she?" She blows her nose loudly.

"What happened, to make her . . . I mean, the fire . . ."

"Steve usually worked nights at the care home," she replies. "The day we visited the home he showed us round, and it was like he was meant to be there to meet me, cos he was covering an early shift. When Mum said there was no way she'd even give the place a try, he offered to pop in on her at home, give me a break. Busman's holiday, he always joked. He'd make her a sandwich, cup of tea, regular as clockwork, and never a word of thanks from Mum of course." She shrugs and glances over. "I was out the day of the fire. Steve had given me some money to buy a new coat. This one." She looks down at her raincoat. "A neighbor called the fire brigade when she saw smoke. She was watching for the blue lights arriving and saw Steve leg it past hers and then go straight inside our house. Never made it out again although he dragged Mum to the door. She died of smoke inhalation, and he was a charred mess by the time the paramedics got to him. They gave me the wedding rings they'd found in his pocket. No box, so I think that must have melted. I reckon he must have had them there to show Mum. He always saw the best in her. He'd have wanted her blessing."

"That's . . . awful. I'm so very sorry."

"Yeah, it is." She gets up. "I should go."

"Just before you do," I say, stopping her with a gentle squeeze to her arm. She looks at my hand and I withdraw it. "Can I show you something?"

She sits and I hand her my phone, the map page open, a red marker centered on screen. "This place looks a likely candidate, but there are a surprising number of abandoned cable car stations in the Alps, and you said I'd got the wrong airport, so—"

"That's not it," she replies, looking up from the phone.

"Oh? Any other ideas then?"

She looks around and then types a long and incomprehensible word in the search box of the map page. "Not the best at spelling, but I think that's close enough. Yes, there's the village shop down in the base of the valley." She holds up my phone. "They put the village name on the labels for the bread. It's the closest humanity, if you can call it that. Miles away, and deserted most of the time."

I'm impressed. It's the first concrete fact she's offered.

The map has shifted by at least thirty miles to a part of the valley I'd discounted as far too inaccessible. I expand the image with a thumb and forefinger to zoom in on a pixelated wooden structure. "Here?" I ask, holding up the image. "Are you sure that's the right place?"

She looks at the phone as I hold it between us, leaning so close I can smell her scent. It reminds me of my childhood, specifically the carpeted bathroom we shared; Mum's talc all over the tufted bath mat. Patient A scrolls with a stubby thumbnail and hands back a satellite image that is pure white until I spot a few small wooden structures in the sea of thick glossy snow, and then, more exciting, an ugly curved structure just visible at the top of a cluster of peaks.

"That's Mount Dunkler," she says, pointing out the highest peak. "Darker Mountain." She rubs the back of her neck. "That's where the avalanches start and that is the Memory Foundation's headquarters."

"Wow," I say transfixed. "Hang on, avalanches?"

"Oh, don't panic, the big ones were years ago. And don't share that location with anyone. It's top secret."

"No, of course not." I drop a pin on the screen, and then she asks for my phone again. I pass it over, afraid she's going to delete the marker, but she leaves it in place and expands the map.

"I'm always picked up at this airport with the other volunteers," she says, showing me a small runway, just one building and a car park beside it, at least another twenty miles from the dropped pin. "And then we're driven up the mountain by Dr. Hunter," she explains. "He's the only one who can safely navigate that road, even in summer, and no way in the snow, although hopefully you will still be lucky and miss the first fall if I can get to Dr. Hunter before—" She stops speaking and looks around, her gaze landing on

Nova who is awake but content to watch the ducks and gulls from her buggy. "You're not thinking of just going there, are you? I mean, driving yourself?"

"Would that be possible?" I ask, my heart thudding beneath my raincoat. "I mean, if time is of the essence before the bad weather arrives . . . And it seems to take an age to get communications going."

"Yeah, that's true, but seriously, I wouldn't recommend it."

"But if I did, just hypothetically, then I'm the idiot who drove up a mountain and either got turned away, or delivered on your mission to send a handpicked journalist there for the exclusive."

She looks at the buggy and Nova stares back, no trace of any smiles on either side. "Or the mother of a newborn who ended up skidding off the side of a mountain, never to see her baby again."

"How long is the drive from the airport?" I ask, ignoring her dramatics. I've trekked through deserts to meet billionaires, hiked forests for drug dealers, and climbed up some admittedly much smaller mountains, all willingly and in pursuit of a story. That's not the part that daunts me, though, because she's right, it's the thought of leaving Nova that pierces my heart.

She looks at the map again, her bitten nail tracing a line up from the valley floor as she follows the twisting road higher and higher into the mountains. "That's definitely it," she says, smiling to herself, then looking at me. "That's the road to the Memory Foundation. I'd know it anywhere. But, seriously, it's a bloody dangerous drive and I don't expect he would let you in, not unannounced. He's very careful about security. You'd have had a wasted journey, even if you—no, leave it with me and I'll see what I can do to get things arranged in time before the bad weather sets in. He will reply, just depends on if he's working or not, which he usually is."

"And if not?"

She grimaces. "Then it'll be next spring, earliest. Which is a real bummer, but you know, hopefully still okay."

"It is a bummer and, in my experience, as soon as one journalist is on the trail, others follow."

She shrugs. "Yeah, but what can you do?"

I trudge home, weary and mind buzzing. Keys dropped on the table, shoes kicked off, kettle on, before I spot the note on the mat. My heart sinks. Another complaint about Nova. This one hand delivered. The thin slip of paper must have been pushed under the door by an angry neighbor. But it's not that.

This is your first and your last warning, Tash. Is that clear? Leave this story well alone.

A Friend.

CHAPTER

16

Lydia

BRIGHT LIGHT FLOODS the laboratory, the relief of being on firm ground immense as Lydia is at last able to step across the threshold. The door closes on the wild weather, and they are all inside the quiet calm of Wade's lab. A place Lydia rarely visits these days—Wade has been far too busy preparing the guests' flights to run hers—but she has come to love with its view to the heavens through the glass-domed roof. Rachel clearly feels the same as she looks up and smiles.

"What the heck is that?" asks Nick, pointing at the elliptical structure the size of a small camper van that sits in the center of the long lab. A pale silver monolith with smooth lines.

"That, my friend," Wade replies with considerable hubris, "is the pod."

Rachel is still captivated by the vista of stars, staring up at the canopy of glass that spans the first half of the lab and is largely clear of snow, sheltered as it is by the rock behind.

"Beautiful, isn't it?" Lydia says, recalling the nights she and Wade lay on the dusty floor staring up at the vastness of the unknown universe. "With no light pollution the view is always spectacular."

Wade is explaining the pod's assembly to the man who builds skyscrapers. Nick runs his hand over the hand-built egg-shaped structure, finding the edge of the self-sealing door. The pod is Wade's absolute pride and joy. She used to joke it was her competition, it took up so much of his time and attention.

"Yeah, right," Nick says, looking at Wade for a fraction longer than feels necessary as he finally concludes his explanation of the pod's multilayered soundproofing. "Gonna give us a demo, then?"

"Um, how about a guided tour instead?" Wade replies, looking at Lydia. "You okay to go back now, Lidds? Don't want to leave the other guests on their own for too long."

"Oh, I thought I would help Rachel on the return crossing."

"You weren't much help last time," Nick says, laughing to himself.

"Rachel will be fine now, won't you?" Wade asks, glancing over to Rachel who is wandering around, touching things. Wade hates anyone unsupervised in his lab. It's his space, and he demands that everyone, including his wife, respects that. Nick's also on the move, at Wade's desk now, wiggling his pudgy finger on the trackpad of the laptop, which lights up, while Rachel is headed toward the back of the lab where the accommodation for the volunteers is housed, as well as a storeroom.

"Um, if you could leave that alone, please?" Wade asks, his comment directed at Nick. "And Rachel, can you stay in here, please? Confidential records back there."

Wade rounds up the Bentleys, directing them back toward the pod. Then he looks at Lydia. "The other guests have been on their own for a while now, Lidds."

"Yes, sorry, of course."

Wade taps the app on his phone and types in a code that unlocks the door, then he kisses her on the cheek. "We won't be far behind you, promise. Just don't look down."

She practically runs over, or at least power walks. The wind has dropped, but the snow is still just as heavy, and the dip feels even more pronounced than on the way over, although it can't be. Not in such a short time.

Then another worry presents itself.

The door at the other end is also locked, and while she has her phone with her, app loaded, she cannot rely on her recall of the code. Thankfully the door opens as she nears it. Wade must have unlocked it for her; ever thoughtful.

Zoe and Jack are waiting on the other side, as if they have been there the whole time.

"Hi, so sorry about that," she says, breathless. Then she catches the beat of silence, and the way they both look away, avoiding eye contact. "Everything okay?"

Jack clears his throat and Zoe stares at her, mouth open, but neither of them responds. The silence that continues is prolonged, the kind that comes when you have interrupted a conversation partway through that you weren't supposed to hear. One that was about you. Not that Lydia ever experiences that with only Wade for company, although she does sometimes feel she is talking to herself, but she has a feeling that's what is going on now.

"Everything okay?" she repeats.

"Yeah, except we were left out of the school trip," Zoe says, arms folded. "What's going on over there?"

"Oh, just a quick tour. Your turn tomorrow."

Jack nods, but Zoe sighs again.

"Maybe you'd like to make yourselves comfortable in your rooms for a few minutes while I make a start on the food?" she suggests. "I'll get Wade to message you both when he's on his way back, shouldn't be long, and then we can all have a nice dinner."

"Getting rid of us again?" Zoe says, but Jack encourages her to follow his lead and they both head up the stairs.

* * *

Wade is gone for a long forty-five minutes, the door from the walkway finally opening to allow in a gust of cold air that rushes into the hot cramped kitchen and alerts Lydia to his return. The Bentleys are in a congratulatory mood as she meets them all in the hallway, but it's hard to hide her frustration as Wade slaps Nick on the back and laughs heartily at a shared joke that she is not a part of.

"Lidds, so sorry we were a while longer than I said," Wade says, noticing her at last. "Where are the others?"

Lydia wipes her brow with a tea towel and forces a smile. "Waiting in their rooms. Can you message them, please, and then start opening wine? Dinner is burning."

"Yes, of course, sorry. We lost track of time."

Nick pulls a face as if Wade's been unfairly told off, but it's Rachel's expression that is most surprising. She is a different woman than the reluctant participant Lydia helped across the walkway less than an hour before. The tight ponytail has been taken down, luscious chestnut-brown curls falling about her swanlike neck, and the angular shoulders are relaxed as Nick massages them. A smile wrinkles Rachel's closed eyes and spreads across her face, changing her whole demeanor, particularly toward Nick. Attentive and adoring, she is rapt by his every word and receptive to his touch, and Nick is looking much happier too as he gives Rachel's shoulders a final firm squeeze, then announces he's starving and asks what's for dinner. "All I've had is a couple of those tiny canapé things. Could eat my own arm."

Wade points out the dining room, candles lit. "You go through, I'll grab the first wine pairing, a cheeky Sauvignon, I believe, and I'll message Jack and Zoe to join us. Get this party started, eh?"

"What happened to you?" she whispers to Wade as the Bentleys go into the dining room and they head back into the kitchen. "And more importantly, what's happened to Rachel? She looks like a different woman."

Wade grins as he taps a message on his phone, then he opens the small fridge. "I'd say job done as far as the Bentleys are concerned," he says, grabbing a bottle of chilled white, then straightening up. "They were both extremely impressed."

"It went well, then?" she whispers, unwrapping a loaf of rye bread, baked at the village store down in the valley. "The tour," she prompts, sawing into the dense loaf.

"Oh yes, all good." Wade concentrates his efforts on finding a corkscrew in the messy drawer. The galley kitchen is cramped, and he's in her way. She reaches round and hands him the corkscrew, juggling the serrated knife that flashes past him so he dramatically ducks, laughing again.

"So what did you do or say to affect this transformation in Rachel?" she asks. "I mean, the lab is fine, but it's not exactly . . ." He looks up from his efforts to uncork the wine. "It's a working lab, Wade, and frankly a bit of a mess."

"True."

Lydia walks to the kitchen door and closes it. "And you were gone a long while, Wade."

"Damn this!" Wade shoves a finger into the neck of the bottle to clear the bits of broken cork he's left behind in his clumsy attempts to open the wine.

Lydia takes a carafe from the shelf and a tea strainer from by the kettle. Then she takes the wine bottle from her husband and strains the contents into the carafe, looking up at him. "Can you please share with me what happened over there?"

"Okay, don't be mad, but I gave Rachel a quick demo," he says, catching her eye.

"A demo of what?"

"It was nothing, really. Just a bit of fun. But it clearly did the trick."

She hands the carafe to him. "You mean a proper memory flight?"

"Look, I'll explain later, okay?" he says, grabbing the carafe by the neck. "We have guests to think of now."

The dining room is impressive as she follows her husband in, the blush-pink taper candles burning down fast but creating a warm sugary haze in the intimate room she'd painted a subtle shade of green to match the newly upholstered chairs. The Bentleys are seated to the left and Zoe and Jack on the right. Old photos she found in the basement line the walls in mismatched frames: pictures of long wooden skis stuck in the snow and shiny faces poking out of bright padded suits, ungloved hands raising glasses of glühwein to the camera. She'd wanted to make the room feel more homely, but now those smiles serve as an unwanted reminder of Zoe's comments about "all those deaths" in the valley.

Wade takes the head of the table, while she will sit closest to the door so she can slip in and out to the kitchen next door and see to timers and finishing touches as she plates up the various courses. A daunting proposition, but everyone seems happy enough now wine is being poured. Especially Rachel who keeps flicking her hair as she tells everyone how amazing the lab was, especially the pod. Wade reminds her that what takes place in the pod remains private, and she places a pointed nail to her lips, eyes wide. Lydia hovers by the door, uncertain whether to take her seat or head back to the kitchen. She compromises by holding the back of her chair and smiling.

"You went on a memory flight, Rachel?" Zoe asks, frowning and covering her wineglass as Wade offers her the bottle. "Just now?"

"It was only a quick demo," Wade replies. "Rachel, Nick, some local Sauvignon to get the evening started? Lidds, can you get that bread you were cutting?"

Lydia grabs the bread basket from the kitchen and offers it round. Zoe takes the largest slice of warm but heavy bread, while Jack thanks her politely but declines that and the wine, pouring himself some mountain water instead.

"Do you have any gluten free?" Rachel asks, her hand on Nick's thigh under the table, so close to his groin that Lydia blushes.

"Oh yes, sorry, I'll just fetch that."

Lydia rushes out, and slices into the brick of gluten-free. Of course Rachel has to be different. The most expensive champagne. The hardest bread to source. And now a demo flight that had in no way featured on the week's carefully planned schedule. And the question remains, a demo of what? Because if, as Rachel seemed to be saying earlier, she had no clear idea why she was here and was keen to leave, then what could Wade have shown her in that short flight that was so impressive it's completely changed her mind?

"This looks wonderful, Lydia," Rachel says as she takes two slices of the unappetizing bread. "You are so very kind, as is your husband. We are both very lucky ladies to have such amazing men in our lives."

"Yes," Lydia replies, glancing at Wade for further explanation of Rachel's metamorphosis and trying not to look down at Rachel's hand, now kneading Nick's crotch under the table.

Wade pulls a face as if he has no idea why their most reluctant guest is now so enthused.

Zoe slathers her sourdough with bright yellow butter, knife glinting as she scissors it back and forth, then she tears off a hunk with gritted teeth. Their scholarship's mood is much less accommodating than Rachel's. A reversal of sorts, which again, Lydia doesn't understand. Zoe is probably still feeling left out after the impromptu trip to the lab, but she is on a freebie, so maybe she could be a little more grateful? And a little less disruptive.

"I take it you're staying for a bit longer, then?" Zoe asks Rachel.

"Oh yes, very much so," Rachel replies. "I'm fully on board. This place is, as you said, Wade, just magic!"

CHAPTER

17

Tash

The tube is crowded and damp. Rush hour a way off yet, but the train is filling up fast. I don't want to be on this journey with my baby, or at all if I'm honest. The visits to the care home come round too fast, although I still feel guilty that I'm not there every day, and I'm ashamed to admit I dread seeing Mum.

It's been almost a fortnight since my last meeting with Patient A. The same day that I came home to a threatening note pushed under the door of my apartment. I thought it was from a disgruntled neighbor until I read the contents and decided it was time to come to my senses and give up on this wild and impossible dream of interviewing Dr. Wade Hunter in his alpine lair. I've never been one to give in to intimidation, particularly cowardly threats that hide behind anonymity, but I've been told to enough times now that this story is a bad idea. Firstly by Ro and now an unseen presence at my door. The latter of which is unnerving in the extreme. The elevators require a key card, only issued to residents and guests, and the stairwell is also locked by a code, so I have no idea how they managed to get in. I shudder and the person opposite me on the tube looks up at Nova. Their face reflects a suspicion I also harbor, that I am going crazy. Maybe it's paranoia, but as they say . . . Anyway, I'm not quite crazy enough to make an unwise trip to a remote location on the off chance something remarkable is happening there. That is definitely not an option, however much I crave it.

I've mentally planned the whole trip, of course. Bookmarking flights and a suitable car for the rough terrain. Flirting with the possibility of meeting Dr. Hunter in person. It's all complete madness, I know that, but I cannot resist the thrill as the red light of my webcam winks at me in the dead of night, even though I now know it was Patient A who chose me, not him.

And as Patient A told me, there is only one scheduled flight in and out per week from the closest airport, and the fares are ruinously expensive. I cannot justify the cost and even if I could, it would take the logistical skill of a NASA space mission to get this trip underway. I have no support network and very little spare cash. If I empty my savings and max out my credit cards I can just about cover the travel costs, but I'd still need to leave Nova with someone I trust and make my peace with abandoning Mum for a whole week, with no certainty she'll still be alive when I get back. Plus there's the small matter of a two-hour drive up a dangerous mountain road that apparently only Dr. Hunter can safely navigate. It may technically be summer here, but autumn is round the corner, and I've looked up the chance of snow in that region in the next few weeks and it's now more than possible. In that respect at least, the sooner I go, the better.

The tube stops, and my silent but suspicious observer gets up. I scan for pinstripe suits and find none, but there's a young woman reading a novel with a snowy mountain cover in the next bay. She's relaxed in her reading, book splayed, nails painted in a glittery green, all the time in the world to turn pages and live a vicarious thrill. That's the trouble when you're young, you think you're invincible. Then you get older and realize you're on the clock, ticking down to the inevitable end. It's the things we don't do that we look back and regret, isn't that the perceived wisdom? But then we are also told to be sensible and face up to our responsibilities. It's a tough decision, and one I continue to tussle with. On my own.

* * *

"Mum," I tell her, leaning in to whisper in the cavity of her ear as Matron leaves us alone for a "nice visit." Mum used to wear a pair of classy gold teardrop earrings, or if she was going out somewhere fancy—a rare occurrence—she'd attach a set of pavé diamonds that hung down to the ends of her bobbed hair and dangled in my face when she'd kiss me good night and whisper a warning not to bother the sitter. I've got all her jewelry now, but I rarely wear it. "I need your advice, Mum," I whisper, so quiet even I don't hear it.

She turns her head and looks at me and then at Nova, who is sitting on my lap. I hold my breath, waiting for the moment of connection I have longed for. Then she whispers back, "Is Alan coming today?"

My father died when I was ten. And he was married to another woman, who had three of his children and knew nothing about us. Alan was a loser. But my mother loved him with a passion that never diminished.

The matron comes in and settles Mum, the anguished cries that came after I told her no, he was not coming today or ever, finally abating. It takes two staff to quieten her down, and the distress sets Nova off. I leave with tears I am too exhausted to shed. I should have lied, told her the bastard Alan would visit soon. Anything to keep her calm, that's what the advice is. But I deal in truths. That's my job.

The call comes as I unlock my front door. They think maybe Mum has a UTI, that's what brought on the agitation, not me. They are waiting for paramedics. Her temperature has spiked.

"Shall I come back?" I ask, picking up the keys I just discarded on the kitchen table. This could be it, and my prevailing hope is, truthfully, that it is.

"No, not yet, Tash. Let's see what happens first. You must be exhausted, and you have your baby to think of."

"Yes, yes. I do."

* * *

The hospital ward is noisy when I visit the next day. Mum was "lucky" to be found a bed, but nothing here feels in any way fortunate. Cries of distress, wandering patients, staff who retain a smile and kind word for everyone despite the horrific conditions they work in. There's feces on the visitor toilet floor, but Mum is sleeping and "comfortable" according to the nurse who brings me a cup of tea when I return to sit by Mum's bed. I feed Nova and absorb the frustration that bubbles. I'd thought Mum was going to die, and the relief it might be over was enormous. What is the point of a few more weeks, even months, when she has all but gone? I change Nova before I leave, and as I walk outside everything feels clearer. Mum has no idea whether I am there or not, and she is well looked after, likely to be in the hospital for at least a week, maybe more. After that, who knows how long she might struggle on. I could put this trip off forever, find reasons to stay, but I'd regret it, and ultimately resent it and maybe her. There's a small window of opportunity, and I really want to take it. It won't be easy, there's a lot to think of, but there's a way to accomplish anything if you want it badly enough. And I do. I really do. And if I'm going to go, now is the time. Now or maybe never.

CHAPTER

18

Lydia

LYDIA AVOIDS JACK's gaze as she comes back to the table with the final two plates of food, hers and Wade's. She is pleased to see both Rachel's hands are above the table as she passes Wade their first course: a very lovely dish of delicately poached fish. The candlelit table looks gorgeous too, although it almost killed them to get the slab of pine back here. Wade felled the tree and logged it, a herculean task, and they'd laughed so much as they dragged the pieces home, both dripping in sweat and Wade looking very handsome with the chainsaw slung across his back. She smiles at her husband now and at the recollection of those times, just the two of them. Then she takes her seat, glad of the rest to ease her aching back. Rachel is right, she is lucky, and whatever Wade improvised for the demo, it has clearly worked its magic, which was the whole point of the trip over to the lab. She has a quick sip of her wine, pausing as Wade raises a toast from the other end of the polished pine.

"Drink and be merry, everyone. I'm sure you are going to very much enjoy the gastronomic experience tonight and the wine pairings, but more than that . . ." Wade looks at Nick. "I can confidently predict that your time here will prove to be a mutually rewarding experience. Cheers!"

Nick raises his glass. "Hear, hear!"

Lydia bolts her food and excuses herself to see to the next course. Catering is so much harder than she'd expected, especially on her own, although all she's doing is reheating and garnishing, but it gives her a moment to gather her thoughts as she pan-fries prepacked garlic mushrooms. It's overwhelming being in so much company after years of only seeing Wade. Everything feels like it's in technicolor, volume turned up loud, like the horror movies Wade loves to watch on his laptop and she just about tolerates through splayed fingers. Jump-scares round every corner as she hides behind a cushion or pillow.

The instructions on the mushroom packet suggest a slug of brandy in the creamy sauce. Crossing the hallway fast she doesn't notice Jack is missing from the dining room until he pops up from behind the bar.

"Sorry, I didn't mean to make you jump," he tells her. "I came to grab a beer, if that's okay?"

"Oh yes, of course, sorry." She picks up the brandy decanter. "I just need some of this."

She catches the flicker of surprise in Jack's kind eyes. There and then gone as he levers the metal cap off his beer with a twist of his left hand.

"Oh, this is for a recipe, not me," she explains. "I'm not much of a drinker."

"Yes, that's what I'd thought. Headaches, wasn't it?"

She nods. "The altitude doesn't help."

"Two beers is my limit. And wine . . . Now, that is not a good idea for a clear head in the morning, although each to their own." Jack looks across to the dining room where Nick's voice booms. Jack smiles when she says nothing. "This must all be very new to you," he says, taking a swig of beer as laughter rings out from the dining room. "And some big personalities in there." He gestures with the beer bottle across the hallway. "Quite an onslaught for you after it being the two of you."

"That obvious, is it?"

"Having strangers in your home can't be easy."

"No, but we are pleased to have you. Do you travel much outside the US?" she asks, as they walk back together, the decanter cradled in her hands.

"Yeah, I've traveled in Europe a lot," he replies. "Especially in the last five years or so. How about you, much of a traveler?"

"Not really."

"Any reason for that?" Jack asks, pausing so she is forced to stop as well. They are halfway across the hallway: no man's land.

"Oh, I just love it here," she says, pointing to the snowy scape beyond the glass entrance doors, the tops of snow-dusted firs trees visible in the distance. "It has everything I need."

"Yes," Jack replies. "Except, does it?"

"You took your time getting that beer." Wade is at the dining room door, the emptied wine carafe in his hand.

"Oh right, sorry," Jack says, holding it up. "I bumped into your lovely wife and we were chatting."

Wade's eyes narrow. "Maybe I'll take over from here."

* * *

"That was rude," she tells Wade as she follows him into the kitchen. She sets the brandy decanter down so roughly by the carafe she's afraid one or both will smash.

"So I'm in the wrong here?" Wade asks, pulling a second bottle of expensive wine from the fridge. "You two looked pretty cozy."

"Wade, stop it. That's ridiculous. What's the matter with you?"

He pauses and listens. Their guests are talking loudly. They sound happy, unlike Wade who looks at her with unblinking eyes. "What was Jack asking you about?"

"Nothing. I don't know what you mean. Are you jealous?"

Wade shrugs as if it were the most ridiculous question. "I don't have time for this."

"Wade, wait. Where are you going? You forgot the wine." She catches up with him in the hallway, hoping to stop him before he rejoins their guests, but he's not headed for the dining room as she'd anticipated.

"Wade, wait. Where are you going?"

"Sorry, folks," he says, raising a hand to the concerned faces that swivel in their direction from the dining table. "I am going to have to leave you in my amazing wife's most capable hands as duty calls. Lots to prep for tomorrow."

Nick nods as if he understands.

"Everything okay?" Jack asks, tall in his chair.

"Yes," Wade replies, abruptly. "All good, just a lot to go over for tomorrow's flights."

Rachel grabs Nick's hand and squeezes it on the table, then smiling at Wade. "Thank you. I so appreciate you both."

"Wade, please, don't go to your lab," Lydia says under her breath, desperate now to stop him. He will be gone for hours. He always is. "I need you here. I can't do the entire evening on my own, it's too much."

Wade opens his mouth to say something and that's when the lights go off, just for a second. And when they come back on, they are dimmed.

"Shit!" Wade says, looking up to the spotlights, which now emit little more than a faint glow. "The generator must be on the blink; that's the backup kicking in."

"Do you need my help to fix it?" she asks, glancing over to the basement door on the opposite side of the hallway. It's where the generator is housed, along with all the tools Wade uses to keep it going.

"I don't have time for that now, Lidds!" Wade says, tapping on his phone. "I have to get to the data from Rachel's flight. It's not backed up."

The seal on the heavy door to the walkway pops open and with a whoosh of cold air he yanks it fully open, exposing the sagging bridge.

"Wade, no!" she says as he steps out. "You need to fix the generator first."

"Hey, what's happened to the lights?" Nick asks, coming out of the dining room. "You going over to your lab to fix it, Wade?"

"Generator's in the basement," Zoe says, coming out too.

"Yes, and I'll attend to that soon as . . ." Wade replies, avoiding Lydia's stare. "Sorry, I just need to see to something in my lab first."

Nick nods, as if he has any idea what Wade is talking about.

"Wade, the generator," Lydia reminds him. "That's the priority. Surely?"

Wade lets go of the door, and Lydia throws out her hand to keep it from slamming. "Wade, wait!"

The covered walkway is listing even more alarmingly now as Lydia steps into it, the wind angrier than she can ever recall, snow hammering against the glass. Wade thuds across regardless of her pleas to come back, her husband running to get away from her as she fights the door with one hand, the other wrapped protectively across her, but he doesn't even look back. If the generator fails completely, it will be catastrophic, not only for his data, which was only an improvised demo, after all, but all the food stored in the basement. With no power they'd have no heat and no way to cook, let alone run the weeklong program of memory flights. The fridge would stay cold for a while, but the freezers would soon defrost. As Wade shrinks to a moving dot she lets the door close and turns to the concerned faces of her four guests.

"Sorry about that, the price of being married to a genius."

"Man of many talents," Rachel says.

"Bloody genius!" Zoe adds.

"Are you okay?" Jack asks.

"Yes, of course, and Wade will only be two minutes, so if you'll all just return to the dining room for a—"

The spotlights in the hallway ceiling flash bright for a second, blinding them, then they dim again. The tiny backup generator is doing its job, but it won't last long. Maybe a few minutes. It's designed to cover small gaps in the supply and allow a few minutes for a repair.

"What the fuck is going on with the power?" Nick demands.

Rachel takes his hand and reminds him of his blood pressure.

"Yes, please, all just stay calm and give us a minute," Lydia says, directing them back into the candlelit dining room as Nick enquires after the next wine pairing that Wade mentioned.

"I'll fetch that for you," Lydia says, forcing a smile. "Just take your seats, please."

Two of the four candles on the table have either burned down or were maybe snuffed out by the through draft from the walkway, but the guests do finally sit back down.

"Clearly everything is not all right, though, is it?" Jack observes. "Without power this place is a ticking time bomb."

Nick curses, dropping the dripping candle he'd picked up to relight the others. Zoe stamps on the carpet with her boot and averts a fire, but they are now down to one candle. Then the weak light in the hallway spotlights fails too, plunging them into near-total darkness.

CHAPTER

19

Tash

Mum is out of hospital by the time I'm packed and ready to go. Beds are in short supply, so as soon as the antibiotics kick in she is returned to the nursing home. I'm pleased to hear she's stabilized, but in all honesty the ups and downs of her condition over the last few days have made no difference to my plans. I'd have gone ahead whatever the outcome. I collect up everything Nova might possibly need for the journey, then I strap her in the car seat in the back of the London rental car, the cost added to my depleted credit cards. It is an inauspicious and mizzly Tuesday afternoon. Not the best day to begin our adventure but this is it. We are on our way, although the doubts come with us as we set off.

Concerns that I am a stone-coldhearted daughter as well as a selfish mother. Reckless and quite possibly negligent too. Or perhaps I'm a woman of thirty-eight who has been shown that life is short and taking chances while you can is not always the moral choice, but often the right one. My view on that shifts by the second as I negotiate the city traffic, but

I've always been a maverick. An only child of an only child, Mum and I were a tight unit but also outliers. We would take off on a whim, missing a school day to splash in the sea and eat ice cream for breakfast, lunch, and dinner. Other mums were normal, stable, but mine was different. No less loving or kind, but feisty and unpredictable. Her own woman. She taught me to be brave, independent, fearless. Antidote, or maybe compensation, for all she couldn't provide, like money and a positive male role model. Armor against a path that has led us to a place of solitude where decisions have to be made by one not two parents. There must be a silver lining to being answerable solely to yourself, and I guess autonomy is it.

Driving through London is scary when I haven't been behind the wheel in a long time. Taxis with no patience, pedestrians with a death wish, and cyclists who whiz past faster than I care to drive. I don't know why I thought it would be preferable to taking an Uber, but the flexibility of my own transport, especially with Nova and all her paraphernalia, will likely be the best and most economical means of travel. Especially as we have a stop to make en route. I can't even think ahead to the drive at the other end, but neither can I bear the thought of seeing the exposé on Wade Hunter published by someone else. I threw the threatening note in the bin along with some past its due date oat milk before we left. The first decision of many I'll make in the coming days, I'm sure, but it seems my choice to drive myself was at least a good one. Nova hasn't slept this soundly in . . . well, forever.

I pull into the quietish street in Chiswick that I haven't visited in months, and a wave of nostalgia immediately engulfs me. It's a lovely residential square, the four-story houses worth a bomb. Number 17 faces a beautiful park which is strictly for residents only, the green space much coveted in such a central and urban location. I manage to find a parking space and sort of parallel park although I scrape the wheels in the process. I should have paid the accidental damage waiver fee, but I'll deal with that on my return.

Ro and Kitty's house is one the grandest in the square. I know it better than I know my own apartment. Not that I have one now. My possessions in storage and the keys handed back. But here, with my best friends, this was always home. The blue painted door of number 17 opened to me at all hours, and the smell of coffee and cigarettes always wafted out. I shouldn't have left it this long, but pride is a stubborn thing, and so am I. My heart hurts at the thought of what's been lost in that stupid argument with Ro.

I came to stay here when I got my first ever death threat, over a decade ago now. Slept in the basement for seven nights surrounded by open and messy suitcases, because I was never going back to my empty apartment. Kitty looked after me, home cooking and scalding cups of tea, while Ro made me laugh with her no-nonsense attitude and snarky remarks about "growing some balls" that I knew were half tongue in cheek but helped. She made me brave and she had my back, always. Together we poured the wine and chain-smoked as we sat in the locked residents' garden and set the world to rights. I miss that. More than I had realized. But that's not why I'm here.

I decided not to message that I was coming over. There was no point. Ro will be at the office, and hopefully Kitty won't be home. She's always at some charity or friend's, helping out. If not, I'll hand over the letter and leave. I don't want to deal with the inevitable questions or hash out the reasons for the prolonged silence. My friendship with Ro is over as far as I'm concerned. This is simply an insurance policy. I am trying to be sensible, or at least as much as I can be in the circumstances. I don't need to be second-guessed at this late stage. I just need someone to know where I'm going. Because I am going. I've made my mind up.

I leave Nova sleeping in the back of the locked car. I'll only be a minute, two tops, and it's a cooler day, the scent of autumn coming in on the breeze. She'll be fine. I walk fast, checking round for any sign of a traffic warden or some do-gooder who might call me out on my bad parenting, or parking. I'm in a residents' only area, but I really won't be long.

Then I notice it. The sign outside number 17.

"Tash?"

A neighbor I've passed the time of day with a few times is pushing her bike down the pavement toward me.

"They should take down that sign," she remarks, leaning her bike against the front wall of Ro and Kitty's house.

"It's in the wrong place?" I ask, looking up at the *To Let* sign.

She frowns. "No, I mean the new tenants moved in last week. Are you here to pick up the post or something?"

"They've moved?" I ask, looking again at the sign. "I mean, of course they have," I add, slipping back into my reporter's role. It's best to never show your ignorance, or your hand.

She gives me another quizzical look. "Rented it to a diplomat and her husband. Have a dog too, a big thing. Nice couple, though."

I look at the house again and notice subtle changes. A potted fig by the door, a large dog in the window, observing us, head tilted, ears alert. "To go where?" I ask. "I mean, remind me?"

"Thailand, I think, or maybe Singapore. Ro didn't say?"

"Aren't they the same thing?" I ask, although I've no idea why I felt the need to point out her lack of geographical knowledge. Except that it's true. "Still can't believe they've gone," I say, deploying the style of questioning that's useful when you're winging it. As if I already know what's happened and we are simply comparing notes. "But I guess it was a good time."

"Yes, what with the magazine folding and everything." She tilts her head like the dog, as if I should know, but I'm still absorbing the fact the magazine is apparently no more. Ro was telling the truth when I challenged her in that awful run-in at the office.

"Have you found a new job yet, Tash?" the chatty neighbor asks. "Ro said she'd given you a heads-up, even though she wasn't supposed to until the receivership was official."

"No, not yet, I'm . . . Doesn't matter. Thanks." I turn to go, then remember something. "Where's Agatha?"

The neighbor looks confused. "Oh, the stinky dog? She went with them. On the plane." She laughs at the thought and then wheels the bike up the path to her house.

I pocket the envelope I had planned to post through the letter box of number 17 and run back to my car, relieved to see Nova is still asleep. The car seat appears to have magical powers. I scroll through Ro's messages, looking for anything she might have mentioned about the magazine closing, but she didn't say a word, just asked to talk with me and I never responded. I google the magazine and the website comes up, still live, but when I widen my searches I find a trade comment piece about the demise of yet another "old-school publication" that's been driven to bankruptcy by the emergence of AI bots and the public's lack of willingness to pay for long-form journalism in this age of "clickbait dopamine-inducing soundbites."

I head out of London toward the airport, stung by the news about my beloved magazine, but also with a heavy heart that I ignored Ro in her darkest hour. That magazine was her baby. She'd built it up from nothing in a misogynistic age of bigotry and prejudice. Championing women and their struggles. It's been weeks since our terrible argument by the elevator. I can't believe I called her a coldhearted bitch when she had tried to warn me as a friend to look for other work. And now she's gone and I have no idea where, other than possibly Singapore if the neighbor is to be trusted. Kitty always wanted to travel, but Ro could never spare the time. But Ro won't last long doing nothing. She needs a project. I start to compose a message as I wait at yet another set of lights, but they change to green and anyway, a text feels inadequate. I'll call her from the airport. But would she pick up after all these months and I don't even know what the time is in Thailand. Maybe it's a conversation to have once I'm back home and I can share some good news about my scoop on Wade Hunter and the foundation. We can strategize together where I can pitch it, or maybe even start a new publication showcasing this as our first story? I hope we can rebuild something together, as well as our friendship.

* * *

"You going somewhere nice?" Matron asks as I explain I'm at the airport, hence the noise of a plane as I pull into the car park. The woman is ubiquitous. Always on hand when I visit or at the end of the phone when I call.

"No, just a work thing in the middle of nowhere, so I won't be contactable for a week or so. But maybe I should cancel my travel plans?" I ask, feeling the need to be a good daughter in the presence of this caring professional's ever-patient voice that fills the hot car and weighs down my already heavy heart.

"It's up to you, of course, Tash," Matron replies, the background noise at her end now. Raised voices and a very loud radio or TV. "What I can tell you is it won't make any difference to your mother either way, so if you do change your plans, do it for you, not her."

She's right, of course, about Mum at least, but the pang of a guilty conscience is hard to ignore. "Right, thanks, and can I ask something else?"

"Yes, of course, anything, you know that, Tash."

"It's not about Mum. At least, not directly. Did you employ a care worker called Steve, or maybe Stephen? Could have been a while ago now, but I think he met my mum on night shifts when she first came to you."

"Possibly," she says. "Would have been before my time, but not a name I recognize, although the staff churn is sadly a big issue in social care. I could try to find out if you give me some more details. Was there a problem?"

"Oh no, nothing like that, just curious as his name came up as someone who'd bonded with Mum."

"I'll see what I can dig up," she replies, ending the call with a polite goodbye as an alarm sounds somewhere in the background. A resident in distress. Maybe Mum.

I pull into a parking space and unstrap Nova from her car seat, lifting my still sleeping daughter into her buggy and then pushing her and my case toward the departures lounge, a changing bag slung over my shoulder along with my laptop case. As the doors part I pray I have made the right decision, but the doubts creep in, getting louder with each step of the process as I check my bags and carry a tired and then distressed Nova through security. The woman I have just abandoned to the care of virtual strangers would never have left me alone in my hour of need. I am a fraction of the mother she was. I know this and yet I press on, running toward my destiny and my flight, more determined now than ever.

Just a week and I will gladly return and be all the things expected of me. That's not too much to ask, is it? One more week to be Natasha Walker, Investigative Journalist. I show my boarding pass and we board the plane, Nova on my lap as we strap in for takeoff. No going back now.

CHAPTER

20

Lydia

THE INTENSE DARKNESS in the hallway after the power fails is disorientating. Lydia feels her way across the void, arms stretched out into a black hole of confusion, looking for any defining features and hoping her eyes will soon adjust. She doesn't even know where she is going. Maybe a vague sense that the generator is in the basement and she should head there to try and restore power, but she has no idea how to fix it. That's Wade's domain. She left the dining room because she had to do something, but now she is unsure what that might be. She pulls out her phone, the screen bright as she taps her contacts, just one, and calls Wade, but there's no answer. She drops the phone and then cannot find it in the pitch black as the screen darkens. Surely he will come to her rescue soon. He must have noticed the building is now without any power. The lab will be dark too, and he can't back up anything until he's sorted the generator, which is the only priority, and that means going down into the basement.

The guests have followed her out of the dining room and are asking much the same questions. Nick sounds angry, Rachel less so but frustrated, then Zoe's voice comes, claiming Dr. Hunter will sort everything and they need to stop panicking. Nick is holding up the last candle, a tremor in his hand she hadn't picked up on before the guttering flame illuminated it so clearly. Jack, tall at the back, is the only one silent.

"Sorry, I'm just trying to—" she begins, unsure what else to say.

All she wants to do is close her eyes and disappear. Or for the guests to disappear. She pulls in deep breaths and taps her thumb to her finger while counting, but there are four people across the hallway expecting her to do something. Breathing becomes harder as anxiety sets in and then, with spectacular bad timing, she is back on that mountain road and the avalanche is thundering toward her car. She drops to the cold parquet floor and squeezes her eyes tight against the memory, ears covered, mouth open in a low moan.

"Lydia?"

Jack's voice comes from above her. She is on her knees and almost loses balance as she looks up to a light, dazzling now. He's holding up a lit phone. The tall silhouette of him moves even closer, his face illuminated by the screen as he crouches beside her. She can make out his gentle smile by the phone's light and the concern in his enquiring eyes.

"You have a phone?" she asks, as if that were the point.

"It's yours," he replies. "You dropped it."

"Oh," she says, taking the phone. "Thank you."

"Don't try and get up on your own," Jacks says, hands outstretched now. "I'm going to help you get up, if that is okay?"

She nods. The darkness, her isolation, the responsibility of looking after the guests, Wade's absence, making her anxiety into a towering cliff she's about to stumble off. Everything is alien, except for Jack's brief touch as he takes her free hand and peels her from the cold floor. Relief rinses her of the fear of a stranger's touch and the memory that was taking her back to the moment when she woke up in the snow and realized what she had done to survive. She trembles as she trics to push away the recollection, but it's stubborn: the depth of her desire to die in those seconds after Wade found her. The agony of knowing she would never be rid of that guilt. That she is a bad person. An evil person, in fact, who would do anything, literally anything, to survive. She moans again, unable to suppress the anguish as she stumbles into the dark, away from Jack.

"Lydia?" Rachel's voice, full of concern, cuts through, close now. "Are you having another panic attack?"

"*Another*?" Jack asks.

"She was anxious on the walk over the ravine," Rachel tells him, taking Lydia's arm.

"I hope these episodes aren't a side-effect of the memory flights," Nick says, his face ghostly as he holds the candle up. "Wade swore he wouldn't test them on his wife if they weren't safe, but now I'm wondering if I should be worried."

"Nick!" Rachel says, scolding him.

"Well, you have to admit she doesn't look all there," he says, the candle dripping on his hand so he swears and almost drops it. "I don't want my wife to end up like this!"

Rachel apologies for her husband's comments, but it's not Nick's lack of empathy that's offended Lydia. She hadn't expected Wade to tell the guests she is a volunteer. Not that it's a secret, and given Rachel's former reticence maybe Wade was forced to say something, but coming from Nick, it's a shock, and now she has to defend the procedure when all she wants to do is curl up in her husband's arms until the anxiety recedes again.

"The flights are perfectly safe and entirely wonderful," she replies, a little more forcefully than maybe she should have so the statement sounds disingenuous, when it isn't at all. "And nothing to do with this, which was brought on by the stress of . . . Well, it's been quite a day."

"You should rest, and eat something yourself," Jack says, watching her as she holds up her phone, flashlight on, hand shaking. "All you've done is run around after us."

"I'm fine, honestly," she says, leading the way back across the hallway toward the dining room. "Wade will be back any minute and then we'll soon have the power restored and the lights running. Nick, could you go in first, please?"

"What happens if the power stays off?" Nick asks, the candle held aloft as they follow him back to the table. "Do you have a backup system?"

"Of course," she says, switching off the light on her phone. She needs to preserve the battery for now. "There's really no need for alarm."

"I know this is different," Rachel says, leaning into her husband as they sit down. "But the candlelight reminds me of when Nick whisked me off for a ski trip as a surprise first date. Private jet, butler, candles, and snow. He'd even ordered me designer ski wear, everything in the right size. I loved that you chose that memory for me tonight, Nick. And more tomorrow, yeah?"

"That's romantic," Zoe says, "Choosing your wife's memory, I mean."

"Just a little surprise your husband and I cooked up," Nick tells Lydia, meeting her stare as he sets the candle on the table. "Hope that's okay with you, Mrs. Wade Hunter?"

Lydia smiles as if she knew, which she didn't. Not that she should have. The guests' chosen memories are confidential between them and Wade, but that's the point. They are their chosen memory, not someone else's. They require collaboration and full consent, which doesn't chime with "a little surprise your husband and I cooked up." Although Rachel seems happy enough, despite noticeably shivering as she cuddles into Nick. The temperature is dropping fast. Which is more of an immediate worry.

It only takes an hour without power for the Memory Foundation to turn into an icebox in these temperatures. Breaths will soon be visible, even inside, as she and Wade have discovered numerous times over the years when they've had problems with the ancient generator. It terrified her the first time the power cut. A reminder of how vulnerable they are here, just the two of them, totally dependent on their limited resources and one another. They've always found a way to keep warm through the harsh winters, but they can hardly ask their guests to huddle in bed, body heat shared. She could do with adding some extra layers of clothing, they all could, but sending them upstairs does not feel like a good idea in the pitch black, and it gives off a very negative signal.

"I'll call Wade," she announces to the guests, now they're all seated around the table. "See what's happening over there."

"Can you do that without Wi-Fi?" Jack asks. "You have a signal up here?"

"No," she replies, defeated again. "I'll have to go over to the lab, fetch him back. He gets so engrossed he loses track of time."

"On your own?" Jack asks.

"You were not a fan of that bridge," Nick points out.

"I have been over many times before without incident," she says, glancing over to the dining room window.

The view across the ravine confirms that as she'd suspected the weight of compacted snow is what's weighing down the suspended bridge. It snows every winter, but she can't recall it ever causing such a pronounced effect. The walkway has always remained level, or close to. Her stomach drops. The hope that she'd imagined the dip punctured by the reality of what is out there, but it's built to withstand the weather, the steel cables driven into sheer rock on both sides. And then she notices something else that shocks her. "Sorry, please excuse me for a moment."

She holds her phone up to guide her as she crosses the hallway again, then taps on the home security app to unlock the door to the walkway, but of course the app won't work, not without Wi-Fi. Luckily there's a keypad to the side of the door; not all of them have one. She lifts the cover and takes a deep breath before she taps in the four-digit code, hoping she has the right one and that the backup generator will provide enough power for that connection to work. The door unseals, freezing air rushing in and that's when she gets a clear view of the lab, confirming what she'd thought she saw before. The glass dome is lit up like a beacon on the other side of the ravine. Wade must have switched the limited power from the backup generator to his lab so he could save the data from Rachel's memory flight. The one he and Nick "cooked up" together.

"I don't think you should go over alone," Jack says, surprising her. "I'll come with you."

Nick has come out now and brought the candle with him, only a stub left. Rachel and Zoe behind him. They look spectral in the dim light, all four of them watching her.

"Can you please remain seated until power is restored?" she asks. "Much safer for you not to move around."

"I'll go with you," Rachel says, stepping up. "Moral support. Girls together."

"I'll be fine, honestly," Lydia replies. "Please, just sit tight for a moment longer."

"No one should go," Zoe says, standing beside Jack.

"Sorry, Zoe, but I don't think that's your call, is it?" Lydia replies, hoping she doesn't sound too stern, but it is time to take charge.

"Dr. Hunter won't appreciate the interruption when he's working," Zoe says, standing her ground, eyes glinting in the dark, which imbues her with a wild expression. "You should let him do what he needs to. The flight data takes priority."

"Not if we all die of the cold," Nick adds, tucking his slender wife to his side.

"No one is going to die," Lydia tells them, opening the door wider, the iced air making her shiver and snuffing out Nick's candle.

Lydia takes her chance, slipping out and kicking the door closed behind her before anyone can follow, heart beating out of her chest as it slams shut. The echo of reverberating metal travels down the length of the bridge that stretches out ahead of her.

Alone in the near-black of the bitter-cold walkway, she is paralyzed with indecision whether to go on or turn back to their guests, just the other side of that door. Then rage takes over. What right does Zoe have to comment on whether she should disturb Wade in his lab. He's *her* husband. Of course he won't mind. Although maybe the reason she's so furious is that Zoe has touched a nerve. Wade has strict rules about interruptions, which Lydia utterly respects, but this is an emergency. The main generator is out and it's cold and dark. She needs to remind him of his priorities. To her and their guests.

As she crosses, slowly at first, Lydia's anger subsides, allowing for rational thought. Their scholarship place obviously has a crush on Wade. She can empathize with that. Lydia has felt jealous of the volunteers who take up Wade's time and his headspace. It's madness, of course—Wade has no interest in anyone but her, he's told her so many times—but it softens her feelings toward Zoe. Wade is handsome and clever and holds the key to unlock Zoe's past trauma and return her to a happier memory. No wonder she hero-worships him and is desperate to take her flights. It must have felt like a lifeline when Wade reached out and offered her this chance, all expenses paid. Zoe's forthrightness is nothing more than a case of patient-to-doctor transference.

Mind made up, Lydia takes on the crossing, and it soon demands her full concentration. The snowfall is even denser if anything, clumps of it obscuring the view through the large windows she sprints past, as if she were watching the snow from a speeding train. Not that she can recall ever being on a train, but she's seen them in films and imagined the experience from descriptions in books. It's strange as a woman in her late thirties, at a guess, to have no inner library. There are forty rectangular windows, twenty on each side, and if she's not counting her steps she counts them, and tries so very hard not to look down. The door to the lab draws closer, but then another worry takes over. Without Wi-Fi, the app, again, won't work, and there's no concealed keypad this side; Wade wouldn't allow it on security grounds. Volunteers are housed over here, and their records kept in the storeroom after they leave. You cannot take chances with that kind of precious data.

"Lydia!"

Her husband is running toward her, the door to the lab open, light flooding the space between them.

"Wade, thank God," she calls across, although the wind is so loud she has no idea if he's heard her. "The power is—"

"Turn round, Lidds. I'm right behind you. We will go back together."

She doesn't need asking twice, but the wind is tugging at the walkway now, the ground shaking beneath her sneakers. She waits for Wade and tries to explain what's been going on, how the power is still out, and it's cold, asking him why he switched what little power they have to his lab, but he shakes his head and presses on, grabbing her hand and pulling her with him. When they are past the dip Wade drops her hand and taps on his phone. The lights in the walkway buzz and hum to life. Still only working at a fraction of their usual capacity, but it feels like a small miracle. Then the light behind them from the lab is extinguished.

They run fast and together, exhilaration making her lightheaded as the door flies open to greet them.

Her shallow breaths turn to vapor in the icy hallway as Wade closes the door.

Hands to her knees and panting in the half light of the dimmed spotlights, she looks to her husband, desperate for him to say something, anything, to make her feel better. She has so many questions. And for the first time, she feels like he's let her down. Her trust broken.

CHAPTER

21

Tash

THE TINY REGIONAL AIRPORT is little more than a runway and a single-story building. Soulless and devoid of any staff—other than the somewhat lax passport control officer who waves our small cohort through with little to no interest—the arrivals lounge reminds me of the waiting room in the car rental company back in London. That feels like a long time ago now. I stand at the empty baggage carousel after my fellow passengers disperse with their carry-on cases. I find it impossible to travel light these days and can only hope all my paraphernalia makes an appearance soon.

I wish in a way Patient A had come with me, safety in numbers, but despite my continuing efforts to be in touch there has been no further contact. I got the impression she was distancing herself from my plans when we parted that last time, but I hope she is at the foundation when I arrive. It would be nice to see a familiar face, and it would also be confirmation of her credibility as my only source. Plus she could make the introductions, although I do feel a connection to Wade Hunter, despite never having met him. Stupid, really. Like a teenage girl with a crush. I should know better at my age. Maybe it's post-pregnancy hormones, telling me I need a man in my life? Which I absolutely do not.

I have no idea what kind of reception I'll get, turning up out of the blue like this, but I guess I'll soon find out, and at the very least I'll have seen the foundation and be able to grab a couple of photos. Maybe even a quick chat with some of the staff or volunteers. Whatever happens, I'll have tried my best, and that's all any of us can do.

I head toward the exit with my luggage, the doors parting and the slap of chilled alpine air hitting me full in the face. It's even colder than I'd imagined. Far too cold for a baby. My natural instinct is to turn around, plead my case for a seat on the return flight before the plane takes off. I check my watch, bemused by the time difference as I try to work out if Nova is due a feed. Hopefully this week won't be too much of a disruption for her. As soon as we get back I'll settle her into a proper routine. Not that we have a home to return to, but given I won't be in the competitive central London market anymore, it shouldn't be too hard to find somewhere. A fresh start is needed all round, and I'm looking forward to a bit more space and maybe even a garden. I'll book us into a cheap hotel for a few nights to write up the story and start looking for somewhere to rent within a reasonable distance of the care home. I'll still need to visit Mum for a while I hope, but the Elizabeth line goes out as far as Reading, so there are plenty of options and I'll also be able to commute in for work that way. I can't wait for those days of meetings and deadlines and being back in the buzz of it all. Nova at a cute little nursery while I help Ro build up a new publication. The first story will be the exclusive on the Memory Foundation, and if that does well we can build on that. If not, then I'll go freelance. Either way I plan on contacting Ro as soon as I get back to the UK. I owe her an apology for the way I spoke to her, a proper one, in person if possible, or at the very least a long call. I'll know the moment I hear her voice if we're okay. On second thought, I'll call her tonight. As soon as I know where I'm staying, either at the foundation or in some nearby hotel or even with a local family. There's always somewhere to stay if you don't mind asking. It will be good to catch up with Ro, and that way I can let her know what I'm up to. There should be someone besides me on this planet who knows my whereabouts.

I squint toward the distant horizon, a spectacular vista of peaks visible despite the blinding sun. Now I just need to drive toward them.

The rental company over here was much less bothered about paperwork and security. They seemed surprised and delighted that anyone would want to hire a car from this remote location and emailed me the registration explaining it would be parked outside, keys inside. Stating, when I queried the arrangements, that there was zero risk of it being stolen or me not finding it. There is only one car on the far side of the lot. A white SUV. I gather up my courage and head toward it. The plates match the details I was given, and the door is indeed, unlocked. The keys in the glove compartment along with a satnav. I haul my bags into the trunk and that's when I see it, the child seat I'd requested. It's already secured when I check, the straps frayed. What was I thinking? But I wasn't thinking, not when I booked all this in the dead of night, wired with adrenalin and desperate to escape my responsibilities. At any cost. This is no place for a child, let alone a baby.

"It's fine," I tell myself, ignoring those frayed straps as the magnitude of what I'm putting not only myself but also my daughter through hits me full on. "I'm doing the right thing. For both of us."

The roar of a plane overhead jolts me into action. The return flight has taken off. A week until the next one. I have no option but to drive in the direction of those distant peaks. I close the door on the baby seat and climb in the driver's side, on the left. I now need to work out how to clear the windshield and change the language on the satnav to English.

With a quick glance over my shoulder to those frayed straps, I start the engine. It's far too late now to change my mind. The only option is to press on.

CHAPTER

22

Lydia

"SHUSH!" WADE INSTRUCTS Lydia as her questions about the power, and Rachel's memory flight, apparently chosen by Nick, tumble out. "I'm sorry, Lidds, I'll explain later."

Their guests are emerging from the dining room now, blinking into the half light of the hallway that the backup generator is now supplying. But likely not for long.

"All sorted over there?" Nick asks, gesturing in the direction of the lab.

"Yes, all present and correct," Wade replies. "Next job is to fix the main generator. Lidds, can you give me a hand?"

"I can help," Jack offers.

"No need, Lidds and I are old hands at this."

Wade goes down to the basement first, shining his phone light ahead of him on the metal staircase, then he directs the beam back up so she can see her way on the damp and slippery steps.

It's even colder down here, one side largely open to the elements, the only shelter provided by the gradient of the steep ramp up to the forecourt. Wade usually reverses the Tank in. Says it's easier to drive out, especially if the ramp is icy, but with the guests in the car he came straight down, the bull bars of the Tank growling at her as Wade's phone illuminates them.

"What did Nick mean when he asked about your trip over to the lab?" she asks, picking her way toward Wade, careful not to trip in the darkness. The basement is crammed with old furniture, and piles of junk.

"What's that?" Wade asks, in a distracted way that makes her think he's not really listening. He's by the main generator now, holding up his phone light, huge snow drifts reflecting glitter down the metal ramp in the moonlight.

"Sounded like Nick knew something. Something I don't."

"Take this for me," Wade says, passing his phone. "Direct the light there, yeah, that's great."

She holds the phone up, her numb hands trembling, although she feels hot, her back painful. She needs to rest, but no chance of that. Wade squints at the generator's control unit, then he removes a plastic cover and peers in. "Keep that steady, please," he says, his attention still focused on the generator. His tongue is stuck out the corner of his mouth, a pink triangle, which is always a sign he's consumed by the task at hand and there's little valuable conversation to be had until he's done.

"Is it fixable?" she asks, leaning closer.

"Hopefully," Wade replies, grabbing a screwdriver from the tool bench and returning to remove something small and metallic from the control unit, she has no idea what. "It's probably just the pressure valve," he says. "We're really getting through fuel, but we should be fine for the rest of the week."

"Couldn't you have done this before you went to the lab?"

"What?" he asks, refilling the tank with the gloopy diesel.

"Then we'd have had power in the main building too," she says, thinking back to that moment when Jack helped her up. That should have been Wade's job, not a stranger's. "I had another panic attack."

Wade looks at her, alarmed. "Are you okay now?"

"Yes, I'm fine, but I wasn't and you weren't there." She almost adds that Jack was, but tiptoes back from that thought.

"Sorry about that," he says, distracted again, his nose wrinkling with concentration as he replaces the plastic cover, turning the tiny screws. He has never mastered the art of multitasking, which is probably why he's so utterly brilliant at what he does; pure single-minded purpose.

She holds the phone light steady and glances behind her to the oversized fridge and two freezers, their usual hum still missing as Wade focuses on finishing the repair that will hopefully get the generator going again, a tangle of cables in his hands now. It's subzero in the basement, but she'd rather not test out her working hypothesis that even in the cold air they have twelve hours tops until they'd need to consume or discard everything perishable. Rachel's good humor would soon wear off when they are on basic rations. It's not much more encouraging outside, the snow constant in the slice of darkness she can see at the top of the ramp. The road will soon be impassable and no other way to get the guests down the mountain in what looks like a full-blown blizzard. The snow must be almost a foot deep out there, drifting to maybe twice that by the gates. She's never known it as bad this early in the season. At least, she doesn't think so. It's infuriating not to be able to trust herself on anything. The bedrooms will feel damp and inhospitable with cold in a matter of hours, the radiators in there cooling already, if not stone-cold. But that's not what preoccupies her the most.

"Wade, I need to understand what's going on with the Bentleys."

"How do you mean?" he asks as the basement lights come on and the reassuring vibration of the generator is soon joined by the gentle hum of the fridge and freezers. Wade turns to her, grinning. "Sorted, for now, but I will need to keep a closer eye." He holds his hand out and she gives him his phone.

"The demo flight tonight," she prompts, circling her head to loosen the dull ache in her neck that always gets worse in the cold, the snow a reminder of how she sustained her injuries.

He shakes his head, holding out his hand to go. "What about it?"

She backs into the snow-wet car, icy cold water leaching through the layers of her dress. She's struggling now to recall exactly what Nick did say, but she knows it felt important at the time.

"I don't know, I guess it's just a feeling that you and Nick have some kind of understanding. Oh, and Rachel's flight! Sounds like Nick chose the memory."

"You know that I have to keep all our guests happy. Our future here depends on it."

"Which involves what exactly?"

"I told you, I ran a demo flight for Rachel, that's all."

"Based on what?"

"Based on her *many* social media posts. It was very romantic, about their first date, which as you have seen, she loved. It was honestly nothing more or less than that and as I say, it has done the trick, so now that the power is sorted, shall we get back to them?"

"And Rachel gave her full consent?"

"Of course. What is this about, Lidds? Are you still feeling unwell?"

"No, I'm just . . . I don't know, it's just a feeling, but it's as if you're keeping something from me."

"Lidds, darling, you do know I would never lie to you. Or isn't my word enough now you've met the handsome Jack Myrtle?"

"Now you're being ridiculous," she says.

He hesitates, then smiles and gestures for her to head back up the stairs. He waits at the bottom to switch the lights off, then he runs up in the dark to join her by the locked door, so close they share frozen air as he takes her hands in his.

"Lidds, listen, the Bentleys are special. And we absolutely cannot afford to lose them, it would mean you and I closing the foundation, and neither of us wants that, do we?"

"Of course not," she says, panicked by the thought as he drops her hand to unlock the door.

The now brightly lit foyer gives way to the cozy dining room opposite, ambient light flooding toward them, as well as convivial voices. Nick's the loudest.

"We need their money," Wade reminds her, squeezing her hand.

"Yes, I do understand that."

"Good, because I'm going to have to pull an all-nighter to make sure tomorrow is even better than the demo."

"An all-nighter, really?" she asks, fear catching in her throat so she swallows the last word.

Wade turns and talks in a whisper, his head tilted toward hers. "Nick was talking about a refund before the demo, and I wouldn't put it past the pair of them to sue us for everything we've got if they end up leaving the program early."

"I had no idea!"

"I didn't want to worry you." Wade kisses her hand, then he marches toward the dining room and announces his successful repair of the generator, inducing a spontaneous round of applause led by his number one fan, Zoe. Lydia hangs back, watching the guests' reactions. Rachel's smile, slipping a little perhaps? Jack's lack of enthusiasm, or is she imagining that? And Nick, on his feet and back-slapping Wade so hard she fears her husband might stumble.

She excuses herself to salvage what she can of dinner, but like a drowsy fly in summer, the unease she has felt so many times in the last few hours will not be swatted away. And despite the restoration of power, she still has the sense she is left very much in the dark.

CHAPTER

23

Tash

THE ROAD OUT of the airport is wide and deserted, allowing me time to get used to the automatic gearbox and get the feel of the heavy car, but after an hour or so the road turns into a track that then runs through a dense forest. Eventually the trees thin and the road widens again to reveal a desolate but beautiful valley dotted with dilapidated triangular wooden buildings with balconies and empty window boxes. As I drive past, I peer in the dirty windows, some broken and no signs of life behind any of them. The valley is vast, the road through it eerily quiet, although there are clues that this was once a popular spot. Rusting and toppling signs direct skiers up the mountains, and the turnstile of a button lift, the cabling now slack, is lying in the overgrown weed-filled grass. A once grand hotel has been left to rot, the three-story timber structure surrounded with weeds and the faded sign hanging off. I keep going, afraid to stop in case I encounter the ghosts of the past. One of the many victims of the avalanches that ended the region's prosperity. Then I spot the shop with the incomprehensible name that Patient A told me is where the foundation gets their bread supply. My first proper landmark and possible confirmation of her credibility. My heart beats faster as I slow the car, but there is no one about and the windows of the ramshackle building are shuttered.

I drive on, through the valley and out the other side, following the satnav onto a winding road that leads toward the tallest peak, Mount Dunkler. *Darker Mountain.* The driving conditions are immediately more challenging as the road rises, steep drops to my left and hairpin bends at every turn. The only consolation is that there's not a sound. I'm not sure how it will work if I meet another driver—there are no passing places, and no way I want to reverse back down. I keep my eyes forward and concentrate.

The satnav shows I am an hour into the journey, but I think I can safely assume the going will get harder the further up I travel. The views—when I dare to look—are spectacular. White-topped peaks in a dizzying 180-degree montage, and the long valley growing smaller below me on each turn. The sun is dazzling as I take the next bend, temporary blindness until the shadow of Mount Dunkler throws me into shadow again. I blink hard, exhaustion setting in as the road twists once more into the dark side of the mountain. I discard my sunglasses and then find them again, over and over, up and up, round and round.

Then the satnav starts glitching, the map frozen, 5G no longer available in this wilderness of snow-capped peaks and not much else. I start to feel dizzy and nauseous. Am I already succumbing to altitude sickness or maybe it's just nerves as I edge nearer to the summit. I go over my rehearsed introduction to keep myself alert, forgetting much, which is always a worry. Mum was well into her sixties when she began to show the first signs of dementia, which was termed as "early onset." I'm likely just panicking because everything is so alien, so empty, an unfamiliar and dramatic landscape, heart in mouth even as my eyelids droop. I cannot succumb to the drowsy calm of a warm car as Nova does. I must be a safe pair of hands at the wheel, for both of us. I am a mother with responsibilities. I crack a window and resist the exhaustion of such a long journey, trying not to think of the crazy risks I am taking for myself and my daughter in the name of pursuing this story.

As I round the next hairpin bend, my phone rings. The tone loud in the silent car. I glance behind me before I answer it, my first thought of Nova, and the car swerves to the right. I narrowly avoid a plummet over the edge, correcting just in time, but the tires skid on loose shingle. I brake hard, sending the car toward the edge again. The road surface is degraded, rocks the size of boulders up ahead and smaller ones making the heavy tires lose their grip. I overcorrect, adjusting again, narrowly missing a large rock, but the precipice looms fast, another heart-stopping glance into the valley before I manage to bring the car to a halt. Phone still ringing.

The patchy signal has found me, somehow, but I still don't answer, hands gripping the wheel as fear slices through me at what so nearly happened. The car would have plummeted straight down if I'd been any closer to the edge. I should take a break, or turn back, but neither are currently an option. The road is barely wide enough for one car. And my phone rings on.

"Tash, can you hear me?"

It's the matron of the care home. The signal terrible so she delivers the same words twice before I can piece them together into a coherent sentence. I have anticipated, dreaded, and sometimes even wanted this inevitable news. But not when I'm thousands of miles from home with no way to get back for another week.

The broken signal carves up the soundbites as Matron fills the silence.

"I'm so. Very sorry. Your mother passed. Peacefully. About an hour ago. Fever spiked. Doctor called. No pain. Comfortable to end. I was with her. Tash?"

"Yes, I'm here."

"There's no need to cut your trip short," Matron tells me, the signal strong again. "We can sort the arrangements. Call me if you want to talk, Tash, or have any questions. Okay? And give that gorgeous baby a hug from me."

"Yes, I will," I reply. The most inadequate of statements. Nova has lost her grandmother. I have lost my mother. It's unfathomable. I should say something profound, but all I can muster is, "I'm fine. It was expected."

"I'm sure it's still a huge shock. She was a wonderful lady, your mother."

"Yes, she was. Thank you."

It's cold up here, despite the sun, and the window has started to fog, plus the terror of another vehicle coming up or down this road outweighs the sadness pinning me to the spot. Survival instinct outweighs grief, apparently. Trumps everything, in fact.

The map on the satnav now shows the twisting line up the mountain. It is much reduced, but a mist has descended as the cloud line draws closer, making the final section of the drive even more daunting, if that were possible, although there are blue skies above the peaks. I inch forward so slowly it feels as if the road is never-ending. With each bend in the road—if you can call it a road now the surface so degraded it's more like a track—the valley below sinks into the mist, which then turns into a thick fog up here that makes it impossible to know how close the wheels are to the edge. I can't look anywhere but ahead. My hands are numb with the stress of holding on, but I finally break through the cloud line, and a brilliant blue sky is revealed. A startling backdrop to the snow-capped peak of Mount Dunkler.

"Darker Mountain," I say, allowing myself a moment to pause and wonder at what has brought me here and why. Patient A has led me here, of course, and she couldn't have known so much of the drive if she hadn't experienced it firsthand, could she? I prize one hand from the wheel and feel the earring at my left lobe, a beautiful gold teardrop. Mum's favorites, and now mine. She is with me. Willing me on.

I turn up the already noisy heater and press on, hoping Nova is warmer than I am. Hot air blasts, the only sound in the car other than the grind of the tires as the road twists this way and that, circling the mountain, higher and higher until I fear there will be nowhere left to go. The view behind falls away now into a ravine so deep I can no longer see the valley floor through the wispy cloud and mist. The peaks rising sheer on the other side, and evidence of more rock falls at the side of the road and occasionally under the tires as they bump over them. I'm getting close to the top now. I must be. The highest peak is a mirage that at times feels nearer, then I come round the mountain again and it is as far away as ever, and no sign of the large curved building I long to find as evidence this enterprise has not been complete lunacy.

I'm convinced I must be on the wrong road and contemplating the terrifying thought of somehow turning around to drive back down, when I see it. An enormous manmade structure. Just a glimpse: like a magic trick, there and then gone. But it *was* the Memory Foundation. I'm sure of it. Just as Patient A showed me on the satellite image. It must be. I can't believe I'm here. Unless it's a fever dream, or altitude sickness. And now there is another problem, forcing me to stop.

The solid barricade that has halted my progress spans the road. It is made up of sections of heavy plastic clamped together and hung with all sorts of ad hoc signs in multiple languages advising visitors to KEEP OUT!!! And as if that weren't warning enough, it's also topped with lethal-looking razor wire.

I kill the engine and climb out onto the steep track, legs stiff and heart thumping hard as I look back in the car to double check I did leave it in Park mode. The sections of the barrier are padlocked together at the middle, a heavy chain wound round too, securing the five-foot-high structure. I walk up the incline and half-heartedly rattle the ice-cold chain, then shield my eyes from the bright sunlight to look beyond the barrier. The rising track is too steep to see anything other than more track and maybe the top of the building. Someone is very keen on protecting this place from unwelcome eyes.

I glance back, knowing it's a terrible idea to leave the car unattended, even for a few minutes. It's parked on the side of a mountain. Only the brake keeping it from rolling back down. I'm running to the car when a voice stops me in my tracks.

"Hey! Who is that down there?"

I turn to see a shadow coming toward the barrier, ahead of a disheveled skinny man in a dirty pale blue padded jacket, the sides flapping as he picks up the pace. "Hey, you! I asked who you are."

I back away and then I stop. Because I know that voice. I know it well. It's become my preoccupation.

CHAPTER

24

Lydia

It's hot in the tiny galley kitchen as Lydia prepares the guests' first breakfasts. The promise of a glorious sunrise on the horizon.

The welcome change in the weather overnight has also produced an upturn in her mood. Although the path had frozen snow to ice when she went down to collect water from the mountain stream. The near-silence of being outside in the half light was as always a comfort, and the softer snow felt less of an adversary as it melted from branches in heavy plops. It's miraculous how everything can be transformed by a new day, when nothing has really changed. There is still the threat of more snow, and the prospect of that and their second day with the guests saps her spirits again now as she bakes more bread and decants juice. Although she will be surprised if they all stay the week. Rachel was back to expressing her displeasure at this "godforsaken place" as the evening wore on and the snow continued to fall, and Jack seemed less than enthusiastic about his first flight, despite Zoe's fizzing excitement. But it's not Zoe they need to convince.

The Bentleys were the last guests to leave the table. Or in Nick's case, stumble from his chair. Jack made his excuses early, Zoe not far behind once her superhero Dr. Hunter had made his excuses, blaming the fact that he had much work to do in his lab before today's first "proper" flights. Lydia was annoyed with Wade for leaving her to it, but he had warned her he would need to pull an all-nighter, and it looked at that point as if the dinner party was breaking up anyway.

It was gone midnight by the time Nick had finally been persuaded to call it a night. The early hours before Lydia had cleared the table and hand-washed all the dishes and was able to turn in herself. She was exhausted, but then she barely slept, the building alive with unfamiliar sounds and voices. A reminder of last summer when she'd heard someone outside their suite. A woman who'd called out her name and knocked at the locked door, making her heart pound under the covers. Wade was in his lab, and he had assured her there was no way a volunteer could have breached his security system to get away from his lab and over the bridge, but she *had* heard someone. Or thought she did.

The alarm woke her at five-thirty this morning to start work all over again. Water to collect. More food to prepare, then there will be another mess to clear away. How can people eat and drink so much and not die.

Wade spent the whole night in his lab, as he'd predicted he would, where he may or may not have grabbed an hour or two of sleep on the sofa next to the pod. These "destination travel" flights are a pale imitation of the pioneering work he does for trauma victims and dementia sufferers, but Wade still wants to make them as realistic and joyous an experience as possible. He is a perfectionist who takes great pride in his work, and she understands Wade will have been working just as hard as she was, if not more. Creating a perfect memory for each guest to take with them and hopefully fly the flag for the foundation in a wholly positive manner.

The sun rises higher over the nearest mountain, a glowing globe that blazes through the kitchen window and makes her sweat. At least it is melting the drifts. It was reassuringly slushy beyond the gates. Not that there was much of a visible path to the stream, the snow even deeper out there, but she knows the way well, tramping a well-worn route with the empty water cannister slung on her back. A barometer of how far she has come since she was bedridden and weak.

Her strength returned slowly after her brush with death in the avalanche, and with Wade's care and determination she came to see some point to her survival. The day she was finally able to submerge the fifty-liter cannister in the stream and haul it back up to the foundation unaided, had felt like a turning point. She'd wanted to surprise Wade with her accomplishment, sneaking out alone to collect water. He *was* surprised, but not in the way she'd hoped.

"Don't ever do that again! I had no idea where you'd gone."

He'd quickly apologized, blaming his temper on his fear that he might have lost her, and she could see he meant it, and how much she meant to him.

She still can't carry a full cannister on her back as Wade does when the volunteers are here and she's confined indoors, just in case, but she drags and pushes it back home, determined to prove her strength and worth. Although she wouldn't survive a day here without Wade, and she is careful to make sure he always knows where she is. It's important in the mountains where that knowledge can be the difference between life and death. She totally gets that now.

The exertion this morning was a good distraction from her worries about the guests, but another question now returns as she cuts fruit and warms the frozen pastries. The one that is always there and likely will never leave her. *Who am I?*

For years she's tried to find her past self on social media, or through endless Google searches, falling down rabbit holes to stumble on missing persons cases that terrified and fascinated her in equal measure. There's one that's stayed with her more than most, about a peer of the realm who had allegedly murdered the family nanny and then disappeared. This was decades ago, but it was a story that captivated the world as well as her, it seemed. Because how could someone vanish off the face of the earth when everyone on the planet was looking for them? The testimony of the victim's son particularly struck her, his ongoing fight for justice especially poignant. He was given the chance to look at the scene-of-crime photos. Disturbing black-and-white stills of his blood-soaked mother that, the detective warned him, once seen could never be unseen. He chose to look at them anyway, but it had clearly left scars. Maybe it is better to leave the past alone. Even if the deep-seated desire to understand where you came from is ever-present. She has feared her past and yet yearned for it too. But if she saw it, all of it, would she wish she hadn't. Or, like than poor man, know that it is best to face the truth, however appalling, and know where you came from, and what you've lost.

She unlatches the kitchen window, although it's far too cold to leave it open for long.

The snow's starting up again, fresh flakes blowing in. All it will take is another day of continuous fall and the guests will be stuck here indefinitely. An intolerable proposition for so many reasons, but she mustn't spiral. It hasn't happened yet, and this is only day two. She closes the window as the certainty they will not all make it to the end of the week, maybe not even the end of today, washes over her again. She swats the feeling like the imagined fly. Then the timer pings and she's back to making breakfast.

The guests should be getting up now, the app on their bedside tablets gently rousing them with Wade's recorded message advising them to meet in the dining room at seven-thirty sharp. There are four memory flights per day to get through. A crazy schedule that means early starts and late finishes. It will be her job to entertain the remaining guests as they wait for their turn. She places the juice and arranged pastries on the freshly laid dining table, footfall coming down the stairs.

"Morning!" Jack says, as he comes into the dining room. "How are you today?"

"Yeah, good," she says, placing butters and jams on the table. "And you, did you sleep well?"

"Not great, to be honest. Lot on my mind."

"Oh?" she asks, wondering if she should have. "You don't need to be nervous. You'll enjoy your flight, I'm sure." She has no idea of his chosen memory, but is suddenly curious to know. "A chance to relive happy times."

"Yeah, maybe," Jack replies, looking less than convinced. "I chose a beach, silly really, not much going on, but it's my happy place. Just me and the surf."

"Oh, sounds nice."

He shrugs. "Hope so."

He doesn't seem excited about his first flight, despite the price tag he willingly paid.

"Do you know why the schedule's been rearranged?" he asks, reaching for the jug and pouring himself a juice. "Not that I mind, but I thought I was up first?"

"Oh, has it?" she asks, pulling the napkin from a tray of fruit she'd covered, although there was really no need. The fly was only in her imagination. "That's Wade's call, I'm afraid."

"He sent us all a revised schedule late last night. I assumed you'd be copied in too?"

The Bentleys arrive and save her from having to answer. She has no idea why Wade's moved around the schedule he'd been planning for weeks, or why she wasn't notified. Although this is all new territory, for both of them, and he's likely crazy-busy.

The Bentleys' mood is reflective, barely a grunt from Nick as Lydia wishes him a good morning, and Rachel is quiet too. The euphoria from the demo flight had worn off over the course of the previous evening, the comedown making Rachel even less amenable to Nick's drunken reminiscences about their past. He's probably hungover this morning. He certainly should be, the amount of red wine and cognac he put away.

Lydia places a pot of coffee on the table and grabs the juice jug to refill it, bumping into Zoe as she comes out of the dining room.

"Watch where you're going!" Zoe snaps. "This is a clean sweater."

Lydia apologizes, although it was no one's fault and Zoe's fluffy sweater is unscathed.

* * *

"There's your gluten-free toast, Rachel," Lydia says, returning with a separate basket for Rachel and setting the replenished juice jug on the table.

Rachel looks at the toast and turns her nose up, pushing it away. "I feel a bit nauseous this morning. Just coffee, maybe? I also have a terrible headache."

"Oh no, I'm sorry to hear that, do you need painkillers?"

"Yeah, that would be good, thanks, Lydia." Rachel manages a weak smile. "Don't really understand it, I only drank champagne, then a tiny bit of white wine. I'd normally be fine."

"Could be the altitude?" Lydia suggests.

"This is more like it," Zoe says, helping herself to two croissants. "I told Dr. Hunter, don't give me that fancy stuff, I don't like it."

"When did you tell him that?" Lydia asks, pausing at the door. Catering is her domain. Wade must have forgotten to mention Zoe's preferences as well as the schedule rethink.

Zoe pulls a face as if it's none of Lydia's business, and Rachel frowns, rubbing her temples as she asks, "Can I get those painkillers now, Lydia?"

She finds the packet in the back of a cupboard, among the first aid supplies, which are looking somewhat depleted. She should have restocked for the guests, but there was so much to think about. When she returns to the table the conversation has taken another turn for the worse.

"Might as well serve fucking cardboard," Nick remarks, looking at his wife's lightly toasted slices of seeded gluten-free bread that she smears with a scraping of the requested low-fat spread. Rachel nibbles a crust before setting it down on her plate.

"Come on, babe, I'm only joking," Nick says, clearing his throat. "Wade said it was important to keep your strength up for the flights, and maybe if you ate a bit more it might help with—" Nick raises his hands in surrender to Rachel's scowl. "Okay, but it was so nice to see you actually enjoying your food last night."

"Which is why I feel bloated this morning," Rachel replies, pushing the toast away. "Is this headache to do with the memory flight?" she asks Lydia as she pushes two tablets out the blister pack and swallows them with a mouthful of black coffee before handing the pack to Nick.

"I think it's more likely the altitude is causing your headache," Lydia replies. "Although I did feel a bit queasy myself after my first flight. It soon passes."

Jack catches Lydia's eye and opens his mouth as if he's about to ask her more, but then Nick talks over him.

"Where's that husband of yours?" he asks as he throws back painkillers with his coffee. The whites of his eyes are jaundiced and the veins in his cheeks thread a pink patchwork down to a saggy jawline. Rachel looks pasty too. Her face, beautifully made up, is pale and drawn despite the contouring expertly brushed onto her high cheekbones.

"Oh, he's still in his lab," Lydia replies, taking her seat at the end of the table and throwing a napkin over her lap as she pours herself a coffee. She'd decided on a more comfortable outfit for today, jeans and a favorite shirt of Wade's. It smells of him, which is reassuring in his absence.

"We're up first," Nick says, nodding to Lydia. "Wade said it would be fine."

Lydia smiles. "Yes, of course. That's Wade's decision." Although she suspects that Nick, or rather his money, is calling the shots.

"Do I have a say in this?" Rachel asks, looking at her husband.

"Come on, babe," Nick responds. "We've talked about this. You loved what you saw last night, remember?"

"If you say so," Rachel replies. "I can barely recall what happened with this headache."

"So what do we do while we wait?" Jack asks. "I mean, can we go out? Stretch our legs now the sun is out? I'm more of an outdoors person."

"Still looks pretty dicey out there to me," Zoe observes, glancing up at the window and shivering as she chews a croissant, mouth open.

"It was beautiful first thing when I went out," Lydia says, trying to brighten the mood.

"The early-morning naked flit?" Nick asks, a smirk playing his greasy lips as he chews off half a croissant and adds, words thick with buttery pastry, "Sorry to have missed that."

"I like that you collect the water," Rachel says, rubbing her temples. "Shows that we women are strong and empowered."

"More like a Trad wife," Zoe chips in.

"I don't know what that means," Lydia responds. "But yes, I do find it very empowering to be physically strong. And I love being outside too. The stream runs straight down the mountain from the glacier," she explains. "It's rich in minerals and delicious." She gestures toward the carafe of water. "You should all try some, good to keep hydrated."

Jack smiles, raising his juice glass, a reminder of something that happened earlier. She'd been halfway across the forecourt, and dragging the filled water cannister, but when she looked up and saw Jack at his window on the second floor, she could have sworn he was holding a phone. She must try and remember to tell Wade when he finally makes an appearance.

"Maybe you could be my guide for a hike in the mountains this morning?" Jack asks, startling Lydia. "While Nick and Rachel are over with Wade."

"Well, count me out of anything outdoorsy," Zoe says, helping herself to all the alpine strawberries from the fruit plate. They're out of season and were hard to procure. "Not much of a hiker myself."

"It's doesn't have to be a long hike," Lydia explains to Zoe, keen that if they are going, she should come too.

"I'll stay in my room, thanks," Zoe responds. "I want to be ready for Dr. Hunter the moment he needs me."

"The trails around here are beautiful, Zoe, particularly through the trees," Lydia explains, sounding a bit too desperate, but she doesn't want to be alone with Jack. He's nice enough, but still a total stranger, and she has the feeling Wade won't be mad on the idea either. "I'll make sure you are back in plenty of time for your first flight."

Zoe looks at her for a second, maybe two. "Nah, I have a good book." She holds up the paperback which looks like a thriller, a dead body in the snow on the cover. "And I can always look out the window for the view. That's enough for me. Until my turn comes round."

Nick eyerolls Zoe. Not that she seems to notice. Then he reaches for a second croissant. Rachel's hand shoots out and slaps his, the pastry still in his hand. There's a moment of tension when it seems Nick might fight back, but instead he opens his fingers like a small child and allows the croissant to fall to his plate. Rachel removes the offending item with her napkin and places it on her own plate, covered, while Nick is left licking his empty fingers. The whole thing only takes a couple of seconds, but it silences the table.

"My husband has high cholesterol," Rachel explains. "Croissant are filled with trans fats and refined flour. One is more than enough for a man of his age. Can't have you dropping dead on me, Nick. Not yet, at least." She laughs but it's a hollow sound.

Nick grins sheepishly. "What would I do without you, babe? Always looking after me."

"What should we expect?" Zoe asks Rachel, the penguin on the front of Zoe's fluffy cream sweater now covered in flakes of pastry and a spot of jam on her cheek.

"Oh, you mean over there?" Rachel replies, waving vaguely in the direction of the lab.

"Yeah, what happens in this pod thing?" Zoe asks, resting her elbow on the table and her chin on the heel of her hand. "Tell me everything."

"That's private to Rachel," Lydia interjects.

"I don't mind," Rachel replies, looking at her husband. "But like I said, I can't recall that much of the flight."

"But how did it work?" Zoe asks, glancing from Rachel to Lydia.

"Well, I was strapped into a chair inside this pod thingy and—"

"Strapped in?" Jack asks. "Why?"

"Some people move around a lot," Lydia explains, putting her coffee mug down. "But I really don't think we should be discussing—"

"I'll definitely need those straps," Zoe says, interrupting Lydia. "I'm a wriggler. But what's it like, Rachel? I mean," Zoe glances at Lydia. "What *actually* happens?"

"Well, you wear lenses, like contacts except black," Rachel explains, wiping at the corners of her mouth with a fresh napkin. "And earbuds, nice and neat, and then you relax into this reclining chair in the soundproofed pod, and that's about all I recall now." Rachel smiles, just briefly, then rubs at the back of her neck. "That's weird, isn't it? I can't remember much else at all. Is it hot in here, or is that just me?"

"I have to hand it to your husband," Nick adds, looking at Lydia. "Man is a fucking genius."

"He is," Zoe says, clapping her sticky hands together. "Cannot wait until my turn."

"The first time is very exciting," Lydia tells them all, recalling again how amazed and impressed she had been when Wade had run that first flight for her. "And the more you experience the same memory, the more it's imprinted. A bit like running ink over a Lino cut, or at least that's how Wade first described it to me. I had to look it up, but it's a good analogy."

"And when was your first time?" Jack asks.

"Oh, such a long time ago," she replies, wrongfooted by the specific nature of his question. "Anyone want more coffee?"

She picks up the half-full coffee pot and offers it round, pouring for Nick who is mainlining caffeine as if his life depended on it.

"Any chance of a word with that genius husband of yours before we get going?" Nick asks, as she refills his cup. "Need to discuss something with him, and he's gone quiet on the iPad."

"He'll be making his last-minute checks," Lydia replies. "Can I help?"

"No, this is between us," Nick says, tapping the side of his bulbous nose.

"Oh, yes?" Rachel asks, taking a top-up of coffee too as she surveys her husband. "No more surprises, I hope. You promised."

"You used to love them," Nick replies, downing the hot coffee. "The cars, the jewelry, the holidays."

"Yeah, well, things change," Rachel says, matching Nick's stern expression like-for-like. "*People* change."

"Wade will talk you through everything he's prepared," Lydia assures Rachel. "Make sure it's what you asked for."

"What I—?"

"Come on, Rach," Nick says, grabbing her hand. "If you're done?"

Nick and Rachel go upstairs, while Zoe helps herself to another pain au chocolat, the last one, and takes it and her book up to her room, adamant that no, she won't go on the hike as her thriller is much more compelling than the stunning scenery.

"So it's just the two of us?" Jack asks, as she starts to clear the table. "Is that okay?"

"Yes, of course," she replies.

"Great. I'll see you down here in five minutes then?" Jack says. "Unless you'd like some help clearing up?"

"No, that's fine, but maybe make it more like ten. And you'll need to wrap up, thick coat and layers. Pretty cold out there."

"Yeah, sure, sounds good," he says, giving her a double thumbs-up as he heads out.

"Oh, and wear snow boots," she says, calling after him. "It can be pretty challenging terrain, especially in bad weather."

"Oh?" Jack says, smiling as he looks back. "I thought it was a short forest walk?"

"Would you rather not go?"

"No, not at all. I'm looking forward to it, and I have a trusty guide to keep me safe."

Lydia waits until Jack disappears up the stairs, her smile fixed in place. This hike already feels like a terrible idea. And why isn't Wade helping her deal with the guests? He could have joined them for breakfast or at least replied to her many messages. He's never here, and yet he seems to be controlling everything, or rather Nick is dictating everything, she suspects, including Rachel's reluctant participation in the memory flights.

CHAPTER

25

Tash

THE MAN FACING me on the other side of the roadblock is wearing snow boots, although the ground up here is clear of snow, just bracken and shingle beneath my new hiking boots, which have already rubbed the skin off my heels. I glance back to my car, worried to have left it this long. The air is pine scented but thin as I exhale fast, cold breaths.

"Who are you?" he demands. "This is private property. Did you drive up here on your own?" He has a wild look in his eyes, but I do recognize his voice, I'm sure of it.

"My name is Natasha Walker. I'm a—"

"You're Tash?" he asks, his hollowed-out features softening. "The reporter?"

"Yes," I reply, relief flooding my shivering body as I hug my arms around my shoulders. "You know who I am? I thought I . . . Are you . . . Are you Dr. Hunter?"

He smiles, his blue eyes lighting up, and then he laughs. The sound is loud and incongruous, echoing around the mountains. I'm so tired I could cry, but with relief. It can't be him, can it? He looks so different and yet . . .

"I can't believe you're here, Tash," he says. "No one can make that drive but me."

"It was a challenge," I reply, checking behind me again to the rental car. I left it on a particularly steep section of track. If it were to roll back . . . My stomach flips over at the thought. The sun is shining on the windshield, dazzling me. I tussle with the desperate urge to drive away, back home, to my real life. But the return flight is a week away, and Wade Hunter is here. I'm almost certain of that now.

He is sizing me up when I look back, staring at me as if I'm not real either, but it is definitely him. Take away the beard, tidy his hair a bit, maybe add a few pounds . . . "You're Dr. Wade Hunter, right?"

He pulls at his beard, rubbing his chin with elegant fingers. "I wasn't expecting you, was I?"

"No and it's very presumptuous of me, but I've given up a lot to make this journey." I hear Ro's voice, berating me for sharing too much personal information. "And I think you wanted to meet me. At least I hope you did."

"Get back in your car, Tash."

"Please, I've come all this way, and I promise I will be fair in my—"

"No, you misunderstand," he says, looking at my car. "You okay to drive that thing in? It's the size of a small tank!"

"Oh, right, yeah, thanks." I wipe away the stupid tears that fall as I walk back to the car.

He unlocks the chain and kicks away sections of barrier to make just enough room to drive through. It's tight, and I need all my concentration not to hit him or the barrier, but I do note his quizzical expression as he looks in the back of the car. I wait as he reinstates the barrier and runs up behind, waving me on.

I'm desperate to snap my first photo of the building, or him, but then there's another obstacle. A set of tall metal gates that only offer me an obscured view of the enormous building between the thick bars. The gates open slowly and the magnitude of what I am doing hits me again, but this time I'm lightheaded with excitement and positively giddy. I can't believe this place is real. Everything Patient A told me was true.

I drive through the gates and park the car. Then I climb out and raise my phone as Dr. Hunter walks toward me. "Okay if I—?"

He blocks the photo with a splayed palm, then holds out his hand. "I'll need you to surrender your phone for your stay."

"Sorry, I won't take any more photos, if you'd prefer."

"And I'll need any other devices you brought with you."

I hand over my phone, and Wade puts it in his jacket pocket. I can argue the case for keeping my laptop once I'm inside. I'll need it for the interview. The most important thing now is to get inside, although the thought of that sends a shiver through me.

"You ready?" he asks, pocketing my phone.

It's just a week. That's all. A week to turn my fortunes around, maybe not even that. I can bag the interview and leave tomorrow. Wait by the airport for the next flight out of here. There must be somewhere in the valley to stay. And then once Nova and I are home I can sell the exclusive, which is already shaping up to be more than I could have hoped for.

I'm doing this for all of us: Nova and me, Mum, of course, and everyone else who needs some hope for the future. It's my turn to be brave. So I try not to panic as the gates close behind us, the sound of metal against metal echoing around the valley.

CHAPTER

26

Lydia

SHE MUST HAVE been standing in the hallway for at least a minute since Jack went upstairs, maybe two, worrying about the fact she will soon be hiking with a stranger in the snowy wilderness. It's a terrible idea. Although still the best way to keep at least one of their guests occupied while Wade sees to the Bentleys this morning and hopefully ensures Rachel's second flight is just as pleasurable as the first. Imprinting memories takes time and repetition and lots of preparation. Which is why the person she needs to talk to the most is still conspicuous by his absence.

She dumps the dirty plates in the kitchen sink and checks her phone. Wade hasn't read her messages. Maybe it's a Wi-Fi issue. She rushes into the guest lounge where the phone signal is stronger, the thick walls of the Memory Foundation less of a barrier to communication in here with the three huge windows looking out across the valley. She hits the only contact in her phone and listens, the ring tones coming one after the other as she watches the bridge across to the lab, now swaying in the gathering gusts. It's definitely sagging, maybe a little less than before, or maybe more, hard to tell from this angle. She sinks into the sofa under the window and types yet another message.

I need to talk with you. Leaving in five for a hike with Jack. Call me asap! Not sure if we should go. Just the two of us.

One tick, then two, appear beside her words, but the ticks don't turn blue. She can never remember if that means the message has been read or just received. She waits again, even though she has no time to, Jack will be back down any minute, then Wade finally replies.

That sounds OK to me. Sorry, up against it over here. Can you cope?

No, I need to cu. Come back, now. x

She backspaces and deletes her reply. She cannot in all conscience justify pulling him away from his lab on the basis she has a bad feeling about Jack. It sounds crazy. It *is* crazy. Jack is a nice guy. Plus her husband thinks it's fine for her to go, which surprises her, but as Wade says, he's up against it. And they won't venture far.

Lidds? You OK? It's to the wire as is, but if you need me? x

No need to come back, just wanted to ask your opinion, all good.

A thumbs-up emoji, that's all she gets and Wade's offline again. It will have to do. She rushes upstairs to find her warmest hoodie, but as she reaches the second floor where the guest suites are, the sound of raised voices draws her in.

The Bentleys' suite is at the end of this floor, past Zoe's and Jack's rooms, but the argument is loud enough to carry down the long corridor. Lydia pauses, undecided what to do. It's almost certainly none of her business. Another marital dispute over Nick's poor hearing or poor diet or controlling behavior or borderline alcoholism. She takes a few steps toward the escalating quarrel, trying to discern what it's about, curiosity making her bold. The door to Jack's room is to her right, and it sounds as if he is talking too, which is odd. The guests all surrendered their electronic devices to Wade at the airport, including phones, but then again she did see Jack with a phone this morning at the window, or thought she had. She listens again, more intently, and catches the sound of his shower running. She could have sworn Jack's hair was damp at breakfast, and he smelled of the expensive shower gel she'd left in all the guest bathrooms. The powerful scent of pine and eucalyptus familiar to her, but maybe she was mistaken about that too. She can't trust her recall one bit. It's patchy, like the phone signal.

She carries on, slowing again as she approaches the door at the far end. The Bentleys are both shouting now, the argument at full throttle. A tennis match of traded insults.

"You won't even give this a chance, babe. It's just a week, Rach. A week to recapture what we had at the start—"

"You mean the way I threw away my youth? The way you bought my affections by hounding me, bamboozling me?"

Lydia raises her hand to tap gently, wondering if she should check on them or leave well enough alone. Either way, her diffident raps are ignored, or not heard.

"What the fuck are you talking about, Rach? You chased me. Broke up my marriage. Promised me everything and now you want a divorce and half my kids' inheritance. Well, tough luck. You have another five years before you get a cent under the prenup, and I intend to enjoy those, even if you don't. You're my wife, so get over it, babe. Or rather, under me!"

Lydia steps back, hand covering her mouth, then she leans in again, the smooth wood touching her cheek as she presses her ear close to hear the lowered voices.

"Your kids know you better than anyone, Nick, and they made their choice. I want out too, and whatever happened last night in that pod was neither wanted, nor—"

"You know, I thought that coming here, reminding you of the good times would make you see sense, but you're not even giving us a chance. You just need to remember how we are together, babe. How good it can be."

"But I do. That's what I'm telling you. I'm sorry, Nick, it's not been all bad, but you must accept my decision and not try and turn back time with some weird . . . I don't even know what that was. Like an acid trip, with the worst come down ever. Do you have any Advil? The pills Lydia gave me haven't touched the sides. And I've hurt my neck sleeping on those crappy pillows."

Lydia leans back from the door, burned by the intimacy of what she's overheard and the consequences of what it could mean. That Rachel has been coerced into coming here by Nick, and Wade is now a part of an arrangement to what, persuade her she still loves her husband? Wade would never agree to that. He can't have known what Nick is up to.

"Rach, honey, come here and let me massage that tension out."

"No, you're not listening. I don't want a massage, or any of this. I just want to start the rest of my life without you. So will you give me a clean divorce with a fair settlement?"

"No, not until you've tried another–"

"But I have tried, Nick, a decade of my life. A whole decade, but this was a step too far, even for you. You can't buy everything in life. You need to accept that and settle now, not make me wait out the prenup when you know it's not what I want. It's not like you can't afford it."

"And you need to do as we agreed and give this week a chance."

"I don't want another weird trip in that—"

Lydia's heard enough. She raps on the door loudly. "Rachel? Hello?"

Nick opens the door. "What?"

Taken aback by his rudeness, Lydia takes a second to formulate a response. "Sorry, I just wondered if I could have a quick word with your wife?"

Lydia looks in. Past Nick.

Rachel is by the window. She glances at Lydia and for a second there is something akin to a connection. Then the steel-gray eyes glaze over and Rachel replies, "All good, thanks, Lydia. Just a marital dispute, private if you don't mind?"

"Yes, but—"

"You heard her," Nick says. "This is none of your fucking business!"

The door closes, leaving Lydia in the empty corridor and wondering what she should do now. Nick is a bully, that much is clear, but Rachel has rejected her offer of help. She is about to knock on the door again, insist she speak with Rachel, alone this time, find out if last night's flight wasn't entirely consensual and if Rachel needs more support from them both, she and Wade, when a door opens behind her.

"I'm ready for our hike," Jack announces as she looks round.

He turns out his large feet to show off his new hiking boots, then spins in his padded jacket, the sides flapping like wings as he holds up a woolly hat and gloves. "All the gear but no idea."

She smiles, but it's not his box-fresh hiking gear that strikes her, although that's odd in itself as that many layers take time to get into. No, the thing she notices is that for a man who was supposedly in the shower barely a minute ago, his thick hair is no more damp than it was at breakfast. In fact, it's now almost dry.

CHAPTER

27

Lydia

"SORRY TO KEEP you waiting," Lydia says when she joins Jack in the entrance hall almost ten minutes later.

"No worries, you all set?"

She nods and Jack gets up from the sofa by the fire, his padded coat displaying the card label still attached to the collar by a ribboned safety pin. His large feet are laced neatly into the pristine tan suede hiking boots and he's holding a pair of ski gloves and matching hat. He looks at her, smiling across the expanse of wooden floor. His expression is open, not a hint of guile. Maybe she was mistaken about him. What she'd thought was talking on the phone could have been anything. A mantra he repeats. Or a prayer. Although she'd thought she saw him earlier with a phone at the window.

"Yes, shall we go?" she says, trying to sound enthusiastic as she checks her phone again. Wade hasn't looked at the messages she sent him about the Bentleys' argument, despite the minutes she's waited for him to read them, pacing their suite.

"That was quite the humdinger of a row earlier by the sounds of it," Jack observes as they head to the sliding glass door that leads outside. "Any idea what the issue is between those two?"

"The Bentleys? You heard that?"

"Just the end, but I'm not keen on Nick's attitude to his wife in general. Can't stand that kind of bullying."

"No, me either, but I guess it's none of our business. And Rachel seems capable of holding her own."

Jack shrugs. "Doesn't always follow, though, does it? I mean, even the most intelligent and astute of women can end up in a coercive relationship and need intervention to get out."

"You think I should have done more?" she asks, fiddling with the hood of her fleece top to avoid his intense stare. Wade's shirt underneath the fleece should be okay for a short hike once she's pulled on the warm jacket and boots she's left by the door. And short is definitely what she's got planned for this excursion.

"You did your best," Jack replies. "But yes, I do feel there is a safeguarding concern."

She looks toward the stairs. It had been quiet on the second floor when she came down, but perhaps that wasn't a good sign. "Maybe I should try again."

"Too late," Jack says. "The Bentleys left for the lab a few minutes ago."

"Really? Well, that's good. Wade will ensure nothing untoward happens."

Jack raises a noncommittal smile. "Let's hope."

In the pit of her stomach something snags, and although she hasn't agreed with Jack, she feels complicit in her silence and therefore disloyal to her husband.

"We have a strict code of ethics here at the foundation," she tells him, kicking off her sneakers by the door to push her socked feet into the fur-lined snow boots. "And Wade is an honorable man," she adds, sensing Jack's resistance. "With a very strong personal and professional moral code."

She turns her back. Keen not to be observed changing, even her footwear, or to deal with Jack's obvious skepticism. Her husband *is* a good man, and the only person she's comfortable spending time with. He has seen everything of her, ugly and raw, but the fact remains that a thumbs-up emoji is all the investment Wade has in this hike into the forest, which is feeling like an increasingly bad idea. She'd much rather go over to the lab and check on Wade and the Bentleys. But that would demonstrate a lack of trust, and she has been tasked with keeping the guests occupied until it's their turn. And Jack is ready and waiting.

She taps in the code on her phone to open the sliding door.

It's close to minus twenty on the outdoor thermometer nailed to the wall, and the snow is heavier than last night. She zips up her pale blue padded coat, a castoff of Wade's, and dons her rabbit fur hat.

"Wow, that's cold," Jack says as he follows her out. "Neat hat."

"Thanks. It's real fur, which is grotesque, but also wonderfully warm."

The hat had been one of her lucky finds in the basement, although it had freaked her out when her bare foot brushed against it. She'd thought she'd stumbled on a dead rodent. The piled up rubbish bags do tend to attract them down there in the summer. The hat had several tails left on it that tickle the back of her neck and make her shiver, but at least the rabbits didn't die on her account, which salves her conscience a bit.

"You'll need those gloves," she says, pulling on hers. "Do you have a hat?"

"Yes, I showed you, remember?" He produces the patterned knitted thing with a large pompom. "Like I said, all the gear and no idea."

"I'm not sure you've even got the right gear," she says, smiling back. "Those are hiking, not snow boots."

"Ah, right." He looks at his feet. "I'm used to hiking through dusty hot canyons, not snow. But wow, look at that view."

The mountains are majestic as always, the heavy snow clouds dotted with patches of bright blue sky between the jagged peaks.

"Watch the ramp," she tells him as they head down to the forecourt. "It's icy."

"You're right," Jack says, grabbing the handrail as his boots slide around. "Bet it was even colder when you went out first thing this morning."

She looks round at him, startled, and catches an impish grin as he slips and trips the last few paces.

"Sorry, I wasn't being weird," he adds as he gathers his composure after almost falling. "Thought I should mention, though, as I had a feeling you looked up at the window and saw me too?"

"I didn't know you'd seen me."

"I was admiring the view," he explains, looking sheepish as he realizes what he's said and quickly adds, "The view of the mountains, not . . . not you. I was enjoying my only caffeine of the day. And the view. Of the—"

"Yes, the mountains, you said." So, that was a coffee cup in his hand. Not a phone. "Let's get going. Too cold to stay still."

She walks ahead, toward the settled drifts at the gates, soon outpacing Jack, who hasn't got the hang of the deep snow packing the forecourt. He slips again, grabbing at thin air as she waits for him and resists a smile at his lack of coordination. As he said, not his natural habitat.

"Wade is very keen on security," Jack observes when he catches her up at the gates.

She's pulled off a glove and holds it in her teeth to load the home security app on her phone. "Yes, we have to be very careful of unwanted visitors."

"You've had intruders then, in the past? Even up here, miles from anywhere?"

"The odd one, but before my time. Wade's ramped up security over the last few years." She angles her phone away from Jack as she punches in the four-digit code, hitting "Gate, Front, open."

Nothing happens.

"Sorry," she says, flustered. "I could have sworn that was the right code, I am a bit . . ."

"A bit what?" Jack asks.

"Oh, just forgetful at times," she says, jabbing at the numbers on screen.

"Is that connected to the migraines?" he asks.

"No, I don't think so." The gates finally open, saving her from further explanation and they stomp down the steep track, knees bent and each step taking them into deeper snow. The flakes are fat and falling hard now, the clouds gathering to spoil the perfect blue. Temperatures have plummeted again, and it's even colder as they lose the windbreak of the curved building. It could well be minus thirty out here.

"Wow," Jack says, breaths visible in the iced air as they reach the point at which the track joins the mountain road. "That is quite the drive down. Didn't really appreciate it from the back of the car, windows all steamed up. Probably a good thing."

Beyond them the road dips before it falls away into a series of tight bends. She tries not to look, resisting the memories that would be triggered. She never walks down that road. Let alone into the base of the valley. It's too far to hike, anyway, and even by car, especially so, that descent only holds terrible secrets and a pile of stones that marks the grave she has never been brave enough to visit. She shudders and turns to the distant peaks off to their left. It is an incredible sight, the sun sprinkling light into the acres of white in the valley, feathers of snow spinning on the currents. In the base of the ravine the cloud often lies heavy, but today cottonwool tufts cluster over the mountains above instead, surrounding the summit of the tallest peak rising up behind the Memory Foundation and encasing it in spun sugar. She is happy that Mount Dunkler is partially hidden today, her spirits lifting and her heart soaring now she is breathing restorative mountain air. Then her eye is drawn to the sagging walkway across the ravine. A reminder of where the Bentleys are. Surely Rachel was mistaken. Wade would never agree to an imposed memory. Nick is a bully as Jack said and clearly coercive, but Wade isn't.

Jack's neck twists like the owls in the forest, taking it all in. "That peak is crazy tall," he says, pointing to Mount Dunkler as the mist shapeshifts and a fragment near the summit is revealed. "Can't even see the top of it."

"No, not today." She shivers.

"That was the source of those deadly avalanches thirty years ago, wasn't it?"

Startled, she looks round at Jack. "You knew what Zoe was talking about last night?"

"I didn't want to make it worse by saying anything, but yes, I do my research. She was right about Ghost Valley too. The village is deserted." He shivers too, exaggerating the spasm through his body. "Not a soul around when we drove through. Why would Wade lie about that?"

"He didn't lie, he clarified," she replies, trying to recall last night's conversation after Zoe's ill-timed comments. "And why, may I ask," she adds, looking at Jack, "would you still come here, knowing all this?"

"It only made me more curious," he says, his gaze meeting hers.

"Curious about what?" she asks, mouth dry.

"The foundation's work, what else?"

"Yes, of course. Shall we keep walking?"

Their feet crunch through virginal snow as they turn from the view over the valley and she sets a course toward the lip of the forest, clear imprints left in their wake, a satisfying trail as she glances back. Nostalgic thoughts of walks with Wade calm her racing pulse as she and Jack settle into a rhythm. So many good times in the last five years to reminisce about, but Jack is a tall and unnerving presence at her side. One she cannot pin down, either as a nice guy or something else entirely. All that talk of coming here for the foundation's work, what did that mean? To steal the secrets to the memory flights once he gets into Wade's lab, or is Jack curious about something else?

"It is very beautiful," Jack remarks, settling into the demands of walking in snow, although his feet are likely soaked in the wrong kind of boots and already numb with cold.

"You have to go with it, not fight it," she says, demonstrating the best way to walk in heavy snow. "Soft knees."

"A good mantra for life too," he suggests.

"Sorry?" she replies, confused.

"Go with it, don't fight it—except sometimes you have to."

"I'm not sure what you mean?"

"No, I'm talking in riddles but some things can't be rushed, can they? Conversations to be had later in the week. When we know one another better."

"Conversations about what?"

Jack smiles. "Shall we keep going?"

Wrong-footed by his response, but sure-footed in the snow, she lets him walk on a few paces, knowing she can easily catch him up and then march on ahead. The exercise is good, heart pumping and muscles worked. She spends way too much time inside, and so does Wade. Particularly in winter. Often in his lab, alone. Then in summer, with the volunteers. She passes Jack and smiles, then her boot catches a tree root and she is propelled forward, landing face first in soft snow.

"Oh my God. Are you okay?" Jack runs after her. "Have you hurt yourself?"

She lifts her head. His eyes are filled with genuine concern as she meets them. A reminder of another time she was found face first in the snow by a stranger. Her future husband.

"Only my pride," she says, jumping up and brushing herself down before the memory of the avalanche takes over. She cannot allow herself to spiral into a panic attack out here, alone with Jack.

He laughs as she spits out snow, and she cannot help but smile too. She checks herself, imagining what it would look like to Wade. There is nothing to be jealous of, but Wade could misconstrue the situation, as he did yesterday. He has absolutely no need to feel threatened by this admittedly charming stranger. She and Wade have an unbreakable bond. She feels that in her bones, her only certainty at times. Her husband has seen her in the bleakest of times, and comforted her in the darkness when she'd truly wanted to die and believed she deserved to. What he did for her is nothing short of devotion. She does not deserve him. Never will. But she will go to her grave knowing she has done her best to repay that debt of selfless kindness and unwavering love, returning it gladly and without limit. Whatever she fears or doubts, it's never his love.

"Shall we?" she asks, leading the way and careful this time not to trip.

* * *

"You and Wade enjoy hiking together?" Jack asks, breathless after less than ten minutes.

They haven't come that far, but at this altitude everything is more effort, especially when you're not acclimatized to the thinner air.

"Yes, although he's often working. I try to get out most days, though. I have a few health issues, so it's good for me to exercise."

"Oh, I'm sorry to hear that, can I ask what is wrong?" Jack asks, looking genuinely concerned, then prompting, "You mentioned an accident."

"Did I?"

"Yes, you said last night the migraines came on as a result of it. Was that a car accident? The roads are clearly treacherous. Or was it something else that caused the injury?"

She shouldn't have brought it up. But everything seems to lead back to the circumstances of her arrival here. No topic, at least in Jack's company, proving a safe one. She opens her mouth to explain as best she can, then changes her mind.

"Sorry," Jack says, gloved hands raised. "None of my business. Please, ignore me. It's just after the argument between the Bentleys . . ."

"Oh God, no, nothing like that! I slipped in the snow, easily done."

"Oh, I see. Sorry about that."

She hits her stride again, walking away from Jack and his questions and worse, her half-baked lies. It's not him she's annoyed with, or least, not really. She's annoyed with herself. She should have trusted her gut and canceled this hike. She knew it was too exposing. She will take Jack as far as the forest, and then turn back. Before she gives something away.

The enjoyable burn of muscles and tendons working against the conditions is again a pleasant distraction as they head into the forest. The exercises Wade devised to strengthen her withered limbs after an extended period of recuperation have worked wonders, but the mental anguish has proved stubborn to this day. There were nights when she would wake screaming, and the panic attacks still come far too often, especially in the last twenty-four hours. It's probably the stress of having strangers here that's brought them on, but still disconcerting and terrible timing. You can't rewrite history, or at least, she thought you couldn't before she came here, but is it crazy to dream that one day, long after these guests have gone home, Wade might find a way to wipe away her pain and eradicate her shame. She'd do anything to forget what she did to survive, but it seems you can't deny your true self, however much you might want to. The truth lives inside you, trapped there, waiting to catch you out. And it's no less than she deserves.

She pauses to catch her breath, the feeling of panic clawing at her as the shadows of the tall pines up ahead envelop them.

"Hey, are you okay?" Jack asks, breathless as he catches up.

"Yes, of course," she says. "And try to keep up. It will keep us both from catching hypothermia."

"Sorry, I'm—Hey, wait!"

They are soon deep in the forest, the sky blocked by the snowy trees until they emerge into a bright clearing.

Jack spins a full circle, face tilted to the sky, tasting falling snow on his tongue. She's pleased to see he's appreciating the clearing as much as she'd hoped. This is her favorite spot. It was where she and Wade exchanged vows. She takes out her phone, but there are no new messages from her husband. Although the signal is nonexistent this far from the building and Wade has the Bentleys with him now. A jolt of fear accompanies that thought. The nagging doubts returning. That's not what the foundation is about. Manipulation. It's about joy and endeavor, research and breakthroughs. It's about hope and above all else, truth. But Wade will represent that, whatever Nick is trying to accomplish.

"It like an enchanted forest with the snow-covered pines," Jack says. "Reminds me of that book, you know the one with a lion and a centaur?"

She shakes her head. "Sorry, I don't know that one."

"You must. It's a kids' classic, and there was a film. It's British, like you." He looks at her in disbelief.

She shrugs, not sure how to reply. Her accent is British, London they think. But she doesn't remember her childhood, or any kids' stories, however famous.

"So where does that path lead?" He points to a space between the trees directly ahead, the trail lined with snow-covered ferns either side. A route that she never takes as it heads straight down the side of the mountain. It would be suicide to even try. Wade told her that.

"Jack, please, don't go that way. It's too steep!"

He jogs to the edge, then turns and walks back, gloves raised in surrender. "You're not kidding, are you?"

"No, I'm not."

"There's no way out of here except by car, then?"

"Are you looking for a way to leave us, Jack? I can ask Wade to drive you down, if that's what you'd like? Although we'd rather you stay, enjoy your flights."

"Would you?"

"Of course we would," she replies, breathless with cold and at the audacity of her challenge and his response. "Both of us want you here, Jack, but it's your choice."

The certainty she's had that not everyone will make it to the end of the week, maybe even the end of today, is back. And in some ways it appeals. They'd have the foundation to themselves again. No tricky questions. No marital disputes. No penguin sweaters and schoolgirl crushes on Wade. But it would be a catastrophic failure of Wade's scheme to save the foundation. Guest refunds would signal a death knell for their future here, with dire consequences for not only the memory flights but also her. She cannot leave the safety of the foundation, the thought of it horrendous. Which means for now, neither can their wealthy paying guests. Jack included.

"Don't worry," Jack says. "I'm not going anywhere. Far too much at stake."

CHAPTER

28

Lydia

JACK AND LYDIA retrace their steps back from the forest. The faltering pace is frustrating, but they are closer now, the gates in sight through the swirling snow.

"You okay?" Lydia asks as she waits for Jack and wonders again if she should have pushed him on what he meant.

She'd thought at first the stakes he referenced were to do with the foundation's work and what it could mean for memory care. Which led her back to the theory he could be a spy or maybe an undercover journalist. Or it could be more personal stakes. A tragedy in his past that he is determined to uncover before he leaves. An excavation of the truth through his chosen memory. Because nostalgia can be bittersweet. She knows that much.

They've been outside for ages now, the walk taking twice as long as it would normally, and the cold is starting to seep inside her jacket, despite the many layers. Her feet are also cold, and Jack's must be frozen. But he doesn't complain. Quite the reverse, he smiles as they fall into step side by side.

She appreciates the slower pace now, her back and neck are killing her, but she'll be glad to get back to the foundation and talk all this through with Wade.

"Do you venture far, I mean beyond the surrounds of the foundation?" Jack asks, flooring her with yet another seemingly innocuous question.

"No, as I said, the trails aren't safe, so it's best to stay close to the building."

"No desire to escape from here?" Jack asks.

"Why would I?" she asks, smiling as much as her racing heartbeat will allow. "We have so much work to do, and we have each other for company of course."

"Yes, you said it was the challenge of the work that brought you here," Jack replies, taking off his hat and wiping sweat from his brow. His shorn hair immediately glistens with droplets of icy snow.

"That's right."

"But it must have been a tough decision?" He pulls the hat back on. "Just getting here is such a challenge. How did you even find it?"

It's a question that's often puzzled her. The former cable car building is completely off-grid and it's not somewhere you'd stumble upon by accident. The road has got worse in the last five years according to Wade, but even back then it was a dangerous drive, as demonstrated by the dramatic nature of her arrival. Although she couldn't have predicted an avalanche. No one can, not with any accuracy.

Wade has no more idea than she does why she was on that road. She wasn't part of the recruitment drive for volunteers, they had all left by the time she turned up, but maybe she was an overly keen student who came here under her own steam, much like the invented backstory they devised together. Although that's never felt right. Not in her gut. She isn't a scientist. She struggles to understand half of what Wade tells her. More than half. And why drive up here in such bad weather? It was a crazy decision whatever the reason, especially with a passenger.

The memory floors her, as it always does. The moment she heard the avalanche coming and knew she only had time to save herself, now more real than the snow beneath her feet and Jack at her side.

"Hey! What is it?" Jack has caught hold of her jacket. The sleeve is thick with goose down, but she can still feel the pressure of his firm grip bringing her back from the brink of another panic attack. "You look like you've seen a ghost."

"I'm fine," she shakes him off. "Aside from the constant interrogation."

She ignores his confused expression and runs ahead, catching the toe of her boot on a rock buried in the snow. She reaches for something to break her fall and finds only icy air, but Jack has run too and he catches her, holding her upright as her back bumps into a tree, an outlier on the edge of the path they're following. The lone pine sheds some of its cargo of snow, soaking them both, and they spring apart. There's a beat, then they both laugh. An impulse she cannot suppress. She's hysterical, and cannot stop, even though Jack has, his eyes sad as he watches her. Not with pity but concern as she wipes away tears of laughter.

"I'm sorry, I don't know what's wrong with me. I'm just exhausted. And I'm sorry if I was rude before. Like you said, you're just being curious. It's so different for me, you see, being with someone other than Wade. I mean. Not like that. But . . . just us two. I can't stop talking now. What is wrong with me?"

"No, I'm sorry if it felt like I was hassling you," Jack says as they start walking again. "We have a week to get to know one another better. I shouldn't be in such a rush."

"So you think you'll stay?" she asks, surprising herself by how strong the desire is that he will.

"Long as I need to," he replies. "And for the record, there is absolutely nothing wrong with you, so please don't ever let anyone make you feel there is."

Sunlight dances off the snow, the aroma of wet pine receding as her cheeks flush. She loves that scent, but with every step the foundation and Wade are getting closer, and that is a reassurance, even if Jack's compliments confuse her into wishing they could stay out here, just a bit longer.

Jack is looking down at his hiking boots. Maybe he's making sure he doesn't trip, but she gets the impression he's as thoughtful as she is. She tries to recall what she knows about him. That he's a workaholic, a self-made multimillionaire. Maybe billionaire. He could be a spy, but he could also be, as he says, just a curious stranger. Maybe even a lonely one. She pushes aside the worries. Always so many of them. The weight on her like the branches that sag with snow. She can't know everything about him yet, and she doesn't need to. She just needs to get back to Wade and then everything will be fine.

She glances over again and Jack's eyes meet hers in a quick shared moment, then darting away again. The charming Californian businessman, who prefers sand to snow and is likely more used to luxury hotels and room service, is finally stumped for the right words. She shakes her head, and the rabbit fur sheds another load of snow. If only the nagging worries about him were as easily shaken off, but she ignores them again, breathing in the alpine air and telling herself to relax. Jack is a nice man. A kind one. Who wants to make her feel special. He probably compliments every woman he meets. A reflex when you are that good looking. He could well have a girlfriend or a wife. Maybe both. Although she'd found neither when she researched him online.

"What is your doctorate in?" Jack asks. "If that's okay to ask?"

"Yes, of course. It was about how we can utilize VR technology to improve memory retention in dementia patients."

"Wow, impressive and right on brand."

"Yes," she says, the unease of lying to him again making her nervous, but she remembered the complicated title of the fabricated PhD, so that's good.

"And you work with the volunteers too?" Jack asks.

"No, not directly. They are only here in the summer, just for a few weeks at a time."

"So you never see anyone but Wade?"

"Wade takes patient-doctor confidentiality very seriously."

Jack raises an eyebrow and smiles. "He certainly does. This place is an enigma."

"He has a duty to protect all of the volunteers, we both do. They are often vulnerable, and present with complex memory issues."

A volunteer once got halfway down the mountain before Wade found him. The poor man wasn't in his right mind, of course, but much like when Wade thought she'd gone missing, her husband was furious. Thank God he managed to get to the man in time. He'd upped security after that, cameras everywhere. In fact, they're about to pass one now.

Attached to a metal post that most wouldn't notice. Jack certainly doesn't, his attention on her as she takes off a glove and rubs at the sore spot at the nape of her neck to relieve the pressure that has built up again.

"You okay?" Jack asks. "I've noticed you do that a few times."

"Yeah, I'm fine. So where's home for you?" she asks, putting the glove back on and hoping to steer him into safer topics until they are back inside the building where she can shake him off for a while and send Wade another message. Maybe even grab a few minutes with her busy husband between memory flights.

"A beach house in Malibu," Jack replies, smiling at the recollection of home. "But I spend most of my time working in LA."

"And work is?" she asks, although she also knows a little of this from her research.

"Investments, mainly eco projects. It's my passion, well, one of them. And I have a daughter."

"Oh!" she responds, surprised at this new information. "I didn't know."

"No, I keep my private life very private. Would you like to see a photo?"

"No," she says, before she's had time to think about it. "I mean, maybe once we're inside. Too cold out here."

She sets off, ignoring the watery feeling in her legs. She shouldn't have come out on this hike in the first place, let alone allow herself to be drawn into such personal discussions. Which might lead to questions about why she and Wade don't have any children.

Wade has always taken responsibility for birth control. He's not interested in being a father. Said he's never seen that as his purpose and he doesn't think he'd be a good one. His father hardly provided him with a loving role model. He admired the eminent professor but also feared him. She forges ahead, almost running now. Running from Jack but also the photo he wants to show her. She can't bear it. To see another man's child and think of what she once had and threw away. As if it never mattered.

"Look where you're going!' Jack says. "You're getting too close to the edge."

She stops just shy of the precipice. Her legs threatening to give way as she sees how close she came to stepping off the side, nothing but sheer rock beneath the toes of her boots and the deadly drop down into the valley. She steps back and tries to catch her breath. Jack's hand touches her back, only the gentle weight of it to tell her he's there. Cold breaths mingling as he stands beside her, reassuring her. The past has caught up with her, as it always does. Five years have passed, but it is here . . . In the snow. Waiting. Always. Telling her she is a bad person. A bad mother. The worst.

She opens her mouth to explain away what she can, but no words come out. Then she is running again, so fast she knows she cannot be caught, not before she reaches the gates. Wade will protect her. He said he would. Always. He promised.

"Wait!" Jack calls after her "Please. What is happening?"

She hurtles toward the locked gates, gloves dropped in the snow and phone ready to key in the code, but her mind is blank. She stares at the app and wills her brain to unfreeze but her panic is obliterating everything. They'd agreed that five years was long enough to invite in a few select and—she'd believed—well-vetted strangers. But how can you legislate for a past you don't remember, except for the one memory that will not let you be? The terrible truth is always there, ready to catch her out. She can never outrun herself. Or the reckoning that will one day come. Maybe even today. Maybe from Jack.

The gates open. She has no idea where the correct code came from, and she doesn't care, only that she can finally get inside and then find Wade. But as she runs across the snowy forecourt her phone starts pinging, a stack of messages downloading one after another.

"What is it?" Jack asks as she stops and stares at her screen. "What's wrong?"

She shakes her head as the remaining messages download. At least a dozen now. They are all the same. Two words. Paired, and repeated over and over. Jack is asking again what is wrong, and can he do anything. Too many demands on her cognition, so it shuts down, as it always does when she tries too hard. She closes her eyes, ignores Jack's hand trying to take hers, his breath in her face as he leans in and asks if she is having another panic attack. What should he do? His voice recedes as she empties her mind. A reset. In the hopes it will make space for Wade's messages, which now take precedence over everything. She knows that much. Because something is terribly wrong if Wade is sending a code red warning. She looks at Jack.

"There's a problem. In the lab. I have to get over there. *Now*!"

CHAPTER

29

Lydia

LYDIA RUNS AT full pelt up the icy slope to the glass entrance door, jabbing in four digits on her phone to unlock it. Jack only just makes it through the door before it closes, but she doesn't stop, dashing across the hallway in her snow boots, no time to shed them. The door to the walkway unseals as she jabs at her phone again, and she barely breaks stride before she is pounding across the suspended walkway toward the lab. It could already be too late, but she must get there in time, that's all she can think about. Not the sag in the bridge or the snow or the wind or what might be waiting at the other end. *Code red.*

Jack calls after her. His voice not far behind. He must have caught the door to the walkway before it slammed and is pursuing her across the bridge, his weight dislodging compacted snow from the roof that adds to the flurries falling past the blurred windows, but she doesn't look back, or down. The bridge rattling and the wind roaring.

The run over to the lab is the stuff of nightmares. Not the usual night terrors she endures, taking her back to those seconds before the avalanche engulfed her car, but the kind of generic horror when you're trying to outrun your fears and your legs won't work. Surreal and slowed down, the final fifty paces feel insurmountable as she tackles the rising gradient and imagines what those stacked messages from Wade might denote. *Code red* is their agreed warning for a medical emergency in the pod. Wade sent those two words too many times for it not to be happening. Sweating and breathless, her next challenge is to type in the code to unlock the lab door.

Jack is right behind her now, looking over her shoulder. "What's going on in there?"

"There's a medical emergency in the pod."

"Oh my God, Rachel?"

"I don't know. Maybe."

The door opens with a pop, the lab swathed in darkness and everything quiet within.

She steps in first, eyes adjusting to the low light.

Wade prefers an ambient light during flights. He says it's better for the participant after the immersion ends, less jarring as they emerge from the pod and come back to reality.

The sofa where she'd expected Nick or Rachel to be waiting, depending on who is taking their flight first, is empty. Wade's desk, over by the window with his monitor on top, is also unoccupied, the desk chair swiveled toward them, and Wade's laptop is missing. He always takes it into the pod to control the memory flights, so he must be in there. They must all be. The egg-shaped construction glistens silver under the glass roof, the door to the pod slightly ajar. Which is also odd. Wade always keeps it locked midflight. And they can't all three fit inside. Can they?

The scent of something sickly hits her nostrils as she edges closer. She curls her fingers around the slight lip and opens the door wide, before turning to Jack. "Wait there!"

It's hot as she steps inside the cramped pod, and the light is even duller in here, every bit of room taken up. Wade is sitting on the floor at the back of the pod, motionless, his head dropped to his open laptop, face greenish from the reflected screen, legs straight out before him and occupying far too much of the limited floor space. He doesn't even look up when she asks, "What's going on, Wade? You sent me a code red message. Multiple times. Wade!"

"I left the door open for you," Wade says, as if that's what she'd asked.

She scans round, taking in the scene. There are two reclined chairs wedged into a pod designed for only one. The new chair they'd had shipped from a retired dentist in Geneva is pushed in tight at the back, next to Wade. That chair is empty. While Rachel is hunched over the old-fashioned leather chair Lydia helped Wade move out and she'd last seen in the storeroom at the back of the lab.

"You need to do something to help him!" Rachel shouts at Lydia, straightening up to reveal Nick who is strapped down and lifeless. "He can't die on me. He just can't."

"Wade, get up!" Lydia shouts, but her husband remains catatonic, staring at his screen. She looks at Rachel. "Why are you all in here? What happened?"

"He collapsed, midflight," Rachel says. "Can someone please *do* something!"

The monitoring equipment—blood pressure, oxygen levels, heart rate—is set up between the two chairs, the screen mounted on a stand. It is designed for one participant only. One set of vital signs. Even if they had two sets of everything, Wade would have needed help to manage the protocols of regular checks for any signs of stress or trauma midflight. There are wires trailing everywhere, some still attached to Rachel's wrist as she holds her husband's hand and sobs. Nick's exposed chest where his shirt is unbuttoned is rising and falling as he fights for breath. It looks like Wade had been trying to spread the sensors between the Bentleys.

"Is he still breathing?" Jack asks from the open door as Nick groans loudly.

"Yes," Rachel replies, looking out at Jack. "But he's not good. Do you have any medical training?"

"First aider, that's all," Jack replies.

"It's been twenty minutes now, maybe thirty," Rachel says between gulps. "He was conscious at first, talking to me, saying how much he loves me, but clearly in terrible pain." Rachel sobs again as she swaps places with Jack. "I don't even know what happened. We were both mid-thingy . . ." She points at Wade. "He was supposedly in charge."

"Both of you in the same flight?" Lydia asks, unable to compute what she's seeing and hearing. "Is that what you're saying? That's not—"

"Yes, that's what I'm saying. And then it happened, whatever this is." Rachel looks back in at Nick and sniffs, shaking her head as she holds the pod door open. "And he has done nothing to help." She jabs a pointed nail down at Wade. "The video I was watching, or whatever it was, started glitching and I came back to the room, and Nick was calling for me. God, I feel so bad. You cannot let him die. Please, do something."

Jack rips Nick's shirt open, buttons flying and exposing a domed hairy stomach. "Describe to me what his symptoms were."

"He said his chest was tight, like a belt pulled in," Rachel tells Jack. "Why isn't your husband doing anything when he's a trained doctor?" she asks Lydia. A perfectly reasonable question.

"I don't know," Lydia replies, crouching down to shake Wade, but he just stares at his laptop, ignoring her. "Wade, you need to help. You're the doctor here."

"Can you check for a regular pulse?" Jack asks Lydia.

"How?" Lydia replies, standing up in the constricted space.

"Like this," he says, grabbing Nick's wrist to demonstrate, two fingers crooked against a prominent vein. "You okay to give next of kin consent for CPR?" Jack asks, looking at Rachel. "I might break a rib, make it worse. I'm only basic first aid trained, but happy to try."

"Yes, yes, of course," Rachel says. "Please. Try anything. Our so-called expert hasn't done a thing." Rachel looks at Wade. "Utter waste of space." Then Jack. "Please don't let him die."

Lydia can't detect a pulse, and she's getting in the way, so she steps out to give Jack the room he needs. She encourages Wade to join her, shouting at him from the door that his legs are in the way, but Wade is clearly in shock and doesn't move, even when Jack accidentally stomps on his shin as he sheds his ski jacket and throws it out of the pod, the two women parting to let it fall on the ground. Then Jack pulls up his shirt, ripping tape from his taut stomach to remove a phone. He throws it to Lydia at the door. She catches it, a reflex action, while Rachel holds the door wide to allow in as much light as possible.

"I knew you were a spy," Wade says, looking up at Jack.

"Call Addison, my PA," Jack tells Lydia, ignoring Wade. "She's listed on my contacts, or if not go into recent calls. Tell her we need the helicopter here now, with paramedics. Suspected heart attack, maybe stroke. Weak pulse, breathing difficulties."

Lydia looks at the black shiny object, smooth as a pebble. She's never seen such a state-of-the-art phone. It has no buttons, not even on the sides.

"Give me that," Rachel says, snatching the phone and tapping in the six-digit passcode with a dexterous thumb as the keypad lights up and Jack calls each number out. Lydia takes the weight of the door.

"Oh shit," Jack says. "He's crashed, I think."

"What?" Rachel asks, hands trembling as she fumbles the phone. "No. That can't happen."

Jack starts administering CPR, alternating the counted pumps of his crossed hands on Nick's chest with breaths into the dying man's blue lips.

Wade is obviously traumatized, but he needs to step up, and Lydia feels she should be doing more too. This is their mess, although what has gone on in the pod to precipitate this life or death emergency, she has no idea. She cannot even begin to imagine how a dual flight would work. Wade's never tried one before, at least to her knowledge. The ethics of a shared memory, if that's what this was, blow her mind, and the consequences look as though they could prove to be deadly. Although she doesn't believe Nick's collapse is attributable to the flight. This is just the most abysmal bad timing.

"Is that Addison?" Rachel says loudly. "Hi, my name is Rachel Bentley, I'm on Jack Myrtle's phone. No, Jack." Rachel turns her back and walks away from the pod, toward the storeroom at the far end of the lab where the volunteer accommodation is housed. "Sorry, can you hear me better now? Yes, I'll hold, of course, but please, this is an emergency. My husband cannot be allowed to die."

If by some miracle Jack's assistant can get a helicopter here and with paramedics on board—and who knows, maybe if you have enough money that's possible—there's no way it can land on the mountain. Even in good weather there's nowhere safe, which had been a reassurance to Lydia for the last five years. Not now, though.

She looks up at the domed roof of the lab. The snow is throwing itself hard against the toughened glass, the wind whipping it up. She's never seen a helicopter fly over, let alone land. A drone once or twice, and that was scary enough. Wade had shouted at her to get away from the windows until it was gone, and she didn't need to be told twice.

"Wade," She looks into the dark pod. "I know you're in shock, but we need your medical expertise."

Wade gets up and looks at Jack. Then, laptop under his arm, her husband steps out of the pod and pushes past her.

"Wade," Lydia says, letting go of the pod door and grabbing his arm. "Why aren't you doing more?"

Wade pauses, looking at her, but also through her. "I don't understand why he . . . There's nothing I can think of that would have, unless it was . . . No. Unconnected. Too much of a thrill if anything. I said it was unnecessary for him to be . . . But Nick was insistent he wanted to be in on it. Living that moment with her."

"No one is blaming you, Wade, but—"

"The hell I'm not blaming you!" Rachel shouts from the far end of the lab, Jack's phone pressed to her ear. "I hold you two fully responsible for this, and if I lose everything because you've brought this on with your half-assed—"

Wade slams the laptop down onto his desk, muttering to himself as Rachel starts talking on the phone again. "There is nothing half-assed about my work, and we both know she only cares about him dying because she wouldn't get a penny if he drops dead now."

Stunned, Lydia says nothing, but she touches Wade arm, trying to bring him back to her. "Wade, you need to help Jack. You're a doctor. A good one. I know you're in shock, but—"

"They were both midflight, you see," Wade explains; again, more to himself than Lydia as she stands at her husband's side, hoping he is looking at his screen for a way to help Nick, not because he is more concerned about capturing the flight data than his patient's well-being. "Exactly synchronized in Nick's memory of their first night together. We'd worked on it for weeks, Nick and me. The last minute he wants something else. Something so—"

"What? You told me it was a demo. You said that—"

"It was going so well, Lidds. Better than well, in fact. It caused a transformation. You saw that for yourself last night. Rachel was a different woman, for a while at least." The monitor comes to life as Wade connects the laptop to it, reams of code appearing. Wade's eyes light up as he focuses on the patterns of code, then he looks at Lydia properly. "You should have seen it today, Lidds. They were both in Nick's memory for thirty-seven minutes. How about that?

Thirty-seven perfectly synchronized minutes. If I'd had more time . . ." Wade's eyes glaze over again as he returns to the data he's downloading. "Who knows what might have been. Bloody shame, it is, but I may be able to salvage something."

"Wade, listen to me. None of this is important right now. Nick is our only concern."

Wade shakes his head, turning to her again. "Don't look at me like that. It's clearly a heart attack or stroke, likely induced by ejaculation."

"Oh my God." Lydia recoils at the thought, hand over her mouth as she backs away from Wade. She glances over to the pod, the door now closed. Poor Jack is on his own in there, no doubt still working hard. The alternated breaths and chest compressions must be exhausting. "You're the only doctor here, Wade. Get in there and help!"

Wade looks at her briefly, then turns his attention back to his laptop. "I need to make sure the dual flight data is saved first. Invaluable stuff, even if it is Nick's interpretation and more like a bad porn movie."

"Seriously?" She stares at her husband, unable to comprehend his reaction. "That's what's important to you now?"

Jack has opened the door and calls out to anyone who cares to respond. "Could do with some help in here. I think I'm losing him."

Lydia looks to Wade, but he is making notes in one of his many online journals as if *his* life depended on it, no more interest in her than in his dying patient. And Rachel has disappeared into the gloom at the back of the lab, presumably in search of a better signal, her words indistinct as she talks to Jack's assistant.

"What can I do?" she asks Jack, propping the door open with a coil of cabling as she joins him.

"If you could grab those wires attached to the monitor," Jack says between shared breaths and heart pumps. "Then connect the loose ends to the sensors on his chest and wrists, see if there are any vital signs. Do you know how to do that?"

She nods, although it's Wade who always takes care of this when she's been in the chair. She gets down on her knees to untangle the crisscross of trailing wires. The sensors that Rachel ripped from her skin are now dangling from the empty chair at the back.

Rachel looks in, Jack's phone clamped to her right ear. "Addison has asked me to wait while she's making more calls. How is he doing? Oh my God, is he—?"

Nick's skin has turned blueish-gray, his lips bloodless, eyes open but rolled back. The black lenses that still cover the irises lend him an alien appearance in the low light. Although mainly he looks like an old man, mouth slack as Jack tries to jump-start him to life, pushing all his weight through his crossed palms and down into Nick's exposed chest, which is crushed by his efforts. Jack must have collapsed the poor guy's ribcage, but what choice did he have. An ear bud pops out of Nick's left ear with the force of Jack's latest compression. Lydia picks it up and wipes earwax from her fingers, revolted. But not as disgusted as she is by her own husband. Wade is out there making notes and backing up data, while in this hot pod Jack fights to save Nick's life. Whatever caused this, their only trained professional is doing nothing to help.

"*Hello*?" Rachel says, leaning against the pod door to keep it open. "Yes, right, hang on. Jack, Addison needs the code word for the helicopter team."

Jack looks up but keeps pumping Nick's chest. "Can you put her on speaker?"

Rachel extends her hand with the phone in it, pointing it toward Jack.

"Hi, Adds, code word is Natasha." Jack switches to mouth-to-mouth and Rachel keeps the phone raised until Jack, out of breath, adds, "Did you hear that? Yes, N-A-T-A-S-H-A. Thanks, Adds, you're the best. Talk soon."

Lydia's breath has caught in her throat. Even in the madness and chaos and fear, that name has resonated. She looks out at Wade and he looks back at her. There's a question in his eyes that reflects her own, but she answers it with a shake of her head, as if she has no idea what he's suggesting. That the name might mean something to her. Which it does. Although she has no idea why. Was that the name of someone who came here? A volunteer, perhaps. But she never meets them. Doesn't even look at their records.

"The patient's name?" Rachel asks, talking loudly into the phone again. "Yes, it's Nicholas Wentworth Bentley. American. Seventy-three . . ." The conversation disappears as she walks away, back toward the better signal. "Nope, no previous incidence of heart attack or stroke."

"Can you grab that?" Jack asks, pointing Lydia to an abandoned blood pressure cuff, hanging from the pedestal that the vital signs monitor is attached to.

Lydia retrieves the blood pressure cuff and passes it around Nick's dead-weight arm, but it's too small and won't fasten.

"That was the one I had on," Rachel says, back at the propped door and now off the phone. "What the fuck were you thinking?" Rachel shouts at Wade, still at his desk. "You can't mess with people like this. I'm a grown woman. Not a doll to be programmed and then brainwashed into submission for another five fucking years of hell."

"Tell that to your husband, not me," Wade responds, his voice chilling. "He was the one who made me do this. He's a bully and you know it, but you're just as bad. You clearly don't care about him at all."

"You don't give a fuck, do you?" Rachel shouts back. "But maybe you will when I sue your ass off."

"This isn't my fault," Wade says, squaring up to Rachel and blocking all the light into the dark pod. "All I was trying to do was—"

"Make a fortune at Nick's expense, and mine too?"

"I'm trying to keep this place going to find a cure for dementia. But you wouldn't care about that either," Wade replies. "Everything is about *you* and trying to get out of the prenup early. So, let me illuminate you, Mrs. Bentley. He was already prepping his legal team for the battle, this was your last chance to make a cent."

"What the—" Rachel replies, letting go of the door. "That's not true."

Lydia flings open the door again and stares at Wade. "We need better light and a larger cuff. Now!"

Wade passes a cuff from the drawer of his desk and holds the door open while she swaps the connectors before securing the Velcro around Nick's fleshy upper arm. His color is improving, or is that wishful thinking? The cuff inflates, and Nick gasps and splutters, a reassuring blip coming from the monitor. *Thank God.*

Rachel pushes her way into the pod as the blood pressure cuff starts inflating for a second time. It must hurt as it squeezes tighter and tighter, but there's no flicker or sign from

Nick, and the reading comes up as an error message. She catches Jack's eye. He'd stopped the compressions at Nick's gasp but starts up again. Rachel looks scared. She feels the same, and why isn't Wade doing something more than holding open the bloody door?

"Hello?" Rachel says, phone to her ear again and voice loud in the tiny pod. "Yes, sorry, hang on, Addison, I'll put you on to someone who can tell you more." Rachel hands Lydia the phone. "She needs detailed location information. Can you help?"

"No. I have no idea. I never leave the mountain. Give it to Wade"

"He's useless. You speak to her." Rachel presses the phone into her palm, and Lydia does her best to respond to the American woman's questions, leaving the pod as the signal is patchy in there. "A landmark? I guess the nearest village. It's a complicated name. I can spell it out. Oh, okay, you have it? Great. There's a shop, in the valley. My husband could drive Nick down, meet the helicopter there."

Wade, now back at his desk, looks up and nods.

"Yes, that would be the closest they can land," she tells the efficient American woman at the other end. "Yes, we will get Nick down there as soon as we can. Just need to stabilize him and then we can move him to the car."

"What's happening?" Rachel asks, looking out of the pod.

"The helicopter is about a thirty-minute flight from here, at the airport you flew into. She's done an amazing job to alert them already, and says they are leaving soon, so we need to get Nick down to the car as soon as we can."

"Thirty minutes?" Rachel asks, looking as panicked by that as Lydia feels.

"I know, but hopefully even sooner and the drive will take at least that long."

"*Hopefully*?" Rachel shouts. Closing in so spittle lands on Lydia's cheek and the pod door slams shut behind her. "You have no backup plan, no infrastructure, and you mess with people's lives, what the fuck is this place? If you've killed my husband I'm going to sue you both until you don't have the clothes you're wearing." Rachel glares at Wade. "You are a monster and I will never forgive you, for any of this. Give me that phone, Lydia!"

Alarmed, Lydia hands it over, and Rachel stuffs the smuggled phone into her trouser pocket.

"No one has killed anyone," Wade responds, perfectly calm. "Your husband was a ticking time bomb. Anyone could see that. I'm guessing that's why you panicked and agreed to this trip. He's not worth a cent to you dead, is he?"

"How dare you!" Rachel says, slapping Wade hard across the face.

"He collapsed reliving the memory of fucking you," Wade replies, rubbing his reddened cheek. "You're nothing more than a—"

Rachel rushes at Wade again, bashing into Lydia, who has tried to block her. Rachel shoves her aside, fists flailing. Wade ducks as the blows rain down. Hands over his head.

"I will make sure the world knows the truth about you and your foundation, you have my word on that," Rachel says. "But first you drive us back down this fucking mountain."

CHAPTER 30

Lydia

THE COURTYARD IS empty as another day hurtles toward night and once again Lydia keeps watch for the Tank's return. Only twenty-four hours since she was last scanning the mountain for headlights. Hard to believe. So much has happened since then.

It's been hours since Wade drove the Bentleys away, the tire tracks now obliterated by the continuing snowstorm, but her worry for Nick's life—that still very much hung in the balance as they left—and so much else besides, remains undiminished. It was awful to witness all that trauma. But the most confusing part is Wade's behavior. She shivers and hugs herself. It feels like she doesn't know her husband anymore, or even herself.

Thank goodness for Jack, who managed to get Nick breathing steadily enough to move him, but that took ages, even with four of them sharing the load. Between the dead weight of Nick, roughly two hundred and fifty pounds, plus the punishing conditions on the compromised walkway, it had been a minor miracle to get him over to the foundation's main building. But it was by then well over an hour post-collapse.

At least Wade seemed to have recovered his composure enough to drive, roaring out the gates with little regard for the poor visibility. He is their absolute best chance of getting Nick the help he needs, although that doesn't excuse his lack of intervention before that hasty exit. She's never seen her husband anything less than in control before. Single-minded, focused, yes, but not paralyzed with fear. Shock can incapacitate a person, but Wade is a doctor. Surely he is used to coping in a crisis. That's what he's trained to do, although he's never worked in trauma, always research. Her questions for Wade will have to wait. All she can hope is that Nick receives the urgent medical attention he so desperately needs, and if not, as Rachel quite rightly pointed out, that is entirely on them.

Nick's motives for that dual flight were clear, to convince his younger wife to stay with him, by any means. And he will have offered an exorbitant sum to Wade, no doubt, which will have played a part in her husband's choices. She's no fool. Everyone has their price, and Wade's desire to save this place is as much for her benefit as the foundation's higher aims. The remote location has provided her with a much-needed sanctuary, but it's absolutely no excuse. They both want the foundation to continue, but not at the expense of every ethical consideration they have jointly lived and worked by. Or the potential death of a guest who, despite his questionable behavior, absolutely does not deserve to die.

What hurts the most is Wade's duplicity. She'd thought until a few hours ago that they shared everything. It scared her how Wade lit up when he explained what he'd achieved in the pod, despite Nick's deteriorating condition.

Imposing Nick's so-called memory on his wife is, as Rachel said herself, little short of brainwashing and entirely repugnant, although Rachel's motives for coming here don't sound entirely innocent either. She agreed to this last-ditch attempt at saving their marriage in order to secure an early divorce settlement. But that doesn't excuse a distortion of the past to somehow trick Rachel into what, falling in love with Nick again? If she ever did love him. Lydia can't bear to think about what was in that memory flight. Wade's description of a sexualized version of their romance sends another shudder through her as she watches for his return. She is so mad at him, but at the same time she agrees with Wade on one vital matter. The Bentleys' memory flight, however stimulating, will not be the direct cause of Nick's collapse. The man was a walking heart attack. This would likely have happened at some point soon regardless. It's just bad luck it was while they were here. The main issue now is whether Nick gets to the hospital in time. She checks her phone again, but still nothing from Wade. She just needs to hear his voice, or see his words, or better still spy the Tank coming up the mountain. They must have reached the rendezvous point at the village store hours ago.

Jack comes down from his shower, the one he'd been reluctant to take in case there was news but desperately needed after the exertion of preserving Nick's life. He's been gone a long while too, but looks refreshed as he joins Lydia and Zoe in the entrance hall, his hair still damp. Maybe he slept for an hour so first. He earned some rest, but shivers now as he sits by the dying embers. Wade only chopped a small basket of logs, and the last one is burning down too fast. It is getting really cold in here now. And the lights are less bright than they were an hour ago too. The generator must be almost through the fuel Wade added last night. Zoe is seated by the fire too, but she barely turns her head to acknowledge Jack's arrival. Lydia's just glad that Zoe's calmed down. It was touch and go there for a while.

The commotion of carrying Nick over from the lab roused Zoe from her room, and it's fair to say she did not handle the sight of a desperately ill man, supported at each limb as they carried him across the hallway, at all well. Zoe started shouting a load of crazy stuff about more ghosts to bury in Ghost Valley, which was unhelpful as they struggled with Nick's bulk between the four of them. Wade suggested Lydia should fetch Zoe a brandy as he and Jack manhandled Nick down the steep steps to the basement, Rachel following behind. Lydia mixed a slug of warming cognac into a can of diet Coke for Zoe and had one herself as they watched Wade drive the Bentleys out the gates at speed, despite the thick snow. Jack refused a drink. He looked exhausted as he'd explained how he had to relinquish his phone to Rachel, to keep in touch for Addison for the helicopter rendezvous. It wasn't the time or place to challenge Jack on the smuggled phone. The many unspoken accusations still there, in the silence, as the three of them wait for news.

"Any updates?" Jack asks her now, rubbing his face with his warmed palms.

"Nope," she replies as she leaves the view to move a little closer to the fire herself. The power is still on, but definitely not running at full capacity, and with night falling and the logs gone, it's a concern. "I'd have told you if there was news," she adds as Jack looks at her hopefully.

She didn't mean to be so abrupt, but with each minute that passes her concern for Nick increases, and her suspicions about Jack being a spy haven't diminished either, despite his incredible intervention with Nick. The lights flicker, but no one comments. Zoe's been silent for a while, and Jack has clearly decided to keep his thoughts to himself. Maybe they are all in shock, as Wade evidently was. She can't get over the way her usually capable husband crumbled so fast, but the foundation is everything to him. To see this week go so badly wrong would have been his worst nightmare. He's been so damaged by his father's poor opinion of him. "If only I could trust you with my legacy, but you always let me down." Dr. Hunter Senior hadn't been in his right mind, but words like that stick. Or at least, they have for Wade.

The lights flicker again, the beat when they are out much longer this time. Zoe looks up.

"It'll be fine," Lydia reassures her. "Wade will be back soon."

Zoe nods. "I know that."

"And thanks again, for all your help with Nick," she says to Jack, declining his offer to make room on the sofa, although Zoe shows no sign of shifting along. "I'm sorry if I was short with you just now. Frayed nerves, but no excuse."

"Forget it. And I only did what anyone with an ounce of medical training would have done," he replies, the inference clear.

"I've never seen my husband like that before," she says, warming her hands on the minimal heat the fire is giving out. Wade had promised to cut more logs as needed. But that was before the snow. Before all this. "In his defense, he was clearly in shock."

Jack shrugs. "We were all shocked by what happened."

"Amazing, though, you getting a helicopter just like that," Lydia says, and Jack nods, as if that's a usual thing. "The foundation will obviously cover the cost."

"That won't be necessary," Jack responds. "But good of you to offer."

She doesn't protest. There's no way they can cover the cost, whatever that might be, especially now this week has fallen apart, just as she felt in her bones it would. They will have to refund all the guests' fees, abandon the program, and if Rachel has her way, face legal action too. The foundation will close and she will have to go home. Except there is no home. Just consequences and a reckoning she's avoided and dreaded, but which now feels closer than at any point in the last five years. She will have to explain the decision that she made in those seconds before the avalanche hit her car. To excuse or explain that instinctive need to survive, if it were even possible to do so. Because who puts themselves before their own flesh and blood. An innocent child. *Her* child. She takes deep breaths, pacing the cold room to distract herself and try to keep warm.

Jack drops his hands between his knees, head down. She can see the strip of skin on the back of his neck above the neatly shaved line of dark damp hair. It's so smooth she wants to run her fingers along it as she passes by. She shakes her head and stifles a shiver at the outlandish thought. No idea where that came from.

Jack looks round at her, the small but flickering flames reflected in his dark eyes. "You sure you don't want to sit here by the fire? There's room."

"No, I'm . . . No. Thank you."

"Shouldn't he be back by now, though?" Jack asks. "It's only a couple of hours round trip."

It's the same thing Lydia's been thinking.

"Maybe waiting for the helicopter to land," she replies. "The weather is bad."

Zoe pulls a face, as if she doesn't agree. "I thought he'd have messaged you."

Lydia checks her phone again and shakes her head. "Nope, not yet. Probably busy helping them get Nick in the helicopter."

She prays it's that and not that something has happened to Wade on the drive back.

Jacks gets up and paces the entrance hall too, eventually coming face to face with Lydia. "I need to talk to you about something, in private."

She glances over to Zoe. In the firelight the penguin's beady eyes on Zoe's sweater are animated. Zoe looks round and stares at them.

"Let's talk about what happened once Wade is back with us," she replies, trying to sidestep Jack.

"Not that," Jack says, leaning closer and holding her arm. "The code name I gave to Adds, did that name mean anything to you?"

"Addison?"

"No, the other name," Jack says, looking over at Zoe and dropping his voice to a whisper. "Natasha."

"Is there something going on with you two?" Zoe asks, looking at Jack, then Lydia. "Feeling like the third wheel over here."

Jack shakes his head and drops his hold on Lydia. "No, nothing. It can wait."

"I'll tell you one thing," Zoe says. "If Nick Bentley has sabotaged my flights then . . . Well, it's not fair, is it? None of this is my fault."

Jack looks as taken aback by Zoe's thoughtless comment as Lydia feels. They exchange a quick glance, standing side by side now.

"I'm not sure any of us should be thinking that right now," Jack says. "We don't even know if he's . . ."

"True," Zoe concurs. "Bad luck all round, though. And of course nothing to do with Dr. Hunter."

"You can't believe that?" Jack asks.

"Of course I do," Zoe continues, undeterred by Jack's expression of disbelief. "Nick's clogged tubes were the cause of this, not the memory flight."

Lydia agrees, but she should be the one saying these things, not Zoe. And when the time is right.

"Nick wasn't being properly monitored," Jack counters. "At the very least it's negligent, not to mention Rachel's obvious lack of consent."

"I wouldn't know about that," Zoe replies getting up. "But I do know that Dr. Hunter would never risk the Memory Foundation's reputation. He's a good man." She stops talking and looks at Lydia. "Isn't that right, *Mrs. Wade Hunter*?"

Zoe's tone is combative, but the sentiment is true. Lydia is about to concur when she hears something outside. She heads straight to the glass door, Jack and Zoe close behind. The Tank is at the locked gates, lights beaming through the steel bars. The drifts are back. The snow relentless. The gates stuck. But Wade's home.

"Stay there!" she yells as she taps in the code and the door slides open.

It's unbelievably cold outside, ice crystals glistening in the moonlight and slippy under the soles of her sneakers as she pelts down the ramp. The Tank is edging through the now opening gates and then across the forecourt, which is awash with powdery drifts. Her feet and hands are numb with cold as she runs toward him. She hasn't even bothered to pull on her coat.

"How is he?" she asks through the window as soon as Wade winds it down. "Did you get to the helicopter in time? Was he still—"

"Go in, it's freezing!" Wade tells her.

"But he *is* alive?"

"He was when I left him."

"Oh, thank God."

* * *

"Nick's on his way," she says, teeth chattering as she comes back inside, greeted by Jack and Zoe's expectant faces. "He was doing okay when Wade handed him over."

"Good," Jack says, looking less than convinced.

"Yes, it is," Zoe replies, with more enthusiasm. "Maybe now we can—"

The basement door flies open and Wade comes through, his hair wild with snow. He looks exhausted, cloaked in sweat and clearly in no mood for questions, but Jack and Zoe have plenty.

"Did you get my phone back from Rachel?" Jack asks.

"Why were you so long, Dr. Hunter?" Zoe demands. Stepping between the two men.

"No, I didn't get your smuggled phone back," Wade says, meeting Jack's stare and ignoring Zoe. "Funnily enough, that wasn't the main priority."

"But Nick *is* okay . . ." Jack says, backing down.

"Yes, of course," Wade replies as he rubs his hands over his face.

"Must have been a tough drive," Lydia says, looking at her wearied husband.

"Yes, it was, darling. Thanks for saying that." Wade offers her a warm smile. "How are you?"

"I guess okay," she says, forcing a smile too. "Sad this has happened. Confused. Lots of questions."

Wade nods and slumps down on the sofa. "Which I will of course answer, but firstly I must thank you, Jack."

"It's what anyone would have done," Jack replies, coldly.

"Well, you did and I didn't. I guess that's something I'll need to address. Years of hibernation have clearly taken their toll. I apologize to you all, but especially my wife." Wade gets up again, as if he cannot sit for long. Too wired, despite or perhaps because of the ordeal. "I thought I'd do better, but I am a man of science predominantly. Not used to such situations."

"No need to explain," Zoe says. "We all get it."

"Good, so if you'll excuse me—" Wade heads for the door to the walkway.

"You're abandoning me already?" Lydia asks, running across the hallway to Wade and the words out before she can filter them.

"I won't be long, I promise," he says, closing his eyes for a second. "I just need to get my head together. It's been, well, rather the eye-opener."

She drops her voice to a whisper and leans in close. "Wade, please don't disappear to your lab. I need you here, not least to check on the power."

"Yes, of course," he says, glancing up to the compromised spotlights. "Just let me clear up the mess in the pod. Gather my thoughts for a moment or two."

"Okay, but I'll come over with you," she says, catching Wade's eye. He owes her an explanation, and he knows it.

"You need to stay with our remaining guests," Wade says, looking at Jack, then finally Zoe. "I'll let you know as soon as we can resume today's flights."

"You don't seriously expect us to continue after—" she says, stunned by what she's hearing. "Nick's not even out of danger yet. Is he?"

"Not now, Lidds!" Wade replies, his voice raised. He relents immediately, taking her hand. "Sorry. You're right. And I promise, I won't be long. Just give me a few minutes, that's all. It's been a lot."

Wade unlocks the heavy door to the walkway and steps out. She can't believe he's leaving again so soon, but he looks crushed and she knows he needs this reset. He glances toward Jack and then Zoe, a quick nod before he allows the door to gently close.

"Is he serious?" Jack storms, pacing the room. "I can't believe the way he treats you, treats all of us."

"He doesn't mean it," Lydia counters. "He's stressed. His work is everything. He won't be long."

"We're all stressed." Jack goes to the glass door and looks out, his breath fogging the pane. "And we all need to get out of here before it's no longer an option."

"There's honestly no need to panic," Lydia tells him, the lights flashing on and off again in defiance of her comment. "Wade will be back any minute and he will fix the power and it will be much better to leave in the morning when—Zoe, what are you doing?"

It all happens at once and in a flash. Zoe runs toward the door to the walkway that Wade just left through and shoves it hard, then their scholarship place steps out into a blizzard.

CHAPTER

31

Lydia

THE DOOR SLAMS hard. Zoe gone. Lydia, stunned, does nothing for a second or two. "I don't understand how she opened the door," she says, looking at Jack. "It would have locked behind Wade."

Lydia takes her phone from her jeans pocket and taps the app to open up the home security system. Jack watches as she enters the combination, then trying other permutations of the four numbers she was convinced were the correct code.

"Shall *I* try?" Jack asks, holding out his hand.

"How would you know the code?" she asks, frustration making her angry. "Were you watching me?"

"No, I was actually watching Wade," Jack says, reaching for her phone.

Lydia cradles it to her. "You are not having my phone. You're clearly a spy."

Jack ignores her comment and runs his hands through his hair, turning away as she jabs in random numbers without success. They don't have the time for this. Zoe will be terrified on the swaying bridge in the dark and with a blizzard blowing across the ravine. "Oh God!"

"What is it?" Jack asks, looking at her again.

"The door at the other end of the bridge will be locked so unless Wade hears her, which is unlikely through the storm—Zoe wasn't even wearing a coat."

Jack nods. "She could freeze out there."

Lydia nods and tries jabbing in a different code, but she was certain she had it right the first time. She gives up on the code and calls Wade, but he doesn't answer. He will be immersed in his work, likely backing up Nick and Rachel's aborted dual flight and analyzing the code. No way he's taking a moment to decompress, that was an excuse. He always escapes to his lab when he's stressed. She sends him a warning message about Zoe, then opens the keypad by the door and tries pressing the code into that. "I don't understand why it's not working."

Jack places a hand on her back, startling her. "Keep trying, but can I please borrow your phone? I need to check with Addison how Nick is. I have a feeling there may be a bigger problem here than Zoe's planned exit."

"Planned?" Lydia says, looking round, a painful twinge in her neck as she does so. "I don't think so!"

"Listen," Jack says, a hand on each shoulder as he turns her to face him, and looks down at her. "Zoe has gone over to meet Wade, and it *was* planned. I saw him give her the nod before he left. He must have opened the door remotely or maybe left it a tiny bit ajar. I thought it was odd how he closed it so slowly when it's usually left to slam shut."

"No, that's crazy," she says, shaking off Jack's unwanted touch. "I mean, Zoe's infatuated with him and the idea of the memory flights, that's obvious, but Wade wouldn't have planned for her to follow him, he just wouldn't—"

"Please, let me call Addison and then I'll prove it to you. Oh, and by the way, I think Wade is changing the codes to confuse you."

"That's absurd. I just forget because . . . I'm forgetful. And it's you who is trying to confuse me with your lies."

"I'm sorry, I know it's hard to take in, but I believe he's messing with your mind as he tried to with Rachel's. He was brainwashing her, just as she said. Just as he—"

"Now you *are* being crazy. Nick is the coercive one. You said so yourself."

Jack doesn't reply, although he looks at her for a long time. His expression, if she had to define it, is one of pity. "You call Addison, then," he says. I need to know if it's too late for the Bentleys before we work out what to do next."

"Wade said Nick was alive. And there is no *we* here." She jabs a finger back and forth between them. "I need to get to Zoe, that is all I care about right now."

Jack holds out his hand for the phone. "Please, one call."

She holds out the phone, then snatches it back. "One call to this Addison, then I want it straight back."

"Thank you." He takes the phone and taps the screen. "Argh! No signal."

"Switch to Wi-Fi calling," she tells him.

"I did. Wade must have turned off the router. Are there cameras in here?"

She looks at the glass door, giving away the location of the tiny CCTV camera next to the coat rack.

"Okay, he's likely watching us," Jack says, following her eyeline. "Turn your back a sec so I can explain."

"No, Wade wouldn't do that, it's the generator again," she says, looking at her useless phone. "The power supply is playing up. That's all."

On cue the lights dim, but thankfully they don't go out completely.

"He's controlling everything, don't you see?" Jack asks, looking at the camera. "The codes, the power, the Wi-Fi—and you."

"That's ridiculous. I have trouble with recall because . . . It doesn't matter."

"What did he do to you?"

"Nothing. I had an accident, I told you. I fell, in the snow."

Jack shakes his head, pacing the cold entrance hall now. "Actually, I don't know about the generator, I think that's just incompetence. He's no more a qualified engineer than he is a medically trained doctor."

"That's enough," she says, trying the keypad again, but the door stays firmly shut. "Poor Zoe, she will be terrified. We have to do something."

Jack runs upstairs, leaving her to it, which she should be grateful for, but she can't deal with this alone. Any company is better than none.

He sprints back down a couple of minutes later. She is still trying to get the code to work, every combination she tries wrong, and despite the dropping temperatures she's burning up, the back of her neck on fire so she feels woozy, like she's floating in the near darkness and is then suddenly freezing cold. She can't let Jack's lies get into her head, making her panic, or the fact the camera is staring at her, a small red light at its base coming on and then disappearing again.

"It's from Zoe's room," he says, shoving an iPad at her. "I had my suspicions, and I was right. Look at the latest messages."

"That is private between Wade and Zoe," she says, pushing it away. "I can't violate doctor-patient confidentiality, and you should not be breaking into her room. How did you even do that? The security system Wade designed is unbreakable."

Jack huffs, a derisory sound as he says, "O-kaay, but please, it's important, read the last few messages."

"If only to prove you wrong," she says, taking the iPad. "And I'll be reporting this to Wade, as soon as I get over there." She brandishes the tablet. "Proves he's been right about you all along."

Jack sighs. "Oh yes, what crackpot theory did he have about me?"

"Just that you were not to be trusted, and he was right." She stares at the lit screen of the iPad, a sudden and even more painful twinge running through her, waves of white hot pain from her neck down her spine that makes her wince and close her eyes.

"Are you all right?" Jack asks. "What's happening? Is he doing this?"

"No, of course not." She shrugs off his concern and rubs her stiff neck and stretches out her aching back.

"You were going to read the latest messages," Jack reminds her, taking the tablet back from her slack grasp and tapping the screen to revive it. "I haven't gone too far back, but there are loads of them."

"Let me see that!" she says, snatching it back.

She has her doubts about her husband's recent behavior, but that doesn't mean she's going to trust a total stranger over the man she loves and has never once questioned from the moment he hauled her out of the snow and carried her to safety five years before. Wade is a good man. Whatever Jack is implying about her husband's interactions with Zoe is pure poison. She squints at the screen, but only to disprove Jack's wild theories. Still not sure what they might be. She starts reading the message at the top of the screen first. One of a few sent today, but not the last.

Hey, you back soon, Dr. H? You must have dumped them both by now.

"Dumped them?" she says, more to herself than Jack.

"The Bentleys," Jack says. "In the snow, I'd imagine, although I pray to God I'm wrong."

"That's crazy. She's just clumsy in her wording. And if she is stuck out there on that bridge to the lab we need to—"

"She isn't stuck, she's with Wade, in the lab, as planned. What I don't know is why."

"Okay, that's enough."

Lydia runs into the guest lounge, dropping the iPad on the bar as she heads to the window. She can't see Zoe on the walkway, but that doesn't mean their traumatized guest isn't cowering somewhere out of sight, concealed in the darkness and shivering now in her sweater. The blizzard makes it very hard to be sure of anything, other than the compacted snow on the roof is weighing it down even more than when they carried Nick over, many hours ago now. It's more like a deep V than a taut line. But what strikes her most as she looks out is that through the snow the glass roof of the lab is a sparkling bright dome. Wade has switched the remaining power back to his lab again, which means he's working and definitely won't hear Zoe at the door.

"She's with him," Jack says, coming in and picking up Zoe's iPad from the bar.

"You can't know that. She could still be on the bridge, cowering. Afraid."

"It's all there, in the messages," he says, brandishing the iPad. "As I suspected it would be when I went upstairs to check."

"You're delusional, that much is obvious. And you shouldn't be hacking into—How *did* you hack into Wade's system? It's pin-protected for each guest."

"Wade's app wasn't exactly hard to crack either. I'm a software engineer, or rather was, it's had to take a backseat of late." He hands her the tablet again and encourages her to scroll through. She takes it. If only to shut him up, because Zoe needs their help.

There are a lot of messages, mainly from Zoe. She scans through them, getting the gist. Zoe is asking "Dr. Hunter" when he will be back. She wants to get on with her flights. Can't wait to try out "the new stuff." So exciting. All pretty much as expected. A troublesome, or maybe troubled, woman with only her own needs in mind. Then Wade's response comes.

OMW, back soon. You'll need to follow me over to the lab. Only chance. Don't let me down. This is your last chance too. I'll give you a signal. Don't fuck this up!

Lydia looks up, heart pounding as Jack meets her gaze. "See?" he asks.

"See what? That she's traumatized, on antidepressants, clearly not well. Wade is humoring her, that's all." It feels as if she's clutching at straws, but she cannot stop, and despite the cold, she's burning up again.

"Okay, then answer me this, if Wade knows that Zoe is mentally unwell, why did he accept her as a volunteer?"

"For that very reason. She was a deserving case and my husband is a compassionate man who wants to give back. The scholarship was an act of kindness."

"Okay, assuming that's true, which I doubt, why allow the flights to continue after this morning's medical emergency?"

"We don't know that is the case, and *if* he is helping Zoe, it will be to try and do just that, *help* the poor woman. The flights are totally safe."

Jack sighs. "You can't believe that. He's proven himself, and them, completely fallible."

"I know it's hard to relate to Wade's single-mindedness," Lydia explains, as much to herself as Jack. "But that focus is what got him this far. He wants to help people like Zoe, and Nick's situation was in no way—"

"And I understand that it's hard for you to accept the reality of what's happening here, you've been under this man's coercive control for five years now—"

"Wade and I love one another, Jack. Everything he's done, literally everything, has been for me and the foundation. You have no idea how much he's helped me, and countless others. Zoe is new to all this, but she too—"

"Zoe and your husband have a relationship of many years." Jack points at the tablet. "It's there, in their exchanges."

"An affair? Is that what you're trying to convince me of?" She laughs. "Wade loves me."

Jack shakes his head. "Look at what she calls herself in the earlier messages. His Patient A. She's been a volunteer for years."

"I don't have time for this," she says, walking out. "We need to help Zoe, she could be stranded out there in minus thirty."

"Zoe knows this place, understands how it works," Jack says, following her into the dimly lit hallway and holding up the iPad as his so-called proof. "She was visiting long before you arrived. That's why she was provoking you. She resents you, resents all of us. Wanted to scare us off to have this place, and him, to herself."

Lydia spins round to face Jack. "I'd have known her, if that was the case."

"Would you? You said you never meet the volunteers."

"Well, she'd have known about me."

"I think she does. She loves to challenge you."

"Okay, so tell me, mister former software specialist, why are *you* here? Come to steal our secrets with your questions and a smuggled phone and a helicopter close by. You clearly have an agenda."

"Not in the way you mean, no."

She glances at her phone. No response from Wade, but her head has cleared and the pain and heat in her neck are finally gone, a cool clarity returned despite the mess that Jack has tried to fill it with. She taps in the correct code and the door to the walkway unseals.

"You stay here," she tells Jack, pushing him back from the door as she steps out.

The blizzard is horrific, the tunnel dark, but as far as she can see there's no sign of Zoe.

CHAPTER

32

Lydia

THE FLOOR SHAKES as Lydia runs over. She's never felt it do that before, and the lights in the tunnel are strobing. Plus the temperature has dropped again, just as she'd feared it would have. The funnel of cold air is so icy it's hard to catch her breath. And the wind is finding its way in through the thin walls and rattling windows. She looks up, terrified to see how the roof is visibly bowing under the weight of more compacted snow. The whole structure is compromised as it creaks and groans against the metal ties holding it in place at each end. Alarming cracks are opening up in the thin sides too, letting in even fiercer drafts. All she is wearing is jeans, sneakers, and the shirt of Wade's she'd covered with a fresh hoodie during the long wait for him to return in the Tank. If Zoe is somewhere up ahead, concealed in the darkness, she could well be suffering with hypothermia.

A blue light reflects from the white that blankets everything below. The helicopter taking Nick to the hospital. No, that would have left ages ago. She daren't look down to check, forcing her gaze up and her focus forward. The blue light is simply the reflection of so much snow in the ravine. The lab glows bright in the distance, her prize. If she can get over there, see Wade, then everything will be all right. She's never known so much snow to fall in such a short space of time and so early in winter, the windows packed with it, and flurries tumbling past, the wind screaming now. It's all an unwelcome reminder of the night she'd arrived at the top of the mountain and got caught in an avalanche, but she can't give in to that memory and the inevitable panic attack that would follow. She must keep going, although she still can't see Zoe up ahead. Then she looks down, just for a second, but that's all it takes.

A blinding pain in the top of her head, behind her eyes, down her spine, stops her in her tracks. She is more than halfway, on the upward stretch, but she can't go on. She closes her eyes and she's back there in her rental car five years before, clambering into the back to free the child restraints. She has seconds at most to release the buckles, but the clasps are resistant and her hands tremble. A familiar pain punctures her chest as she realizes she won't be able to save her baby in time and yet she tries in the vain hope she can unfasten him and throw him to safety. The roar of the avalanche grows deafening. She has seconds left and she knows this is it. The moment she will regret to her dying day. She covers her ears and drops to her knees as the familiar ear-splitting sound fills her head. A sound so loud it easily eclipses her cries, but this time the keening sound is not coming from her, but from the past. The screams of her child, the one she left behind in her car. High pitched, desperate, then gone as the car that she'd flung herself from seconds before is dragged into the ravine in a river of snow.

She opens her eyes to meet Jack's. They are kind eyes. Filled with concern. He's crouched on the floor of the walkway beside her, and she is ridiculously, illogically, pleased to see him. He must have followed her, catching the door before it slammed and there all the time, a few paces behind.

He looks past her, to the end of the tunnel, which is very clearly empty. Zoe must have gone through the locked door at the end and into the lab. Either that or she has vanished.

"She's with Wade," she says, stating the obvious before Jack does. "That's good."

"Maybe," Jack replies, frowning, although he resists saying that he'd told her so, offering a hand to help her up. "Are you okay to go on?"

"Yes, thanks. But you can go back now."

Jack shakes his head. "No way. And we should move fast, this thing looks ready to collapse."

She leads the way, no time to argue her case or reassure him that despite appearances there's no way the bridge will detach from the rock its attached to at each end. It's been here decades, withstood all weathers, but the effort of the steep gradient and the constantly moving walkway make it much harder to walk at speed, let alone run, especially when the wind rocks the moorings, a grind of metal that slices through her. She takes the last few hard-won paces, phone in hand to unlock the door, but then she stops, feet planted to steady herself.

"What's wrong?" Jack asks.

"There's no signal. There never is out here, but the Wi-Fi won't connect either." She hammers on the sealed door. "Wade, open up!" She looks at Jack. "He can't hear us."

"Is there another way in?" Jack asks, hammering too.

"No, and it's soundproofed in the pod so if they are in there—"

Jack is feeling around the door in the dark. "No emergency handle on the outside?" he asks, scanning back down the moving dark tunnel as the wind screams at them. She shakes her head. "Right, course not, that would involve an element of safeguarding your husband clearly does not—"

"So what do we do?"

Jack shrugs and her heart sinks, then he takes Zoe's iPad from the back of his jeans, wedged there under his shirt.

"The guest app doesn't unlock these doors," she tells him, anticipating his thought. "And if the router isn't working . . ." She returns to her thumps on the door, the heel of her hand painful against the metal. "Wade. It's Lydia!"

The walkway suddenly drops, a few feet or more, displacing them both so they end up grabbing one another to stay upright. "What's happening?" she asks, looking out the closest window to the crystalline rock face, sheer and as smooth as the ice that covers it.

Jack looks out his side, to the view over the wide ravine. "The bridge is collapsing, minutes left, if that."

"Are you kidding me?" she asks, hugging herself as she shivers, her body if not her mind believing him. "We need to get in there and warn them."

"Give me your phone," he says. "Let me try to connect it."

"How?"

"Just let me try."

She hesitates, then the walkway drops again, and she shoves the phone into his hand.

Jack taps on the screen and a few seconds later he hands it back, the Wi-Fi connected.

"How did you do that?" she asks.

"There is another network over here, I'm guessing you didn't know about it?"

"No," she says, tapping in the code. There's a delay, agonizing, then the door opens. She hauls herself up the steep incline first, Jack following.

The lab is bright and apparently empty, the door to the pod sealed tight. No signs of life as Lydia scans the length of the lab and then runs down to the storeroom. Also empty.

"I guess they're in there?" Jack asks, pointing to the pod as she returns.

"I guess they are."

"How do we get in?" Jack asks, feeling round the almost invisible edges of the door.

"There's no way to open it from the outside."

"Now you are kidding *me*?" Jack asks, raising his hands. "What if there was an emergency?"

"Wade can open it from inside."

"For God's sake, can you hear yourself?" Jack replies. "I'm sorry, but this place is a death trap." The sound of the creaking bridge competes with the wail of the wind as he pauses to think. "Is there another way back, other than the bridge?"

She shakes her head. "It's sheer rock on every side of the lab, so that's not an option, believe me."

"Which means we're all marooned once the walkway collapses?"

"But it won't. It's as solid as the rock its attached to, I know it is."

Jack closes his eyes and puts his hands on his head, then he draws a deep breath and looks at her again. "I know it's not your fault. He's done this to you. But please acknowledge that the foundation is falling down around us."

"No, I do not accept that. And no one has *done* anything to me, least of all my husband."

Jack goes back to his attempts at prizing open the pod door, his nails pulling at the sealed edges.

She turns her back and types a message to Wade, concealing her efforts to alert her husband by pocketing her phone as soon as Jack gives up on the pod door and starts hunting around the lab.

"What are you looking for?" she asks him.

"Something to break into that pod," Jack says, heading toward the back of the lab.

"It's just a storeroom back there," she replies, following him. "And the volunteer accommodation."

Lydia's had no reason to come back here since the renovations of the accommodation were completed. The predigital patient notes are locked in a tall cabinet at the back of the storeroom, each drawer labeled alphabetically, the top one dedicated to just one volunteer: Patient A. The name stands out after Jack's comments about Zoe referencing herself as Wade's Patient A in their exchange of messages. The longest-standing volunteer. But that cannot be the case. She was a scholarship. First time here. It's just an affectation Zoe adopted. Lydia thought Wade had shredded the paper records after they moved them from the Crow's Nest to make room for her desk up there in the eaves. Flight data is digitally stored and backed up now, has been for years. Video testimony replacing transcripts. Some of these volunteer records could be getting on for a decade old now, when Wade took over his father's research. Dr. Hunter Senior's attempts at memory capture and retrieval had, as Wade put it, produced "mixed results," but all data is useful, both good and bad. She tries the cabinet, but it's locked. She checks her phone again, but there's still no response from Wade, so she follows Jack through to the volunteer accommodation. The noise he's making as he rifles through cupboards and drawers in the kitchenette, is irritating her now.

"You won't find anything sharp," she tells him as he starts searching a nightstand beside the lower bunk of one of the metal framed beds.

"Won't I?" Jack says, holding up a penknife.

Jack tries hard to force the pod door open with the blunt knife, but his efforts prove a waste of his time. He throws the knife aside, and then the door springs open, winding Jack who is knocked to the floor.

"What's going on, Lidds?" Wade asks, looking at Jack who is struggling to his feet.

"I could ask you the same thing," she replies.

Wade glances behind him into the semi-dark of the pod where Zoe is strapped into the nearest chair, unmoving and silent.

"We don't have time for explanations now," Jack says, pointing up to the glass dome, which is now completely covered in thick snow. "The walkway is about to collapse, and I am concerned the whole building is compromised too."

"For God's sake, Lidds. Haven't you explained to our guest that it's been there for half a decade or more?"

"I think he may be right, Wade," she says, swallowing the hurt and recriminations that, as Jack said, will have to wait until later, when they are all safe. "About the bridge, at least."

Whatever Wade may or may not have planned with Zoe, and whoever Zoe may or may not be to him and the foundation, the priority now is everyone's safety.

"We need to leave now, while we can," Jack says. "Including Zoe."

"That won't be possible," Wade says. "As you know, Lidds. We could be looking at further trauma and PTSD, other contraindications if I end the flight now."

"Or certain death when the bridge collapses and none of us can get back!" Jack says.

"What's going on, Wade?" Lydia asks, unable to hold back in the face of Wade's intransigence. "Are you two . . ." She swallows. "Are you having an affair with Zoe?"

"God, no." Wade laughs, looking appalled. "You don't honestly believe—Zoe has serious mental health issues. I've been trying to support her as any good medical practitioner would. I can't believe you'd—"

"But you're not a doctor, are you?" Jack says.

"Of course he's a doctor," Lydia replies, tired now of Jack's pathetic attempts to discredit her husband. "And he's explained to us what he's doing, trying to help Zoe, which is exactly what I said he would—"

"You're an academic, Wade, and a failed one at that," Jack says, interrupting her. "More of an engineer at heart, you claim, although not a particularly talented one. You flunked your grad course and got fired by your appalling father for incompetence verging on—"

"Whatever you are trying to do, Jack, I suggest this stops now," Wade replies.

"I couldn't agree more!" Jack shouts, barging past Wade and into the pod.

CHAPTER

33

Lydia

"JACK, NO!" LYDIA shouts, blocking him as he approaches Zoe. "Wade's right, we can't just stop the flight. It could permanently damage her."

"Really?" Jack asks, looking shaken. "Then what do we do?"

"Nothing," Wade tells Jack, pushing him aside as he resumes his position at his laptop beside Zoe. "And if you don't mind kindly fucking off out of my pod now, or I'll have to forcibly remove you for the safety of my patient."

Zoe is strapped down but looks calm to Lydia as she leans over her. In fact, Zoe's in a state of bliss, her mouth curved into a smile. Even the penguin on her sweater looks happy.

"We need to get her out of here," Jack says to Lydia. "What can you do?"

"Wade, I do think you should abort the flight for now," Lydia says, looking at Wade across Zoe's prone body. "At the very least until the weather improves and the bridge is more stable."

"I've had enough of this scaremongering," Wade says, looking up from his laptop. "The bridge is fine. Zoe is fine. I just need you both to leave."

"Really?" she asks, incredulous. "You'd risk Zoe's life, and yours, to carry on the flight?"

"There is no risk," he says, checking the vital signs monitor, then back at his laptop.

"The bridge was dropping by feet, you must have noticed," she tells him, touching his arm to try and bring him back to her. "You can extract Zoe gently, like you used to with me if I was upset. That would be okay, wouldn't it?"

Jack catches her eye, but Wade either doesn't hear or pretends not to, then he mutters, "I can't, no. Not in this case."

"What's going on, Wade?" she asks, heart skittering almost as fast as Zoe's. The blips on the monitor speeding up.

Wade looks at her then, his eyes shining. "Can you believe it, Lidds?"

"Believe what?"

"I'm sorry I kept my plans from you, but it really is a game-changer. Permanent immersion, or at least, the start of it. And not only that, but a credible alteration of her history."

"What? No! That's incredibly dangerous, Wade."

"As is always the case in uncharted waters. That's why it's pioneering work."

"What's permanent . . . whatever that was?" Jack asks, fiddling with wires attached to Zoe's temples now.

"Don't do that, Jack!" Lydia warns him. "Please. You can't unplug her. Not if—"

She turns back to Wade, shaking his shoulder as he hunches over his laptop. Zoe hasn't stirred, but there's a reassuring blip of her racing heartbeat on the monitor. "You said we were years from that. You said it was too risky, too soon to try."

"Well, clearly not, because it's happening," Wade says, triumphant.

"No, this is wrong," Lydia replies, panicked now. "It's not worth it, Wade. She could—"

"She knows what she signed up for. Practically begged me for it, even more so after what happened with Nick," Wade replies, puffed up with pride as he looks at Zoe, still replete in her cocoon of muted delight. "And so far, so good."

"You said permanent immersion was a dream for years in the future, maybe beyond our lifetime. That's what you told me when *I* begged you to—"

"Permanent?" Jack repeats, looking at her. "What does that mean?"

"And simultaneous memory alteration," Wade tells Lydia. "I'm running an alternate narrative for her as we speak."

Stunned, Lydia steps back and hits her head hard against the curved wall of the pod. "I begged you for that for me, but you maintained it was a conceptual nirvana!" She grabs Wade by the shoulder and tries to make him to look at her.

"Can someone please explain to me what's happening," Jack asks. "Or I will pull the plug."

"The safety concerns and moral issues of immersion in an alternate reality need robust interrogation and much more thought, that's what you said," Lydia continues, ignoring Jack. "Nutrition, muscle wastage for long-term flights.

Confusion and brain trauma even on short ones. It's too dangerous and far beyond us. Beyond anyone. You outright refused when I said I was happy to be the first one to try. You said it was playing God." Lydia points at Zoe. "I can't believe she is the first one to try this, not your wife!"

Wade had mentioned the possibility of a completely fresh start about a year after she'd arrived. She'd urged him to try his untested and risky tech on her, she'd have done anything to erase her one persistent memory, but he wouldn't countenance it. Said it could lead to catastrophic brain damage. Or worse.

"I would never have exposed you to this first, my love," Wade says, glancing at her, then back to his screen. "Zoe has always been my Patient A. A pioneer in many ways. Although not exactly the first."

"Are you saying this could kill her?" Jack says, pointing at Zoe, who is laughing now, eyes blinkered by dark lenses and ears plugged.

Zoe isn't in a pod in a lab in a snowstorm. She is in her chosen place, far from here, reliving her life in an alternate and by the looks of her, much happier way.

"She wanted it, Lidds," Wade says. "Just as you did, my love. Wanted it so badly she was prepared to accept all the risks."

"You think she was in her right mind to make that call?" Lydia asks, knowing or at least suspecting the answer.

"This could well be academic soon," Jack says. "We'll all be dead if we don't get out of here before the bridge collapses."

"Wade, this is madness!" Lydia shouts, trying to work out what she might do to help Zoe. She could wrestle the laptop from Wade, but that is unlikely given he's holding it tight to his chest. And even if she did, she has no idea how to reverse the journey for Zoe, or if that's in any way a possibility. She suspects not. As Wade says, this is uncharted waters. The fully immersive experience, as far as she understands it, is too intense, too stimulating. Even setting aside the physical concerns of trauma and readjustment in long-term immersion, which this hasn't been as yet, the brain atrophies, and more worryingly, Wade told her that any kind of alteration, or deletion of traumatic events, can cause permanent and potentially fatal damage. The volunteer's brain function damaged by the conflicting data and unable to compute the changes. Even minor alterations to the truth take their toll, hence the headaches, nausea, blank spots. It's risky in the extreme and totally untested. Rumors of attempts to produce alternate immersive futures have been covered up, but there are unverified reports of volunteers suffering calamitous side effects and immense trauma, and most likely death. Zoe is a sacrificial lamb, that much is clear. Headed to slaughter. Albeit willingly. If consent was within her capability. Lydia has no idea how long they've got, or how to get Zoe out of this safely, and in time. But they must try.

"You have to do something," she tells her husband. "This is madness."

"Madness or visionary?" Wade asks. "Zoe and I have created a perfect narrative of what her life would have been like had it not been for certain *traumatic* events beyond her control. Much preferable to the one she was experiencing in her so-called 'real life.' Isn't that a kindness? She is with the man she loved who died in a fire. Very tragic."

"And if it kills her?" she replies, appalled when he shrugs. "You don't care about that?"

Wade sets the laptop down on the podium. "I know you are feeling left out, my love. But when this is proven, we can try it on you, I promise."

"Get her out of this program," Jack says, holding up the blunt knife. "I mean it. I'll kill you if you don't!"

Wade looks unnerved, then he smiles. "You think I'd leave anything even vaguely sharp with the volunteers? I don't think so."

"Get her out!" Jack repeats, throwing the knife to the floor.

Lydia checks the monitor. Zoe's pulse is now weak and her blood pressure dangerously high. Time is running out. For Zoe, and possibly them all.

"Do something," Lydia tells Wade.

Jack's fist comes out of the darkness and connects with Wade's jaw. Wade reels, dropping the laptop as he crumbles to the floor. He lies still, then he opens his eyes and smiles, clearly dazed. The monitor beeps loudly, and Zoe thrashes under the restraints. Then the heart monitor falls silent, a single line across the screen.

Jack grabs hold of Zoe's wrist, then lays his head gently on her chest. He looks at Lydia and shakes his head.

"Do something," Lydia says to Jack this time. "Save her like you did Nick."

Jack looks doubtful, but he tries anyway, pumping the penguin hard, and trying to breathe life into Zoe's still smiling lips. It's so clearly wasted effort, but he keeps going.

"I thought we were a team, Wade?" she says, tears cascading down her cheeks as she crouches by him on the floor.

He's only semiconscious, the laptop beside him. "I thought we made choices together. Tested ideas together. How could you do this? You killed her. You killed her and . . . Oh my God! You've killed others too, haven't you?"

Wade looks at her then and wipes a thumb under each of her brimming eyes. "Zoe and the other volunteers knew what they were doing. Like canaries in a mine. And they all went willingly. It's what she would have wanted. But we can try again, until we get it right for you, my love."

"Don't make this about me!"

Jack pushes Wade aside and grabs the laptop from the floor. Then he pulls Lydia up by her wrist, dragging her out of the pod and slamming the door shut on Wade who had slumped back, eyes wide and mouth open. The wind shrieks above the snow-packed domed roof of the lab. Then the crack of something metallic shreds the stormy night and the glass cracks, a fissure zigzagging from one side to the other and snow tumbling in along with lethal shards of splintered glass and ice. Jack ducks and covers his head as a piece of glass impales him in the shoulder, blood soaking his shirt. She takes her phone from her jeans pocket, punches in the code, and the door unlocks.

"Come on," Jack says, running to the door. "What are you waiting for?"

CHAPTER

34

Lydia

HE HOLDS OUT his hand, but she's not ready to leave. Not yet. This is all she knows . . .

"I can't," she wails, the reality of their escape finally hitting her.

"Are you injured?" Jack asks, as she doubles over. "Did Wade hurt you?"

"I can't leave him," she says, shouting above the blizzard as she straightens up. "I know he's made mistakes, terrible unforgivable ones, but he's my husband and he saved me." She looks at the sealed pod. "I am a bad person too, Jack. You don't know me. I've done unforgiveable things to survive. You go, I have to stay here."

She turns to the pod, then the wind drops and the creaks abate and she hears it: the terrible silence that comes before an avalanche, like a held breath. She resists Jack's pleas to get going as she hears the whumping sound that populates her nightmares and precipitates every panic attack. She looks past Jack, along the compromised bridge and toward the foundation and although she can't see it through the blizzard she knows that the beast that is Mount Dunkler is there, waiting; Darker Mountain. The highest peak, and the source now of the only thing that could ever present a risk to the Memory Foundation's fortress-like structure: an avalanche. The thing she has always feared is headed straight toward them. And this time it's real. And by the deafening sound of it, even worse than the one she met on the other side of the mountain and has relived in every panic attack and nightmare.

Panic takes over again now. She covers her head and squeezes her eyes closed, waiting for the approaching wall of snow to engulf the walkway and the lab, taking them all down into the valley and oblivion. This is where she's always been headed, she's known it from the start, felt it in her gut. She doubles over again, hugging her stomach although the pain in her neck is worse and white hot. She deserves this. It's her destiny.

"It's okay. It's okay." Jack's hand rests on her bent spine. "I'm here, take my hand and step out. There's time. But we have to outrun this avalanche now."

"No, I'll slow you down," She looks into Jack's eyes, dark and soulful, and sees his goodness. Knows he must save himself now. "You go. I'll stay here. You stand a better chance without me."

Jack grabs her hand and pulls her onto the bridge, the door slamming behind them. "We go together or not at all."

She looks out the nearest snow-blinded window. A slide of ice and rocks is about to hit the walkway. Can she truly outrun an avalanche? She's tried before, hundreds of times, and it's never worked. The ear-splitting slide of snow and rocks and ice takes over then, and that selfish need to survive kicks in once more, and she runs. Runs as fast as it feels possible to down the steep incline and toward the dip at the center of the bridge. So fast her sneakers barely connect with the swooping swaying twisting floor.

She looks back. The lab is directly in the path of the avalanche now. There's a crunch of twisting metal, then a beat of terrible silence before the loud cracks of smashing glass as the remains of the lab's domed roof is crushed, then the bolts driven into rock on either side of the door decades before are pulled to breaking point and only hanging by a thread. She stops, appalled as the heavy metal door to the lab tumbles into the maelstrom of snow, down and down into a white powder abyss.

She screams, turning to see the avalanche engulf the rest of laboratory, the whole structure demolished in seconds as Jack watches too. There's no time to process that before the walkway is ripped from its moorings beneath their feet. The end that was attached to the lab swings free, the first half of the bridge they've now dashed across dropping through yards of air, the ground literally disappearing beneath her thudding sneakers. She grabs hold of a window frame and wedges her feet either side of it, just about holding on. The bridge is in freefall, the ravine opening up in swirls of bright white, thousands of acres wide and deep as fathoms, one end of the amputated bridge exposed to the elements, the other taking all its weight. The base of the valley visible far below in the gaping hole. She crawls up toward Jack who has dropped to his stomach and wedged his large feet either side of the floor, his legs long enough to be able to do that. She flips on her stomach now too, an icy water slide below her that leads to the sheared end of the walkway and certain death. She loses her grip and glides. Fast. Like a ride. Jack lets go too and catches her outstretched hand as her legs find cold air, feet dangling into the void. He's jammed his knees against one side of the swinging tunnel, then braces his heavy boots against the wall to prevent a fall into the roaring avalanche below. She screams, holding on to his hand as tightly as she can—it's the only thing she's attached to.

"Throw me your other hand," he tells her, maneuvering round so he's leaning out over the sheared edge, stomach flat to the wet floor, legs behind him, boots wedged against the sides of the walkway. "I need to pull you up."

"No, you'll fall too, let go!"

"No way, I've got you!"

She tries to reach her other hand up, strong in her core, but Jack is barely holding on himself, his chest over the torn metal edge now, so she's afraid she'll pull him down and they'll freefall into the ravine, smashed on the rocks long before they hit the valley floor. Then his other hand finds hers. There's blood on his exposed stomach from sharp metal and broken glass as he winches her up, his body braced hard against hers, smearing her clothes and skin bright red. "Let go of me," she tells him, her feet finding only air. "Save yourself!"

"No way," he shouts as the avalanche closes in, gathering snow and ice as it leaves the trampled lab and then turns back toward the bridge. The landslide is like a wild animal, tumbling rocks in the snow as if they are shingle as it heads straight for them. This is it, the end, just as her nightmares foretold, but then she's yanked up, caught by a tight grasp that drags her to safety, or at least, relative safety.

"Okay?" Jack asks after he hauls her back up into the suspended remains of the bridge. "I need you to crawl toward me, use your feet like I have. Wedge your sneakers against the sides. Yes, that's it."

It's much more of a stretch for her, but she manages. Just. They have seconds at most before this section falls into the ravine too, the metal attaching it to other end, by the Memory Foundation's main building, screeching and grinding so loudly it eclipses the crash of the avalanche, which has narrowly missed them and is making landfall far below in the valley. It's like being on the worst kind of ride she could imagine, stomach-lurching drops and swoops as the detached bridge lurches and falls until it hits the rock and hangs almost vertical, a sheer drop beneath and an impossible climb on ice and broken glass above. She crawls on hands and knees through slush and jagged debris, ignoring the pain of the makeshift foot and handholds she reaches for in the debris. Bits of torn flooring and peeled plastic. Hanging on to Jack's hand as he scrabbles upward too, inch by inch toward the locked door at the other end. The *locked* door. *Shit!*

"What are you doing?" Jack asks, looking back at her as she pulls free of his tight grasp.

"The code," she tells him, feeling for her phone from her jeans pocket where, thank God, she'd stowed it before they left the lab. "Need to unlock the door."

The phone then slips from her hands, ice-wet and numb, and slithers away, a lost heartbeat before it stops, wedged just out of reach by a spike of tangled metal, about six feet below her right foot. She maneuvers herself round, Jack begging her not to, she could fall again, but they need that phone.

Fingertips stretched, she reaches down, but the bridge swings violently to one side, smashing into the rock face. She manages to get her foot against the phone, but it's like chasing a block of ice down a slick mountain, the struggle enormous as she stretches as far as her reach will go without falling. Her back screams in agony, feet gripping on, somehow, as the phone is retrieved with a final lunge of her right hand. She palms it tight and jabs in the code, the door behind Jack unlocking just before the phone slips from her grasp into the frozen mist.

"Shit! Just go!" she tells Jack. "Before the door closes again."

"No, you first."

"Jack, please. I can hold on. I'm strong."

Reluctantly Jack launches himself toward the unlocked door, crashing his lacerated shoulder into it as it threatens to swing shut. The walkway is pulling hard on the final metal cables attaching to the building. It drops again, a few feet this time, as he lands heavily on his back and immediately looks out for her.

"Here," Jack says, rolling onto his stomach and extending his hands over the edge of the open door.

She reaches up for him, but he's too far away. He slides further forward, almost at tipping point. Then the fragile connection the cables have left to the foundation loosens more, compromised by his weight. She screams and he slides back.

"It's okay," she tells him. "I can do this."

She's on her stomach now too, sneakers digging in either side, nails clawing up the incline to the lip of the door. She's nearly there, Jack's hand outstretched and almost touching hers when the cables holding the walkway split apart, pulling away from the thick rock and taking the door with them.

She dodges the falling door and launches herself upward, lunging for Jack's hand, not even knowing if it's there until she finds it. He pulls her hard, her shoulder wrenched so she cries out. Then she lands on top of him in a tangled heap in the entrance foyer. Breathless, soaked, shaking, but alive.

"You okay?" he asks as she rolls onto her back in a puddle of melted snow, shivering more with relief and shock than the ice bath. The Memory Foundation is in total darkness, snow tumbling in from the open mouth of the walkway that took the door and frame with it too. She was seconds from certain death.

"Yeah, I think so," she says as he helps her to her feet. "You?"

"Yeah, I'm fine," he says, brushing himself down.

He isn't, he is bleeding from numerous cuts, as is she, and her shoulder hurts like hell and her back is on fire with spasms of white-hot pain from the rigors of making it this far. And they haven't even left the building. But all of that pales into insignificance when they look out of the gaping hole where the door was. The bridge across the ravine is completely gone, no way to cross to what was once a bright glass-domed laboratory, also eradicated. The mountain has reclaimed both in a matter of minutes, along with her husband. And Zoe. It's inconceivable. And yet it's true.

They stand side by side, transfixed as the avalanche thunders along the valley. Like a raging river, the continued destruction is swift and complete. Houses torn apart, their walls and roofs reduced to matchsticks. She can only hope that whoever was down there somehow got out in time.

"I can't believe it," she says, looking across to the piled snow where the lab once was and imagining Wade and Zoe buried far beneath in the pod. Maybe that was a blessing. They wouldn't have known a thing until it was too late. She should feel something. Pain, grief, loss, but instead she feels numb. Jack hugs her for a moment, then he pulls away and looks up at the ceiling. There's dust falling on his head and shoulders, hers too as the entrance hall quakes. Vibrations through their feet too, and growing stronger.

"Do you know where the car keys are?" Jack asks.

"Yes, Wade keeps them in the car," she tells him, running after him as he heads toward the basement door. A door that is locked, and her phone is another thing the avalanche swallowed up. "We can't unlock it."

"Where are all the other devices that Wade confiscated?" Jack asks.

She shrugs and he sighs. Then he thumps his forehead and reaches round to the back of his jeans waistband and produces Wade's laptop.

"So glad I risked my life getting that phone," she says.

"Sorry, forgot I'd grabbed this before we left the pod." But the laptop is useless, soaked and the screen black.

Jack hands it to her and goes over to the long dead fire. Then he plucks out the axe that Wade had tossed in the log basket. "Stand back."

It takes three, maybe four swings for Jack to hack his way through the lock and kick the metal door open. Then he leads her into the darkness of the basement with a cheery "Come on. Let's get out of here!"

CHAPTER

35

Lydia

"YOU WANNA DRIVE?" Jack asks as they cross the pitch black basement. The elation she felt momentarily as Jack led her to their escape has now turned to dread and a pervading cold that is spreading through her bones and making her shiver uncontrollably, so she almost drops the laptop.

"I don't drive," she replies, teeth chattering as she climbs in the passenger side and tosses the laptop in the back. It's of no use to them. "Not since my accident."

"No worries," Jack says, frowning.

There's no time for an explanation now, the rumblings above growing louder.

He turns the key that was left in the ignition, the throaty engine turning over first time. Then he eyes the gear stick with concern.

"You do know how to drive a manual?" she asks, swallowing the panic that rises as bile. The thought of leaving the foundation is terrifying, even as it shakes and crumbles around them, fissures opening up in the basement walls. Jack is a stranger. It's unthinkable to be doing this, and yet unavoidable.

"Um," he says, grinding the gears. "I guess I'll work it out."

She returns his nervous smile, but the panic she has lived with for five years now, is overpowering. She cannot stop trembling, her hands fumbling the seatbelt to finally fasten it as Jack begins the tricky reverse out.

"Watch that side for me," he says as a horrible grating sound is emitted from somewhere round the back of the Tank. She forces herself to look, warning him to go more slowly as they narrowly miss Wade's work bench. A chainsaw and snow shovel hit the hood as Jack overcorrects.

"Damn." Jack presses the brake. "Hang on, I've got this."

He tries again and the heavy car slowly reverses up the ramp, emerging into the snowy forecourt. Shards of sleet immediately hit the windshield as Jack turns on the wipers and executes a half circle toward the gates. The *locked* gates.

Jack gets out and starts kicking at the snow and rattling the bars, while she watches, helpless. He gives up and climbs in again, rubbing his hands over his face. He looks at her, about to speak, when there's a crashing sound behind them. They both turn to look out the dirty back window in time to see the top floor of the foundation's curved structure, where her beloved Crow's Nest office is, collapse into the floor below. The halfmoon window splintering and falling to the ground just behind the car.

"Okay," Jack says. "Hold on tight."

"What, no, you can't mean—"

The heavy car zooms back in a tight arc, almost to the ramp, dust from falling concrete engulfing them.

"Okay, you ready?" he says.

She nods, the encouraging smile wiped from her face as Jack's boot presses down hard and his blood-soaked hands grip tight. She grips on too, grabbing the sides of the seat as the ancient but thankfully solid car smashes into the metal gates at top speed, bull bars ramming into the center and splitting them apart with a smack that's so loud, she fears it may start another avalanche or obliterate the Tank.

"Go, us!" Jack shouts as they speed down the mountain road.

She looks back in disbelief at the concertina of destruction. The third floor where she and Wade lived and loved for almost five years has collapsed into the guest suites, both floors then crashing into the hallway and lounge on the level below. The whole of the foundation has turned to rubble in a matter of minutes, a dust cloud chasing them down the mountain. They only just made it out in time.

"Not too fast, Jack," she warns as the tires lose traction in the thick snow, lurching toward the next obstacle, a set of roadblocks padlocked together across the narrow mountain track. "Jack, slow down!"

He aims for the center and they crash through, plastic bollards and twisted signs left in their wake as she looks back at the debris now tumbling down the side of the mountain.

"You're crazy," she tells him, half terrified, half hysterical as she laughs, but the road is dropping away again now, so steep she can't see where they are headed, the snow still falling like nails and the rocks and snow from the avalanche making it almost impossible to know what is road and what's not. "Jack, be careful, this is where I had my accident."

She cannot believe she is on this section of road again, the one that claimed her passenger's life five years before. The thought impales her heart with a sadness she cannot disguise. Her hand covers her mouth and she sobs, as silently as she can, although Jack is concentrating on the twisting road and barely seems to notice. She will have to face up to what she did to survive, if they last the journey, because back in the real world someone will know and care about that child. And make sure she pays, just as she should.

Jack's boot covers the brake pedal and he presses down hard, but instead of slowing they are gathering speed.

"It's not responding," he says, fighting to keep control of the wheel. "No traction."

She can only see as far as the length of the headlights, but that's enough to make her gasp. A hairpin bend is taking them round the far side of the mountain, the memory resurfacing so strongly it takes over. She closes her eyes, then a lurch and Jack's panicked shouts make her snap her eyes open again. They are headed toward the edge. They won't make it out. This is it. After all they've been through, this will be the end, and it is no more or less than she has deserved for the last five years. She sees her baby strapped in the back of her rental car, remembers him and craves him. The smell of her son's plump cheek against hers. Gabriel, that's what Wade called him, as she couldn't even remember his name. Only those eyes, imploring her to unstrap him, save him as she would then save herself. She'd tried. She'd tried so hard. But not hard enough.

"Hey," Jack says, bringing the car to a steady stop. "It's okay, you can look, we're fine."

Slowly, she lifts her head and looks out at the valley. The sun is just visible, miles away. A crease of light and the promise of a new day. They are past the dark side of the mountain and the worst of the avalanche's trail of destruction. It's a stunning view. A warm pink on the horizon. She has lost all track of time, but there is hope in that sunrise. She covers her face in shame and sobs into her hands.

CHAPTER

36

Lydia

"HEY," JACK SAYS. "What is it? We're going to be okay now, I promise."

She nods, unable to speak.

"So I'm thinking," Jacks says, still watching her. "We get to wherever I can find a public phone or someone with a cell and call Adds, get some help. All the way to the airport if needs be, we've got enough gas. We'll be okay now, I promise." He starts to drive on, slowly.

"I need to say something first. Before you talk to anyone else."

"Yes, of course," he glances over. "What is it?"

"When I drove up here five years ago, I wasn't alone."

Jack goes to speak, but she silences him with a raised palm, and he soon has to return his eyes to the road, which is still demanding of his full attention, although nothing like the challenge it was.

"I have no idea why I was driving up there, let alone with . . . but I was and then I heard an avalanche." She takes a breath. "I climbed in the back and I tried to release the restraints in the car seat, but the buckles wouldn't come undone, the straps, they were frayed, you see, so I gave up and I jumped. Saved myself." She swallows hard and pushes Jack's hand away. She won't be able to get through this if he's kind to her. "Wade found me a while later, half dead in the snow, and a few days later he found the car, but—" She sobs, covering her mouth. "He buried him in the base of the valley by the wreck of the car, marked the grave with a pile of stones."

"A boy?" Jack asks, as if that were the part he cannot comprehend.

She looks down at her hands, scratched and bloody. "Gabriel, that's what Wade called him. And I let him die, so there's no escape for me, no celebration. You should have left me back there." She points up to the peak of Mount Dunkler. "I deserved to die that day and I wish I had, but I will face up to what I did. And take whatever reckoning is coming. I just wanted you to know first."

Jack reaches deep into his jeans pocket, a maneuver that involves him lifting the seat of his jeans and terrifies her as he drives. The tiny piece of card produced is crumpled and wet. "Take it," he says, handing her a photo of a young girl. It's hard to see in the half light as the sun slowly rises over the distant peaks, but the child has dark soulful eyes and a smile to match Jack's. He says with not inconsiderable pride, "That's my daughter. I told you I had one. She's called Nova."

"I'm pleased for you," Lydia says, handing it back. She doesn't want to look at his child. It's insensitive and unhelpful. And of no comfort to her. However well meant.

"Please, look at it," he says. "Properly this time."

Lydia takes the photo more to ensure they don't skid off the road than because she wants to. She wipes her eyes with the wet sleeve of her sweatshirt, which is blood-smeared and soaked, noticing the cuts on her hands. The girl in the photo is about the age Gabriel would have been now. Maybe five or six.

"She has your eyes," she tells him, keen to hand it back, but then she changes her mind and instead holds it close to her face and stares into those brown eyes as something snags deep inside, painful and yet familiar. Almost exquisite in its longing.

"Her name is Nova," Jack repeats. "I am her father and you," he says, slowly and without any drama as she looks up from the photo to his smiling profile, "are, as I suspect you are now guessing, her mother."

Each word lands softly in the car, now entering the silent valley.

"No, I . . . I came here with a baby boy. I remember him. And he perished."

"You were going to bring Nova with you, but you changed your mind last minute and flew to LA to drop her with me," Jack says as he drives a slow and careful route around the worst of the broken houses and tumbled rocks, and avoiding the deepest parts of powder snow. "No indication where you were going, but you were on a mission, and upset to leave her, of course. And I was in shock. Only wish I'd asked more questions, but when you find out that you're a father, that kind of takes over every other thought." He smiles at her, then drives round a pile of wood that was once, presumably, a house, except then she spots the sign for the village store, still intact at the side of the road.

Lydia drops the tiny photo in her lap as snow from a nearby tree plops on the roof of the car, startling her, but they are safe here, halfway through the valley now. Safe enough to take her time and look again at the little girl on a beach. Or more specifically, the girl's eyes. The same dark brown eyes she saw in every flashback, every panic attack, every nightmare. Pleading with her to unbuckle the straps and save them from a snowy grave. Torturing her for what she did to survive an avalanche.

"Is she . . . ?" she asks, the pronoun still unfamiliar to her. She's thought only of a boy for all these years. "No, Wade found the car, Gabriel, my son, was still inside. He described him. Every feature." She shivers again at the thought. No painful detail spared in Wade's account.

"I'm afraid that Gabriel was an invention," Jack points back up the mountain. "Wade trapped you here with his lies and instilled in you a morbid fear of ever leaving."

"No, that can't be, I had a son. I know I did." But as she looks at the little girl, that certainty is already being rubbed away by a stronger one.

"This wasn't how I envisaged telling you all this," Jack says, glancing at her. "You and I had a short but very impactful encounter that gifted us the miracle of our daughter, five years ago, a little more now, in fact. You flew to LA and left her with me before you came here, and the rest is a fabrication. Wicked evil lies implanted by Wade to trap you at the foundation for his own ends. Which were many, clearly."

Jack slows and stops by an hotel that has survived the avalanche if not the rigors of the last few decades. He pulls her to him and holds her tight as the shock makes her shake, the photo between them in her closed palm, but she soon pulls away. "I want to believe you, I really do."

"You know the truth in your heart, don't you?"

She takes in a gulp of cold air and looks at Jack. "I don't know. I think so. It's a lot."

"I wanted to do this so much better for you. Gain your trust over the week. Bit by bit. But that wasn't to be."

The second half of the valley and everything beyond is virgin white. They are two tiny dots of life in an empty wilderness. Two souls bound together and facing one another now, the relief immense as she allows the truth to wash over her, but Wade's terrible deceit crowds in too. How could the man she loved, or thought she loved, have made her believe she had a baby called Gabriel who she abandoned to save herself. To manipulate her like that, for his twisted pleasure, would be pure evil. It cannot be true. Except that's exactly the kind of manipulation he was helping Nick exact on Rachel. And Zoe was another victim of Wade's obsession, along with goodness knows how many other volunteers. But to invent a perfect frozen little boy, still strapped in the car seat, that's another level. That image has tortured her day and night for five years. She'd howled with pain, in grief, desperate to die, but Wade spared her none of it, no story too wicked to get what he wanted. *Her.* Every intense detail reinforced to trap her here as Jack said, with guilt and fear and presumably to fill up his empty life with an adoring wife and constant willing volunteer who needed him as much as he needed her. Too many benefits for him to ever set her free. It cannot be true, and yet she knows in her heart that it is. She opens the door and leans out over the piled snow. But she can't bring up anything, only emptiness inside of her.

"I was a bad mother, either way," she says, wiping her mouth. The photo in her other hand, gripped tight as she closes the door.

"Not at all."

"I left her to come here," she says, brandishing the photo. "And for what."

"I'll share everything I know about you once we are somewhere warm and safe, okay?"

He's right, they are still a long way from shelter, and totally reliant on one another and the ancient car, plus Jack's driving through the devastation of a recent avalanche.

"We're going to be okay now, aren't we, Jack?" she asks as they head off again, toward the end of the valley.

"Yes, we will, and by the way, my name is Jay. Jay Mason."

"Pleased to meet you, Jay," she says, smiling as he looks over. "My name is . . . What is my name?"

CHAPTER

37

Tash

I AM ALONE IN an empty airport lounge waiting for a private plane that will be several more hours according to Addison, Jack's scarily efficient assistant. Or rather, Jay, as I now know he is called. All I have is the clothes I'm wearing, and Wade's laptop, which has miraculously dried out and finally booted up. I type in Wade's passcode, his late father's date of birth, which came to me easily for some unknown and bizarre reason, and tether to the poor Wi-Fi to begin my continuing search for the truth.

"Sorry, they look awful," Jay says, setting two packets of sandwiches and two coffees on the sticky table twenty minutes later. "Came out of a vending machine. Did you find anything?" he asks, looking at the laptop.

I swivel the screen so it's between us and break into the sandwich, although I have no appetite for it, not after what I've seen. I stroke the trackpad and replay the video for Jay.

A blond-haired woman, slim, with defined cheekbones smiles nervously on the screen. She is holding a glass of black coffee in her elegant if slightly wobbly hands. She looks to be in her mid to late thirties at a guess, and she's wearing a smart shirt and beautiful gold teardrop earrings. She appears tired, exhausted in fact, dark circles under her eyes. She is in front of the enormous curved window in the foundation's guest lounge, blinding sun coming in to burnish her wavy hair. The backdrop is snow-covered peaks, but only the tips are iced, that late summer dusting that was always my favorite time of year, especially when contrasted by a brilliant blue sky as it is here. The lounge is sparse, as I recall it when I first arrived.

"Is that who I think it is?" Jay asks, reaching for my hand.

I nod and pull away, sipping the scalding coffee, which is sweet, laden with sugar. For the shock.

"Hey." Wade's disembodied voice fills the echoing airport lounge as he addresses the nervous woman on screen. *"Can you tell me why you came here today and what you were looking for?"*

I can't look at Jack. I mean Jay. Panic speeding up my thoughts so they trip over one another even though I've watched this clip twice already.

"Did Wade film this?" Jay asks.

I nod. "I'd imagine so. It's his voice."

The woman replies to Wade's question, *"Hi, yes, my name is Natasha Walker, but please call me Tash. I'm a journalist and I thought I was here to interview you, not the other way around."* She laughs, and I wince. I cannot bear how she looks to him off camera as he explains it's a kind of visitors' book, in video form. *"Not that I have many visitors here, so indulge me, I'm a mad scientist."*

She laughs again. *"Okay, I'm thirty-eight years old, and I've come to the Memory Foundation today to find out more, I hope."* She sips her coffee and I sip mine.

"That's how I remember you," Jay says. "From when you dropped Nova with me in LA."

"Can't quite believe I made it here at last, with the great man himself."

"Well," Wade's voice says. *"I'm very pleased you did."*

"Yeah, me too. I'm hoping to find something extremely exciting to share with the rest of the world."

"I look happy, well kind of," I say, tapping the track pad. "Nervous, but excited. It gets worse."

The same woman appears in the next clip, but she is less relaxed, less smiley. Her hair is dirty, and she has stitches in her eyebrow and bruises on her face. When she lifts her right arm, there's a makeshift cast on it, and crutches are propped beside the bed she's lying on, a gray pillow all that's supporting her.

"Hey, my name is Lydia. I don't know who I am, just that I came here in a snowstorm with my—"

"Come on, Lidds," Wade's voice cajoles, still behind the camera. *"Bit more effort please. We've talked about this."*

"Wade Hunter saved my life and I owe him everything."

"You could say it with a bit more enthusiasm than that."

"But it isn't true," she says, anger contorting her face. *"Or I don't think it is. I'm confused, but I know that I need to get out of here and you won't let me go. I'll jump out that fucking window again, I will. You are lying to me, I know it."* She slumps back on the sagging pillow, clearly in pain. *"And I want my phone back. You are a fucking liar trying to make me think I left my baby in the car. I didn't bring her, I left her with her father, and I need to call him."*

"I'll call him, if you'll tell me who he is."

"Never! Liar!"

"Lidds, you're not making this any easier on either of us, are you? I've told you, you're confused, that's all. But I'll take care of you, make you better. Let's leave it there for now."

"I'm so sorry," Jay says, pulling me into a hug.

I can't help but break down in his arms, but there's more to show him so I wipe my nose and press on, clicking on the next name, and the next. So many volunteers, giving their so-called consent. Including Patient A, who is of course Zoe, and who gives her wholehearted wish to be a volunteer for "a fully immersive future alteration memory flight."

"We think Zoe recruited you," Jay says. "Not as a volunteer but as a pro-foundation journalist to get the word out. Wade was obviously panicking about being beaten to the finish line by a rival."

"How do you know all that?"

"Rowena, your editor and a good friend of yours, and now mine, is carrying a huge amount of guilt for passing on an email from a source at the Memory Foundation a few months before you disappeared. We believe you were targeted. By someone called Patient A."

"So why did it take so long to find me?"

"I never stopped looking for you, and neither did Ro," he replies, looking hurt.

"Sorry, it's just five years is a long time."

"You left no details with anyone. Your flat was empty, all your possessions gone. Neither of us are next of kin, and the police did nothing. It was as if you'd vanished off the face of the earth. The email from Patient A was just one line of inquiry, and when we'd exhausted that, sending up drones all over the vast search area, and hiring private detectives who came up with nothing, we widened the search and scoured the four corners of the earth for you."

"So it was luck, in the end?"

"Not exactly. But a couple of lucky breaks did help. Wade's incompetence, for one. I reversed-imaged some stuff on his website."

I must look confused as he nods and says he can explain in more detail later.

"Tell me now."

"Okay." He takes a sip of coffee. "So Ro never gave up on the idea you'd gone to the foundation, said she had a feeling about it because of the way you were so passionate about that story. Not much to go on, but there was a link to a guy who used to work at a care home where your . . ." Jack catches my eye but doesn't finish the thought. "Basically, that linked you, tenuously, to Patient A's fiancé, a guy called Steve who died in a fire. So that wasn't much help as we had no way of tracing him and still no idea where the foundation was."

"You mentioned an image on the website?"

"Yes. I used to watch Wade's videos all the time, so did Ro, and you were caught in the background of his latest one a few months back. A plea for wealthy investors to come to the foundation for an exclusive experience. Just a reflection in a window, so neither of us was sure. You looked different and it had been, as you say, five years, but the only way to be sure was to come here myself. Which again proved tricky, but you know, if there's a desire to do something, you find a way." He smiles. "I was hoping that seeing me would be enough to jog your memory. Not your fault, but you clearly had no idea who I am, and I wasn't a hundred percent so—"

"Why not just ask me?"

"You'd clearly been brainwashed by Wade, and also I've been taking advice from a trained therapist who helps deprogram people and get them out of cults. He told me to win your trust first, bide my time. Or you could react badly. Maybe never believe me. And first I had to be sure it was you."

"I saw you on the phone to them, I think."

"I was actually taking a photo of you, a few in fact. We'd only met twice, so I needed Ro's opinion. I sent it to her and she was a hundred percent certain it was you, straightaway."

I manage a weak smile. "She sounds like a good friend."

"The best. Is there any more video of you?" Jay asks, quickly adding, "Only if you're up to it."

I nod and click on the next clip in the folder, the videos arranged in chronological order. Then the next and the next, as this lost version of me I don't recognize morphs into the person I became: muscular, dark haired, in love with Wade, and extoling his virtues. How he saved me from a fictional avalanche in which he swears I abandoned my son, Gabriel, who was strapped in the back of the car, killed by my negligence and taken away in the snow, then buried by a benevolent Wade. Except for the fact that Gabriel never existed. The baby seat was empty because I left Nova in the safe care of this man beside me, now holding my hand so tight it's like he'll never let go. And I don't want him to.

"What do you think really happened when you arrived?" Jack asks, dropping my hand as he pauses the video on screen. "Because it's not that."

I shake my head. "I don't understand why I was so compelled to go there that I would leave her with you. I mean, I know you're her father, but you didn't know that until I turned up, and you live in LA. I must have had some family closer by, this friend, Rowena, for instance?"

"Ro was traveling and . . . I'm sorry, but I am Nova's only other family."

"Why don't you hate me?"

"Why would I hate you?"

"I dump a baby on you that you didn't know existed and then disappear, and yet you've raised her and searched for me all these years."

"Of course."

"Why?"

"Why do you think?" He pauses, eyes down. "Try and eat something, shouldn't be too long a wait now."

"My only friend is called Ro?" I ask, and he nods. "Can't wait to meet her."

He hesitates again, then reminds me to eat the disgusting sandwich.

I force down a couple of bites of tuna salad on stale bread, but Wade's voice is back. Hard to shake after all these years of only him in my ear. *"Don't believe everything he tells you, Lidds. There are always two sides to every story. Truth is mutable. We all rewrite history, over and over; always have, always will. I only did what you asked of me, and I did it, gladly."*

"I was a bad mother. That much is clear."

"Hey," Jay says, catching my hand as I get up and pulling me back. "He's the bad guy here, for kidnapping and brainwashing you, and I was her father, not a stranger. You did the right thing by her, and by yourself. You were a career woman before the baby. A brilliant journalist."

I look out the viewing window beside our table. The sun is out, distant peaks visible. Near and yet far. "I still don't understand why I was targeted."

"We think Zoe might have had some kind of quid pro quo arrangement with Wade," Jay says. "She was to bring in a sympathetic journalist, which was in all fairness definitely you, and in return she would get to be at the foundation for more flights. But she obviously resented your relationship with Wade and continuing presence."

"She must have been gutted when I became a permanent fixture."

"Yes, I'd imagine so. You were perfect for his needs," Jay explains, looking sad and angry at the same time, his jaw set. "A well-established journalist and also . . ." He stops talking and looks away.

"Also what? Tell me."

Jay squeezes my hand again. "Your mother passed away a few days after you disappeared. She suffered from dementia. Alzheimer's. I'm so sorry, Tash."

I shake my head. It's far too much to process. "So you think Zoe recruited me because of my mother's condition?"

"It's possible. If she'd somehow met you, or heard of you at least, via your mother's care home, possibly. This is still quite new information to us and hard to come by, but we can dig further."

"Do you think—I mean, it doesn't matter now—but do you think they were having an affair?"

"Wade and Zoe? No evidence of that. And she was there to be with her dead fiancé."

"Poor Zoe."

"Yes, same as hundreds of other so-called volunteers."

"Hundreds?"

"I'm gathering names all the time. Missing persons whose trails go cold but with characteristics that unite them. They had few relatives, if any, a connection to dementia, and were often completely alone in the world."

"Like me."

"Yes."

"And where are they now? Oh God, they're not all—?"

"I have a team on it already, mainly private investigators, it's slow going, a lot of opposition to release of information. And fear, but someone will know where the bodies are buried other than Wade, bound to. There was far too much at stake for him to be working entirely alone or to leave an easy trail."

"And the Bentleys, they are victims too?"

"Addsion has confirmed the helicopter waited at the rendezvous point for two hours, but Wade never arrived with the Bentleys."

"Seriously?"

He nods. "My working hypothesis is Wade kept any volunteer casualties in the freezers until the snow arrived and that's likely where we'll also find the Bentleys. Buried in the snow, I mean. There's a shovel in the boot of the car. I saw it when he loaded our bags."

"I had no idea, I swear."

"I know that, Tash."

I shake my head and cover my mouth. Wade had scrubbed out the chest freezer before the catering supplies started to arrive for the guests. I was so grateful to him, but now I feel sick as I think of the vermin that gathered each summer, the bags of rubbish he'd take away in the Tank. I could vomit, but I swallow it down.

"There is no suggestion you are in any way to blame, Tash. Please believe me," Jay says, holding my hand as I push the sandwich away. "You are an innocent victim, the same as everyone else who crossed paths with Wade at the foundation."

"But I was the only one who fell in love with him. Married him. Lived with him for five years."

"He made all those things happen."

The old-fashioned phone Jay bought here at the airport, offering the only member of staff we could find an exorbitant sum for it, buzzes loudly in his jeans pocket. He looks at it and smiles.

"Ah, good old, Adds. Plane is landing in thirty minutes. You ready?"

"I guess," I reply, literally no idea if that's in any way true.

Epilogue

A Year Later—Tash

A BRAND NEW CAR seat is secured in the back of Jay's SUV, and we have both checked the pristine straps and shiny buckles, twice. The occupant is sleeping peacefully. Our one-day-old son is coming home. Nova has apparently created a glittery banner with more enthusiasm than she expressed for its recipient, but no doubt she will fall in love with Rowan on sight. How could she not. He's perfect. Like his big sister.

"We're very good at making gorgeous babies," Jay says, looking over and squeezing my hand. "Shall we do another one soon?"

"Do? How romantic!" I laugh, then wince. As with Nova, I needed an episiotomy and stitches. Serves me right for allowing the tall man beside me to impregnate me, twice. Not that I'm complaining, well, not much, but Jay has passed on broad shoulders to our boy that did not deliver easily.

"No, we shall not do this again. Not ever." I tell Jay, although he's right, we do make beautiful babies. Rowan is the most handsome boy in the whole world, but I'm forty-four years old and therefore according to my hospital notes, a "geriatric" mother. The term makes me shudder.

Jay carries the car seat into his beachfront house, the one we will likely move from soon. It's too small for our growing family, at least according to Jay, who thinks twenty-five hundred square feet is woefully inadequate for our needs. I would like a garden but also to still be near the coast. I like to see the horizon. Monterey appeals. Jay's mom lives there, and he loves his "folks" as he calls them, an unwanted reminder of Wade's adopted faux-friendly vernacular when the guests first arrived at the foundation. There are lots of times I still hear him, but the memories are fading, slowly and in a nonlinear way, but they are. Jay's family has welcomed me, and there are loads of them. We'd love to be closer to be able to visit more often, and LA is too busy, too polluted. Jay is working mainly from home these days, his laptop open on the kitchen table. Another unwanted reminder, this one to Wade's laptop and the testimony I witnessed on it that I can never unsee. The video clips of the days after my arrival at the foundation are devastating to watch, although I have done so many times. Wade broke me down piece by piece with promises and lies. He reinvented my past to fit his own needs with the story of my supposed selfishness at the expense of my child's life. An invented grave for a baby boy who never died. Never even existed. I blamed myself for five years, and that guilt kept me prisoner as much as Wade did. I wasn't the only one to suffer, not by a long way, but I am, as far as we can tell, the only one to get out. I'm tired now, too tired to fight the survivor guilt, so I push it down into a box and snap the lid shut.

"You okay?" Jay asks, as he so often does.

"Yeah, just thinking about Rowena," I tell him, pointing at the photo of our newborn's namesake on the sideboard. My old friend and former boss. "She would have loved him."

"Would she?" Jay asks, pulling a face. "Not a baby person from what I recall."

I always forget that Jay and Ro became good friends. United in their five-year quest to find me. They never gave up, even when the trail went cold. Even though Ro was sick. So sick she had to give up on almost everything, except me. "She'd have loved that he has her name," I say and Jay nods.

I swallow the tears that brim so easily, beleaguered as I am by the enormous effort of birthing my ten-pound boy. Ro will never meet Rowan. My beloved friend passed before his birth, but he will know of her through us, and Kitty, Ro's wife and carer whom I have met and love. Even when the cancer got too invasive for Ro to travel with Jay, she helped him from home, always a whiz at research, which is how she got chatting to the matron at Mum's nursing home, who told her, in passing, that I was at a work thing in the middle of nowhere when she'd called me with the news of Mum's death. That would have meant very little to most people, but it was how Ro and Jay began to join the dots, tenaciously following them for years until I was finally found and the puzzle was complete. That's when Ro gave in to the cancer, or so Kitty tells me. The moment Ro knew I was safe she accepted her fate. I missed seeing her again by two days.

This last year has been filled with much sadness, but there's been happiness too. That's what real life is like, and as with any period of adjustment, the changes have not always been easy. As my therapist says, all change is traumatic, be it good or bad, and I have had much to process. Much to regret and mourn too. Losses that cannot be replaced, like Ro and Mum. Time that cannot be reclaimed. There is heavy and emotional work yet to do, but the nightmares are receding, the real memories slowly teased back. There are gaps, big ones, days when the mental labor feels overwhelming, the brain-freezes all encompassing, but I have been given techniques to help with that. A lot of it is down to acceptance, and the knowledge that time is the best healer. I need to grieve not only for the time I've lost but also the parts of me that may never return. There's been a lot of anger and denial, mostly centered around Wade's appalling treatment of me and other so-called volunteers, like Zoe and many others of course, but I am learning acceptance of that too, if not forgiveness. Not that I will ever get over the scale of Wade Hunter's utter disregard for human life, and nor should I. Nick and Rachel Bentley were sadly two of the many who perished as a result of the Wade's "boundary pushing." Their bodies found bludgeoned and buried in a remote spot where remains of other volunteers have also been located. The aptly named Ghost Valley. The fact that Zoe knew what was going on does not in any way justify what Wade put her through. She was desperate and vulnerable, an addict of sorts. Targeted because of her grief, much as she then targeted me.

Becoming a mother to Nova has been the greatest reward, and challenge. Nova did not take to me for a long time. She clung to her father out of jealousy and distrust and fear. It didn't help that I was in their lives pretty much from day one of our return. A part of this new family because Jay and I had fallen in love hard and fast, bonded by the trauma of what we'd shared. A new normal that Nova neither wanted nor embraced. But she is coming round. Although the pregnancy hasn't helped. Guilt on my side, and resentment, rightly, on hers that when her mom finally returned, she was soon to be shared with a new sibling. Maybe now that Rowan's finally here, two weeks overdue, she will understand that there is love in our hearts to mend the past and look to a better future, together. I only wish my mother could have met both of her beautiful grandchildren.

As far as finding some help for sufferers of dementia like Mum, progress has been hampered in the field of memory retrieval and reconstruction by the revelations of the Memory Foundation's unregulated and deadly practices. The necessary enquiries are underway into what appears to have been a massive cover-up that may go right to the top. At least fifty families have come forward saying their missing loved ones may have been volunteers in Wade Hunter's secret trials, and a dozen bodies have been exhumed from Ghost Valley, but the ravine is hundreds of square miles. There are likely other burial sites yet to be uncovered. It could take years to find them all, and some may never be laid to rest. The process of uncovering who knew what has been met with continuing denials from those who now wash their hands of it, or try to. The faceless, nameless government officials who hide behind the impunity of official secrets and "public interest" and investors who deny ever feeding the greedy machine of the foundation. I fear none of us will ever know the scope of it all. The rumors of webcams being remotely monitored, along with social media harvesting, ring true but remain unproven as yet.

I follow the news stories with journalistic interest but try not to obsess, although one thread that *has* consumed me is the capture and arrest of one of the so-called suits. A thug who used to keep an eye on volunteers who had made it home, like Zoe. It's strange to think that she and I used to meet for coffee and in the park, my source and also my recruiter. I didn't recognize her, but she knew me.

The "man in the pinstripe suit"—who cannot be named for legal reasons and won't admit who he worked for—generates continual speculation of connections between the foundation and high-level government departments with the power to award lucrative publicly funded medical contracts. He has become the vilified if faceless hate-figure of the operation. The press and the public do love someone to blame, and the way he turns up to give "evidence" in his grayed-out diplomatic car, hiding behind a screen in court with only flashes of his pinstripe suit, is a journalist's wet dream.

Both Jay and I have been called as witnesses and no doubt will be again, but for now, that part of our lives is over, other than the memories.

Our charitable work keeps me busy, the foundation Jay set up and funded now my day job. It assists families of those suffering with all forms of profound memory loss. The aim is to offer much-needed hope of a cure one day.

I have no desire to go back to full-time journalism, although a podcast appeals. I'd like to talk about what happened to me, and maybe prevent it ever occurring again. But I'm not ready to unpick all that trauma yet, which is selfish, I know.

"You want some ice water?" Jay asks, setting the car seat on the kitchen floor and heading to the fridge. "It's a hot one today, need to adjust the AC."

"Yes, thanks." I look at the baby, his eyes tight shut, long eyelashes fluttering, and a ghost of a memory stirs. Of another kitchen table, high above London. "Can you bring some painkillers too? Then I'll take a nap."

"Good idea, get some rest while you can." Jay kisses the top of my mussed-up head of white-blond hair, bleached not only by the sun but my desire to look more like I used to. *Before.* Only more so.

"You got another migraine coming on?"

"Maybe, I'll just have a lie down, try to fight it off."

Nova is outside with the nanny, my girl barefoot and in the surf, splashing about. I go out on the veranda to see her better, kicking off my shoes on the sandy deck that wraps around our house. I wave and Katerina, our nanny, waves back. I didn't want any hired help, my trust issues far from resolved, but Jay insisted that the support is good and needed. Our girl is, as Jay told me, incredible, but a full-time job. A Californian through and through like her dad, Nova is indeed a force of nature. Her father, who I met in a bar and have ended up falling in love with, possibly more than once, is much more chill. Maybe it's fate, maybe it's just good fortune to finally have found my soulmate. It's definitely true. But raising two kids will be tough, especially after a traumatic brain injury. I find it almost impossible to trust strangers, but Jay has known Kat his whole life, one of many distant cousins, so that's reassuring, and Nova is feisty and stubborn and brave, which is wonderful and demanding all at once. We do need the help. Well, I do.

I go inside and sit with some caution on the side of the bed. The woman reflected in the mirrored wardrobes looks back. I rub at my aching neck, and regret, as I have a thousand times, probably more, that I allowed this awful thing to be implanted into my neck.

The bean.

Jay and my latest therapist—I decided I would prefer to talk to a woman—have both dismissed any guilt that I express for stupidly allowing Wade to insert an implant into the base of my brain. I was in a coercive situation, held captive and lied to, brainwashed, the truth kept from me at all times and replaced with a litany of heinous stories that made me out to be the monster when it was Wade who was the living embodiment of pure evil. You can analyze why, go back to his father's legacy, maybe even look at his undisputed genius in the field of memory retrieval and talk of "the greater good," but I will never forgive or understand his actions. And although I was not in a position to make informed choices, or offer proper consent, I still blame myself for agreeing to the implant. Wade told me it would increase the effectiveness of the memory flights, and I gave my permission, willingly. I'd have done anything for him and to assuage the guilt of what he made me believe I was capable of doing to survive.

The specialists want to study me, the only living person with such an implant. They speculate how it was inserted—I have no recollection of that—and warn me, after the event, long after, how dangerous it is to mess with an area so close to the spinal cord. I could have been paralyzed, easily, by the rudimentary device that they think was inserted by, of all things, a contraption normally used to microchip animals. It transmits and receives, they have recently discovered, although to what end and how, they have no idea.

I press a flattened palm to the spot on the back of my neck. The bean is hard and hot, pulsating. I am not imagining this. It has come back to life in the last few days and with it the panic and fear that flips my stomach over.

Jay comes in with the car seat. "Sorry to disturb, but this little fella is hungry."

I smile, rub at my neck again and try to cover up the anxiety that feels like I'm toppling off the side of a cliff.

Jay frowns, well used to the signs that I am spiraling, but he has no idea that this time I have every cause. The threat is all too real.

"Is that thing bothering you?" he asks, lifting baby Rowan with two careful hands.

"No, it's fine," I say, rubbing my neck and then taking Rowan and offering him the breast. He feeds easily, guzzling hard. So different than Nova, she was a tough one to get going. I love that small details like that come back. If I relax and allow them to. I just need to stay calm.

Jay places his hand on my neck as he sits beside me. "It's really hot," he says. "What does that mean?"

"Nothing, it means nothing."

He raises his hands and gets up. "Sorry. I'm just worried about you."

"No, I'm sorry. And don't worry, I'm just tired. And hot. Still getting used to this climate." I force a smile as he backs away and starts unpacking my hospital bag. He is still getting to know me too.

I told Jay about my implant two weeks after we'd escaped from the Memory Foundation. We were in London for Ro's funeral, the second we'd attended that month. The first was a hastily put together memorial service for Mum that Jay thought might help bring me some closure.

I broke down on the flight home to LA. What was the point of our escape if all I came home to was death and losses. And then I confessed to Jay that I was damaged, permanently.

"If you want to write . . ." he says now, looking at my pen and notebook on the nightstand. "Or I could bring in your laptop from your office?"

I shake my head, claiming I'm far too tired, which of course I am. The story I began five years ago—no, six—when I drove myself to the top of a mountain on a bright sunny day, no sign of an avalanche, my baby safe with her father, will be written, one day, but for now motherhood is enough, more than enough. I relax and enjoy the pull on my breast, watching Rowan's closed eyes and his tiny kneading hand. The secret to happiness, true happiness, is living in the present. That much I know. I only wish the heat in my neck would dissipate.

After I told Jack about the implant, we went to every specialist in the United States, then a man in Austria who is supposed to be the world expert, but none of them had seen anything like the bean. Every scan confirmed that it had burrowed into my spinal column, probably the cause of my horrendous back pain. It cannot be removed, even by gamma knife, not without risk of paralysis, brain injury, probable stroke, even death. In fact, death is most likely, an eighty percent chance. I have no option but to leave the bean in situ. And as the months have passed and then I found out I was pregnant, another surprise, especially at my age, and

Nova was finally coming round to the idea of having me as her mom, I allowed myself to believe the bean was inert. Believe in what the doctors and Jay are convinced of too, that the implant is as dead as its creator. And yet fear, hard as granite, grips my gut and twists as the bean burns. I scratch hard, feeling it beneath the skin and wishing I could rip it out.

"You sure you're okay?" Jay asks, dropping my blood-stained hospital nightgown into the laundry hamper. "I can call the doctor."

I smile, put on a brave face as I tell him there's no need. I have no fever. No buzzing red-hot bean in the back of my neck. Because that would be impossible. The only man who could have reactivated it is dead.

THE END

ACKNOWLEDGMENTS

FIRST THANKS GO to my agent, Joanna Swainson, who shared my passion for this story from the moment she read it. Her enthusiasm and commitment have restored my faith in so many things, not least myself. I cannot thank her enough for her tremendous hard work on my behalf. She is kind, honest, and a brilliant advocate. I am honoured to have her represent me.

And to Marcia Markland, my superb editor at Crooked Lane, who loved this story, and especially the twist, and has been instrumental in shaping *The Memory Foundation* to be the book now in your hands. It is all the better for her expertise.

I'm also immensely grateful to the teams at Hardman and Swainson and Crooked Lane Books. I know how hard everyone has worked on this publication—from pitches to cover design, to copy edit, to proof read, to publicity and promotion, and many other things besides. I'd like to thank every single one of them.

On a personal level, many fellow authors have been with me on this journey. To Hayley, Kate, Jackie, and Jane, you always understand as only a fellow writer can, and we laugh so much it's medicine. To Rachel for being the best host and true friend as well as an inspiring woman and writer. And to all the Ladykillers for their moral support and informed opinion as well as the daily distractions, much needed. And to my colleagues and all the writers at the Novelry who create such an energising place to work. Sharing thoughts on the craft of storytelling is always a privilege.

To Chris, Beth, Dan, and George, my gratitude and love as always for your amazing support of my crazy decision to make stuff up for a living, and to my dad for showing positivity and courage in what has been a very tough year.

And to all my friends and family for being interested and encouraging, and reading my books. And to all my readers. Without you, there is no story. I am endlessly surprised and delighted by your support.

This book is dedicated to my mum. I'm glad she knew about *The Memory Foundation*, and I hope she'd be just as proud of this book as she was of all the others.